My dearest Mary Ellen,

You asked me about all those trips to the doctor. Well, he's been doing tests on my heart, and the results aren't too good. He thinks I should go to Pasadena for six months to see a specialist.

I'm going because I'm not quite tired of life. You and Ramsey have been after me for so long to have work done on the house, I'm giving you this golden opportunity. Spend the next six months fixing up the place however you like. I trust your love of it to make it turn out well. The only catch is, you have to do it with Ramsey.

Don't tell me you won't. If he does it alone, the old place will be obliterated by all that form and function, or whatever he calls it. I hate to be inflexible, but this could be my last wish. Please don't thwart me.

Your loving aunt

ABOUT THE AUTHOR

Like most authors, Leigh Roberts has firsthand experience in her subject matter. "I've been undergoing a remodel on my house, remotely akin to a religious experience, except that it goes on for a couple of years. It changed me, scarred me deeply. Writing *Built To Last* helped me get some perspective on the matter," Leigh says, revealing the same sense of humor readers have come to expect from her characters. They won't be disappointed in *Built To Last,* which is full of adventure, intrigue, humor and romance.

Leigh Roberts lives with her husband, Jerry, and children Matthew and Jeremy in Palo Alto, California.

Books by Leigh Roberts

HARLEQUIN SUPERROMANCE
81—MOONLIGHT SPLENDOR
390—A PIECE OF CAKE

BUILT TO LAST

Leigh Roberts

Harlequin Books

TORONTO • NEW YORK • LONDON
AMSTERDAM • PARIS • SYDNEY • HAMBURG
STOCKHOLM • ATHENS • TOKYO • MILAN
MADRID • WARSAW • BUDAPEST • AUCKLAND

Published April 1993

ISBN 0-373-70543-3

BUILT TO LAST

For those who came through the fire
and built their dreams again

CHAPTER ONE

HIS PICKUP TRUCK roared into the circular driveway, sounding louder than the gas-powered compressor she used to run the nail gun when there wasn't enough electricity on a construction site.

Her heart rate instantly accelerated. It made enough racket to mute even the rumble of Ramsey MacIver's pickup.

Mary Ellen Saunderson clutched an armful of underwear to her chest and told herself to calm down. This was just another job. She would handle it the way she handled all the jobs in her general contracting business. With tact, expertise, aplomb.

Herself wasn't listening.

She was at the window before she knew it, peering cautiously through the yellowed lace curtains. The truck ground to a stop, and Ramsey got out. He stood in the driveway for a moment, looking at the old house. She ducked back before his gaze swept up to her window, and then felt silly. Of course he knew she was there. For one thing, her truck—small, neat, with Victorian Visions painted on the door panel—was parked just ahead of his.

Mary Ellen scurried back to the bureau to put away the armload of underwear. The practical white cotton bore little resemblance to the slinky, silky things she'd worn for him six years ago. If he saw the bundle, he'd know that her love life was on hold. He couldn't know that it had been that way for quite a while. But somehow she minded him even guessing that no man had succeeded in permanently replacing him.

The bureau drawer stuck, as old things will, and she spent an undignified moment cursing at it before it would cooperate. She smoothed her dark blond hair and took a few deep breaths. "It's no big deal," she told her reflection in the bureau mirror. She'd managed to avoid Ramsey for the past five years, but she'd always known that sooner or later they'd have to see each other again and even try to be civil. She'd just never dreamed that, when she did see him, it would be because her favorite relative, her mother's sister-in-law, Aunt Alma Saunderson MacIver, had finally found a foolproof plan for throwing them back together.

Ramsey's footsteps thundered over the porch and through the front door. The sound took her into the past, when she'd been newly in love with him, starry-eyed, waiting for him to arrive. They had spent evenings cruising the main street of Dusty Springs, California, going to movies in the town's one ancient theater, parking at the top of Spring Hill. But that was before she'd moved in with him, before love got nudged out by disagreements and disillusion.

Now she stood with her back to the mirror, waiting to confront the man who'd taught her so much—about carpentry and construction, about love and its loss.

He came around the curve of the staircase and strode down the hall toward her open bedroom door. Judging from his scowl, he was in no pleasant mood.

Mary Ellen watched him warily when he halted in the doorway. For a moment there was a measured silence between them.

"So. You've finally engineered our reunion," he said at last. His gravelly, growling voice was instantly familiar, as though the five years that had passed since that last quarrel had been no time.

Also familiar was the surge of temper that his words sent through her. Only Ramsey had ever been able to make her truly angry. Normally, she considered herself a peaceable, consensus-building kind of woman. Around him, something more primitive came to the surface.

This time, she vowed, fighting back the anger, she was not going to let him goad her. This time, she at least would behave as a mature person. She hadn't been able to handle him when she was twenty-four, but at twenty-nine, she was in control of her emotions.

Relaxing her death grip on the edge of the bureau top behind her, she managed a pleasant smile. "Why, Ramsey, it was my understanding that you were behind this ludicrous proposal."

His eyes narrowed, acknowledging a hit. "You didn't put it into Aunt Alma's head?"

"Are you crazy?" After the heated words were out, she remembered her vow of control and pinned the smile back on. "Why in the world would I do that? I've got work piled up in Berkeley. It's going to be very inconvenient, having to live here." She felt her smile slipping, and struggled to keep it in place. "I tried to get Mr. Featherstone to let me live at home, but he just said he couldn't change her mind about any of it. I'll be lucky to make it back to Berkeley a couple of times a week."

Ramsey smiled, too—a superior smirk that made her long to wipe it off his face. "I've cleared my calendar," he remarked. "Thought it was only right that I give Aunt Alma's place my total attention."

"Ha," she said, not believing him for a minute. Ramsey devote himself to one job? He'd always worked from dawn to dusk on a succession of remodeling jobs.

His grin widened. She knew he was just trying to provoke her; he was just waiting for her to complain about the way his work habits caused him to neglect the people who loved him. The same old triggers would start the same old arguments.

So she kept smiling, wondering if her jaw would fall off, if her nose would grow longer from all this bogus politeness. "Things must not be going too well for you," she murmured with false sympathy. "Too bad. Has the competition finally gotten tougher out here in the sticks?"

"People are falling over themselves to hire me," he snapped, stung. "I've got as much work as I can handle."

"So you didn't really clear your calendar." She pounced on that little slip triumphantly. "I thought so."

He waved her observation away. "I meant that I'm just not taking on anything new until this whole mess is straightened out."

"It could have been straightened out in no time if you'd refused to play," she grumbled, losing the smile. What was the point in pretending? They both still knew how to needle each other.

"What, and let you call the shots? No way." He laughed, and the sound gave her that same familiar frisson. Shivering, she brushed it off. The most important thing to remember for the next few months, or however long it took to get through this nightmare, was that Ramsey was a walking disaster for a woman. He looked good, she had to admit, sneaking a glance at that tall, rugged body, those lean hips and broad shoulders. His dark hair was still too long, hanging straight and shiny down the back of his neck. His eyebrows still met in the center of his forehead when he was annoyed, and that had happened more and more frequently during the year they had lived together. Compromise was not in his vocabulary. She'd thought he'd loved her, but he'd never brought himself to say the words. He was bossy, overbearing, condescending and arrogant. Hunkiness just didn't compensate for all those problems.

"This isn't funny," she said fiercely, her facade of tolerance abandoned. "You've encouraged Aunt Alma to set the situation up, but whatever it is you planned to get out of it won't happen, Ramsey. So you can just talk her out of it."

"I didn't talk her into it." He returned her glare. "I don't even know how to get in touch with her. Why don't you tell her to stop playing Cupid?"

"I would in a second if *I* knew where she was." Mary Ellen jerked another bureau drawer open and put a stack of sweatshirts into it.

She caught Ramsey's gaze in the mirror. He was staring at her, his anger arrested. "You mean you don't know either?"

Shaking her head, Mary Ellen stared back. Ramsey was the first to turn away. Running one hand through his hair, he banged the door frame with the other one. "Damn it to hell," he growled. "I figured there'd be some way to call the whole thing off." He let his breath out in an explosive sigh. "Guess I was wrong."

Mary Ellen sighed, too, and went back to her suitcase. The next six months loomed ahead of her, full of uncertainty and emotional stress. She liked having everything neatly planned, each job calculated in advance. Now her whole schedule would be disrupted. When she saw her aunt again, she'd have more than a few things to get off her chest.

Unless Alma MacIver didn't come back.

Mary Ellen refused even to let herself think that. A world without Aunt Alma in it? Impossible.

Behind her, Ramsey echoed her thoughts. "You think this clinic or whatever it is will fix her up?"

"They'd better," Mary Ellen said, a catch in her voice. "I never realized it was so bad. Did you?"

"Hell, no." He came a few more paces into the room and absently leaned against one of the bedposts. "She kept putting me off when I asked her about all those doctor visits. Said she was taking part in some study."

"She told me the same thing." Mary Ellen blinked hard and put a pair of ragged sweatpants into a drawer. "I knew she was slowing down, but after all, she's in her mid-seventies."

"She's a tough bird," Ramsey averred, turning away for a minute. "She'll pull through fine." He glanced at her. "You don't think this whole scheme might be a sign of—well, of her brain going soft, do you?"

"Ramsey MacIver!" Mary Ellen stared at him. "Don't you ever let *her* hear you say that. Besides, no one who was losing her marbles could have pulled off this monumental coup." She shook her head. "She's got us right where she wanted us."

"The master manipulator." Ramsey sounded resigned. "Guess you're right. This is just the culmination of months of strategic planning."

"She wanted us to get married five years ago." Mary Ellen glanced at him sideways.

Ramsey snorted. "Fat chance. As if two people who argued like we did would have even dreamed of marriage."

"Right." Mary Ellen laughed hollowly. "A woman would have to have her head examined to marry a man like you."

Ramsey scowled again. "That's just your opinion," he muttered. His heavy work boots left little blobs of dirt on the floor when he stomped away from her. "Well, we'd better decide what to do."

"I've already decided." Mary Ellen got a stack of jeans out of her suitcase and marched to the bureau. "I'm going to do what Aunt Alma asked me to. And right now, I'm going to finish unpacking and go over some paperwork. So if you'll excuse me?"

There was no response to this sally except for ominous silence. She looked in the mirror and saw him still standing in the doorway, one hand braced against the jamb. He looked cool now, the perturbation wiped away, as if he was prepared to stay there for hours.

She shut all the drawers, arranged her zippered bag of toilet articles on the dresser scarf, and closed her suitcase. Still Ramsey didn't move.

Swinging around, she picked up the empty suitcase and put it in the closet, right next to the room's entrance. "Is this entertaining you?" she asked politely, shutting the closet door a little harder than was necessary.

"Oh, yes." He held out one hand to stop her when she would have turned away. "We should discuss the situation. Set some ground rules."

"Aunt Alma already set the ground rules," Mary Ellen said, amusement replacing some of the anxiety she'd been feeling. Much as she hated the situation they found themselves in, she would bet that Ramsey hated it more. He always had to be in charge. The thought of being a pawn in his aunt's game must be galling him, too. "But if you want to discuss things, it'll have to be the living room. I don't want you in my bedroom."

The frown was replaced by a look far more dangerous to Mary Ellen's peace of mind. She knew that intentness, the way those dark brown eyes could heat until the warmth in them drew you, like fires drew moths. "That's not the way I remember it."

Mary Ellen stepped back another pace, and stopped herself, breathing deeply. "Okay, ground rules," she snapped, annoyed with her voice for sounding so...shaky. "No dragging up the past. No fighting all those fights over again. I said I'd do this, and I will, but so help me, Ramsey, if you start—"

"Okay, okay." He shrugged, those wide shoulders nearly filling the door of her room. "I get the picture. No guys allowed."

"Right." She grabbed the doorknob.

"We'll meet in the living room. Fifteen minutes."

"Fifteen minutes?" Mary Ellen clutched at her hair, and the tortoiseshell combs that were holding it back from her face promptly fell out. "Maybe I won't be ready then."

Ramsey picked up the combs, turning them over in his big hands as if he couldn't imagine what they were for. "Well, whenever you say." He gave her a false, toothy smile. "Let's have meaningful dialogue, Emmy," he said, calling her the childhood nickname that came from combining her first two initials. "Let's get in touch with our inner children. Let's—"

"Okay, fifteen minutes." Mary Ellen struggled not to grin, and didn't succeed. "I didn't think people talked like that in Dusty Springs. Have you been going to sensitivity classes?"

"Me? Heck no." Ramsey snorted. "But there is a family counselor in town now. She does psychotherapy and all that. I've been wondering about my inner child ever since I heard her blathering about it in the Food Mart."

Mary Ellen couldn't help laughing. "Your inner child is pounding nails into a block of wood. Or maybe squirting everyone else with a hose."

"For that, you only get ten minutes."

"Fifteen, and not a second less."

"Fine." He took her hand and turned it palm up to drop the combs into it. "See you then."

She snatched her hand away and shut the door after him with more force than she meant to. Then she remembered something, and jerked the door open again. Ramsey was still standing there, his face split in an unaccustomed grin. The sight paralyzed her for a moment. In her memory he was usually dour, critical.

"You're not moving into the house?" She crossed her arms over her chest, striving to regain a dignified footing.

"I don't have to," Ramsey pointed out. "I only live ten minutes away. I can stay at home."

"I could stay home, too, and just drive up every day," Mary Ellen muttered.

"Great," he responded instantly. "The terms of this dumb scenario clearly state that we have to work together, full time or as near to it as we can manage. If you don't live here, I'll get the whole say-so." The annoying smirk was back on his face again.

Scowling, she turned away and shut the door, more gently this time. *So much for maturity,* she reflected, listening to Ramsey stomp downstairs.

She jammed the combs into her hair without looking in the mirror, and opened her briefcase. It seemed there was always a lot of paperwork to do. And now she'd be doing it from a distance, having had to abandon her crew to come sixty miles to work on this lunatic project.

The letter from Aunt Alma lay on top of the papers in her briefcase. She took it out to read once more, hoping to find some loophole to help her get out of a situation that promised to be intolerable.

Dearest Emmy,
You asked when you visited last month about all these trips to the doctor. Well, he's been doing a lot of tests on my heart, and the results aren't too good. He thinks I should go to Pasadena, where there's a specialist who puts people like me on a six-month regimen of diet, drugs and exercise. Sounds dreadful, doesn't it?

I'm going, anyway, because I'm not quite tired of life, though I will be 76 next month. You've been after me for so long to have work done on the house—you and Ramsey, too. So I'm giving you this golden opportunity. Spend the next six months fixing up the place for me—however you like. I trust your love of it will make it turn out well. The only catch is, you have to do it with Ramsey.

Don't tell me you won't, either. If he does it alone, I know what will happen; the old place will be obliterated by all that modernity and form and function, or whatever he calls it. You're both contractors...you should be able to get it done in double-quick time.

I hate to be inflexible, but I'm afraid you'll have to do this, sweetie. I do feel a teensy bit guilty at interrupting your life, so I've asked Jamie Featherstone to handle everything for me. Please don't try to get in touch with me. If you want to write, Jamie will forward letters for you. This could be my last wish, you know. Please don't thwart me.

Your loving aunt

When she'd received the letter two weeks earlier, Mary Ellen had been worried, but also amused by Aunt Alma's perennial attempts to get her and Ramsey back together. She'd wanted them to get married, and hadn't really approved of their living together without doing so.

Then Aunt Alma's lawyer, James Featherstone, had actually shown up at Mary Ellen's Berkeley apartment house, and after that she had lost that tolerant amusement for her aunt's machinations.

Mary Ellen looked around the room, the tower bedroom that had been hers when she'd lived with her aunt. She loved it, from the leaded casements in the tower windows to the cedar chest at the foot of the old spool bed. Every crack in the plaster, every chip in the picture molding, was familiar to her.

But she had her own place in Berkeley now, her own business, a life away from Dusty Springs. It was wrenching to come back for six months, let alone having to work with Ramsey. "You had better get well, Aunty," she said into the air, frowning. "Because I've got some heavy-duty bones to pick with you."

RAMSEY PROWLED THROUGH the living room, feeling at loose ends until Mary Ellen deigned to come down for their conference. The big room seemed very empty without Aunt Alma's commanding presence there. Hard to believe she was four hundred miles away in Pasadena, when she could pull the strings so well. Trust her to come up with a plan like this one, guaranteed to turn sensible contractors into gibbering idiots before it was over.

Well, he wouldn't gibber. But Mary Ellen might. With the merest bit of goading, she'd gotten very irritated. A satisfied smile touched the corners of his mouth. It was like finding a favorite hammer after having lost and done without it for a long time, to rile Mary Ellen and have her spark at him. She'd started off in control, but she hadn't stayed that way. To his mind, that meant she wasn't indifferent.

He opened the French doors at one end of the room and stood on the veranda for a moment. The sun was warm, but there was a crispness to the air that cried out for the scent of burning leaves. From the veranda, he could see down the hill toward the small

Dusty Springs business district. On the other side of town his crew was building a house on speculation. And he was hanging around dancing attendance on his absent aunt, and getting ready to do battle with a woman he'd never really gotten over.

He squashed down that realization right away. There was no point in that line of thought. Mary Ellen had made it clear for the past five years, and even before, that she would have nothing to do with him. She'd left him empty-handed once. He wouldn't be put through that again.

But he knew Aunt Alma was right: he had made a mess of it the last time. Hell, he'd done the worst job of holding on to a woman than any man had ever done. It just hadn't occurred to him that it was such a dicey proposition—or that he would care so much about the outcome.

So could he consider this another chance? Ramsey turned his back on the view of Dusty Springs and went into the house. He knew that was what Aunt Alma had had in mind, though she hadn't seen fit to consult him about it.

Well, he wouldn't crawl to any woman. So he'd made mistakes the last time. Mary Ellen had, too. But maybe for her they hadn't had the repercussions they'd had for him. In all the years since she'd left, he hadn't found anyone to take her place. He'd checked a few women out, but the spark had never operated like it had with his feisty former love.

He stared up at the portrait that hung above the native stone fireplace. It was his father's brother, Ramsey "Scottie" MacIver, for whom he'd been named. His uncle stared back from under fierce, bristling eyebrows. Scottie didn't look like a man who'd take guff from anyone, and yet according to all reports Alma Saunderson had been able to wrap him around her finger.

Grimacing, Ramsey wandered through the room. Being wrapped around someone's finger sounded pretty uncomfortable. He refused to even contemplate it. But he wouldn't mind being on speaking terms with Mary Ellen again.

It wouldn't be easy to patch things up; that much was obvious. Simply asking Mary Ellen to let bygones be bygones wouldn't work. Not after the things they'd said five years ago. Not when he could see the memory of those last bitter days in her eyes when she looked at him. He, too, felt anger, betrayal, hurt. Those emotions had kept him from trying to make up all these years, from acknowledging that what they'd had together was more special than either of them had known at the time.

He sat down on the overstuffed sofa, and waited for the wave of pain and self-criticism to subside. He'd spent two of those five years suppressing every thought of her, just to avoid confronting how badly he'd behaved. Maybe no one would ever have called Ramsey MacIver a prince of a guy, but at least he'd never felt like a creep until Mary Ellen had left him, citing his stubbornness, his inflexibility, his unwillingness to listen to another point of view and his condescension toward her.

Twisting uneasily on the sofa, Ramsey brought out all the defenses he'd spent the last five years assembling. "She didn't know beans about the construction business until I taught her," he mumbled, trying to ignore the memory of how he'd taught her. *"Not like that, Emmy! A five-year-old could do it better!*

Here, hold it this way, if you think you can manage it." Certainly he wouldn't have taken that kind of treatment from anyone without blowing up. But she'd taken it—at first. She'd been so damned sweet and awkward and anxious to learn how to help him.

He jumped to his feet, shoving those bittersweet memories away, and stomped into the hall. Why was he going through with this ridiculous plan? Aunt Alma was off her noggin. The floorboards creaked loudly under his feet. He knew what that meant; going down to the spider-infested cellar to shim the floor joists. The wallpaper bulged ominously on one side of the hall, indicating rotten plaster underneath, and he knew if he dropped a marble it would make a beeline for the low spot near the kitchen door. There wasn't a level floor in the whole damned place.

The squeak of the swinging door that led into the kitchen set his teeth on edge. The old place was a firetrap, or worse. He'd been nagging his aunt for years to let him come in and fix it. He'd offered to take it to the ground and build her a fine new house from the foundation up.

She'd been horrified. He filled the kettle with water and searched through the cupboards for some coffee, tea—any kind of stimulant that would knock him out of this hell of recollection. He seemed doomed to disappoint women—his woman, his aunt, even a few of the local ladies who saw him as that rare character, a financially stable unmarried man. Dating them had gotten old fast.

At least Lenore hadn't turned on him when Mary Ellen had left town, even though the two women were close friends. He and Lenore had settled into a comfortable friendship. When he needed a date, he took her. When she wanted a male escort, she called him. They didn't make any romantic demands on each other. He knew gossip had them between the sheets, but gossip was way ahead of itself in this case.

He'd been wondering if he was just getting old, if his libido had been put into cold storage. But one look at Mary Ellen, and parts of him that had been quiescent had sprung to immediate attention.

Now, while he waited for the water to boil, he was uncomfortably aware that his jeans felt too tight. There was a jar of instant coffee on the shelf behind the stove. He seized it eagerly and spooned a mound of it into a cup. Tapping his fingers impatiently on the counter, his gaze fell on a big tin, ornamented with faded pink scrolls and gilt curlicues. He pulled it closer and curved his fingers around the lid, and it came off with a familiar whoosh that took him back to childhood, when Mary Ellen and her mother had lived with Aunt Alma. He had a vision of Emmy sitting at the table, her feet not yet reaching the floor; Aunt Alma, bustling around pouring juice for them; himself, parceling out the vanilla wafers, cramming one surreptitiously into his mouth when he thought no one was looking.

The tin still exhaled the familiar fragrance of vanilla and sugar, although it was empty. Staring into it, he faced the knowledge that Aunt Alma might not come back from her visit to Pasadena. If only he'd known about her health before. He could have made sure she saw the right specialist, talked her out of this bizarre plan.

He put the lid of the tin back on with unsteady fingers. Who was he kidding? Aunt Alma would never have let him take charge of things for her. She had done exactly as she wanted her whole life, and Scottie had been the only man who'd ever had the slightest influence on her. His uncle was but a dim memory for Ramsey—a big, booming voice that had been silenced in the same quarry accident that took his father's life. Alma had carried on valiantly after his death, but she still spoke of Scottie as if he'd just gone round the corner to wait for her.

"Don't join him yet, Aunt Alma," Ramsey whispered, clasping the tin to his chest for a brief, shaken moment. "I'm not ready for that."

The door squeaked open behind him and he shoved the tin hastily against the counter back splash, rubbing the back of his hand over his eyes. He poured hot water into his cup and stirred it vigorously, not turning when Mary Ellen approached.

"There's some more hot water if you want something," he said gruffly, stirring harder than ever.

She touched his arm, just for a second. He wondered if it had happened, even as he felt the warmth of it spread from his arm through his bloodstream. "She'll be all right." Mary Ellen's voice was soft.

"I know." He wanted her to touch him again so badly he couldn't stand next to her. He took his cup of coffee to the old kitchen table and sat down, morosely blowing into it.

Mary Ellen fished a tea bag out of one of the canisters on the warming shelf. He could tell by the set of her shoulders that she was annoyed, that she thought he'd brushed off her sympathy. But if he didn't, he'd start bawling like a little kid, and he had no intention of doing that.

He stared at Mary Ellen, noticing the changes five years had brought. She was still slender but sturdy, still came up to his shoulder. Her dishwater-blond hair was shorter now, held off her face with those comb things instead of being pulled back in a French twist. He remembered how she used to dress to go to her job in the bank, in those neat little suits and white blouses. She looked more comfortable now, wearing worn blue jeans and an oversized T-shirt. Her eyes were the same, a steady greenish-blue, with the same thick, fair lashes surrounding them. She still didn't go in for makeup, he could tell.

He felt that hormonal stir within him, and tamped it down firmly. She probably wouldn't welcome any tender speeches from him, even if he made a groveling apology for past faults. Truth was, he had all those faults still, maybe more, and he didn't particularly feel like getting rid of perfectly comfortable bad habits if there wasn't any point. Despite what his body wanted, Mary Ellen showed no sign of uncontrollable passion for him. If she made the first move, he'd reciprocate.

"I said, hadn't we better get a work schedule agreed on?" Mary Ellen was scowling at him from across the table, and he pulled his few wits back.

"Good idea, but first we'd better get some plans together, figure out the scope of the project." He pushed his coffee cup aside, fishing for the little notebook he carried in the pocket of his flannel shirt.

Mary Ellen was looking smug. "No need," she said airily. "I already have plans. I did them a couple of years ago when Aunt Alma sounded like she might really let me fix the place up. She liked them, but I could never get her to agree to actually start the work."

"You have—" He stared at her, waiting for the familiar rush of anger at being out-generaled. He liked being in charge, everyone knew that. He'd just assumed he'd be in charge here, too.

Mary Ellen was waiting for him to blow up. She sat back in her chair, her arms crossed over her breasts, a glint of triumph in her eyes. Because she clearly expected him to lose it, he swallowed his first reaction. "Let's see the plans," he suggested mildly, hoping she couldn't tell that his teeth were clenched.

Evidently she couldn't. She was puzzled, he knew. He discovered that he liked keeping her off balance. Maybe if she got off balance often enough, she'd stumble in his direction.

He shoved that thought hastily away before the sensations it aroused took over his body, and smiled blandly, waiting for her to produce her plans.

"They're in the truck," she said, pushing her chair back. "You'll like them, I'm sure."

"Maybe." He followed her to the door, reaching forward to open it for her. It was not the kind of little courtesy to which he usually succumbed. Women, he figured, had liberated themselves from such meaningless gestures. It rattled Mary Ellen, he could tell. He was beginning to enjoy himself.

She led the way outside to her truck, a compact little pickup with nice built-in toolboxes along the sides of the bed. The whole truck was amazingly clean. He'd forgotten that passion for order she had. Shaking his head, he wondered what sort of general contractor she was. None of his other colleagues kept their trucks so neat. Certainly his big old Ford, parked behind her little import, was no sterling example.

She unlocked one of the tool bays, and he saw that it was filled with tidily rolled sets of blueprints. He raised his eyebrows. If those were her current jobs, she was doing very well, indeed.

Selecting one of the rolls, Mary Ellen glanced around. "We can take it on the porch," she decided, heading back up the sidewalk. Ramsey followed her, scuffling his feet in the crisp yellow leaves from the elms that flanked the walk and admiring the rear view of Mary Ellen. Her bright T-shirt matched the soft blue of the autumn sky. Late roses climbed the walls of the old house and bloomed around its casement windows, while the sun highlighted the elaborate swags of carved ornaments. He had to admit the place had charm, especially with Mary Ellen climbing the steps. She sat on the top one and spread the blueprints out along the porch floor. He grabbed the opposite edge of them before they could roll back up, and sat down, too.

The plans were neatly drawn, with all the details spelled out. He supposed they were fine if you liked restoration work. He didn't.

"This is a hell of a lot of trouble," he said after going through each floor plan and the attendant technical drawings. "I've told Alma a million times, the best thing to do is gut the place. That way you don't have to worry about dry rot and termites and unsound foundations."

Mary Ellen's face hardened, but she kept her voice level. "By gutting, I presume you mean tearing down the house? Otherwise, the foundation is still of some concern."

"Leave up one wall, say," he suggested, glad to hear her sound so reasonable. "Leave up the front wall, and take the rest down. If she can't afford that, we can pick up the slack—or at least, I can. I have a few chips I could cash in."

"The money is not the biggest problem," Mary Ellen said, glaring at him. "It's your idea that's totally out of line. Aunt Alma was right. You'd create some monstrous modern horror and think it was just as good as this lovely old place, with all its history and fine craftsmanship—"

"Just a minute," he protested, glaring back, oblivious to the sound of a car turning into the drive. "When it comes to craftsmanship, I know more about it than you've even guessed exists. I'm a realist, Emmy. This place is old and falling down. It'll take ages and cost a fortune to renovate it—"

"Excuse me." The words were preceded by the sound of a throat clearing, and followed by an apologetic cough. Mary Ellen swiveled to look at the interloper, and Ramsey followed suit.

"Oh, it's you, Featherstone." He wondered how much the old lawyer had heard. "We were just discussing the plans."

"So I inferred." Mr. James Featherstone looked amused. "I wondered if I might take a little of your time, both of you."

"Certainly." Mary Ellen got to her feet, twitching the blueprints out of Ramsey's grasp and rolling them up protectively. "Let's go inside."

She led the way to the living room. Mr. Featherstone stood politely until she waved him into his chair. "Would you care for some coffee or tea?"

Ramsey took the sofa again, wondering what bombshell Featherstone would drop this time. Mr. Featherstone did not appear overjoyed to be in the middle of this situation, but everyone knew he'd been carrying a torch for Alma MacIver since the days when she was still Alma Saunderson.

"Your aunt," he said now, looking at each of them in turn, "has asked me to tell you that she will write you both here. She asks that each of you send her a weekly report—or rather, that you give the report to me, to forward to her. You know that she does not want you to get in touch with her directly."

Mary Ellen's face crumpled. "Why?" She wiped her eyes with her sleeve, and blinked hard. Ramsey felt a knot in his own throat and concentrated fiercely on the plaster flowers that circled the central light fixture. "Why doesn't she want us to know where she is? Is she really all right?"

"I understand your distress," Mr. Featherstone said soothingly. "Perhaps she was afraid this scheme would be distasteful to you both, and is simply ducking the possibility of receiving a lot of irate phone calls."

"Touché," Ramsey muttered. He'd composed several steaming sentences in his mind. Judging from the look on Mary Ellen's face, she'd done the same.

"You must remember, your aunt is not in good health," Mr. Featherstone continued with his usual lawyerly understatement. "I know you will both be sure not to upset her in your weekly reports. I will let you know when I hear from her how she is doing." Anxiety shadowed his face momentarily.

"Will she be all right?" Mary Ellen twisted her hands together. "This is all so unlike her—so final, somehow. I'm worried."

"According to the medical reports she showed me, Alma has a good chance," Mr. Featherstone replied carefully. Ramsey glanced sideways at Mary Ellen.

Her eyes glittered, but she blinked fiercely, maintaining control.

Mr. Featherstone broke the short silence that followed his words. "Alma has also asked me to give you this memo about her wishes for the house. She especially wanted me to tell you that she preferred Ramsey to be in charge of the structural work, and Mary Ellen to be in charge of design and finish. If these terms are not acceptable, either of you is welcome to withdraw. In that case, as you know, the other one gets complete and final authority over the project."

Ramsey wondered why he didn't just withdraw now. He knew Mary Ellen would do an adequate job of restoration, which wasn't really his thing at all. He could concede gracefully, leave it in her hands, and go back to his own business, where he was truly needed.

He opened his mouth, but the words just wouldn't come out. Aunt Alma had pegged him too accurately. He didn't want to walk away from this and let someone else be in total charge. He didn't want to walk away from one more chance to work with Mary Ellen—maybe even work things out with her.

They were both looking at him, he realized, Mary Ellen and the lawyer. He closed his mouth and shrugged.

"I'm glad that's agreeable to you, Ramsey," Mr. Featherstone said smoothly, with a faint smile. He turned the smile on Mary Ellen, and opened his briefcase. "Here are the papers she asked me to give you. I've made a copy for each of you." He brought out two paper-clipped bundles. "In accordance with these instructions, I've arranged a construction account at the Springview Bank, and you are welcome to draw on it. All checks must be cosigned by each of you. In matters of crew and timetable, Alma leaves it up to you, but hopes that you can finish the work in the specified six months. She asks that each of you accept a monthly stipend, to recompense you for the work you are turning down on her account.''

There was another brief silence. ''Does Aunt Alma know how much this will cost?'' Mary Ellen spoke wonderingly. ''Can she afford it?''

''Your aunt,'' Mr. Featherstone said with a faint smile, ''has always had an eye for the stock market. She's done very well over the years since selling Scottie's quarry—very well, indeed. She can afford it.''

He packed up his briefcase and stood, and Ramsey stood, too, holding out his hand. Mr. Featherstone shook it, and then Mary Ellen's, and dropped his lawyerly persona for an instant. ''I must say you're both very brave to do this,'' he said, smiling at them conspiratorially. ''But it's wonderful that you are. The anticipation of getting your weekly reports is obviously doing Alma a great deal of good. Thank you.''

''Thank you, Mr. Featherstone,'' Mary Ellen murmured, seeing him to the door. Ramsey just stood in the living room, wondering at the hollow feeling that filled him. Every minute that went by made him more and more wary of his aunt's obvious scheming. And every new revelation made it more and more difficult to draw back.

CHAPTER TWO

MARY ELLEN TURNED away from the door and found Ramsey watching her. She tried a nonchalant smile. "Aunt Alma is certainly making a big mystery out of all this."

Ramsey's dark brown eyes examined her. "We could probably find out where she is pretty easily. There can't be all that many heart clinics in Pasadena."

"I don't know," Mary Ellen said slowly. "She doesn't want us to get in touch. Guess we'd better go along with that."

"Just like we're going along with this whole ridiculous scheme?" Ramsey shoved his hands through his hair and swung away impatiently. "It's nuts. She's manipulating us." Ramsey turned back to her, amusement and irritation struggling in his face. "She knows neither of us could stand to let the other one be in charge."

Mary Ellen reflected that it was humiliating to find Aunt Alma assessing their individual hot buttons so accurately.

"She hooked us both, anyway," she said aloud. "Now we just have to get it over with. What will we do for crew?"

Ramsey sat down on the sofa, gesturing for the plans, and Mary Ellen sat beside him, spreading the blueprints on the coffee table. "Let's look at this again," he said grudgingly. "It'll take a huge crew if we're going to maintain the original fabric of the house."

"That's the way Aunt Alma wants it," Mary Ellen said stubbornly. "And me, too. I think you'll find the basic structure is sound, after we do a little demo."

"You agree to demolition?" Ramsey assumed a thunderstruck expression. "Gracious me! I thought we were going to have to save every little crumb of plaster, every little stop-molding—"

"We'll save as much as we can of the woodwork," Mary Ellen interrupted crisply, trying to tamp down her annoyance. She remembered this attitude of Ramsey's very well; in the past he would make fun of her ideas and belittle them until she gave up and let him do what he wanted. Since those days, however, she'd learned a great deal. And on this job, she meant to have her way. "Woodwork is difficult to match unless you have it custom milled, and that takes time and money. There'll have to be a certain amount of that, but we'll reuse everything we can."

Ramsey shook his head disparagingly, but he didn't say anything more. Mary Ellen went on, tempering the firmness in her voice, but not by much.

"The objective here is to maintain the atmosphere of the house. I'm not ruling out innovations and modernity, within reason. If you look at the kitchen plans, you'll see I've brought it up to date without sacrificing charm—or at least I like to think so."

She leafed through the blueprints until she found the right page, and waited for him to examine it. He'd make more sarcastic remarks, she was sure, but she would stand her ground. The kitchen plans had taken a lot of thought, plus a couple of consultations with a designer she often used, and she was proud of them.

To her surprise, Ramsey didn't say anything. He perused the plans, his eyebrows going up in surprised approval a couple of times, but at the end he just grunted and moved on to the next page.

"This new bathroom you've added upstairs. What about the septic tank?"

"I checked the capacity, and it'll have to be replaced. In fact, I want to redo the sewer lines and replace all the galvanized pipes with copper."

Ramsey rubbed his chin with one hand, but not before she'd seen the grin he tried to suppress. "And you're going to live here! Great fun."

Mary Ellen frowned. "It doesn't seem fair. You'll be living in the lap of luxury, and I'll be shrouded with plaster dust."

"Well," Ramsey said, the grin widening, "you can always bunk with me if it gets to be too much for you."

"In your wildest dreams, MacIver." Mary Ellen glowered at him. "I can only be manipulated to a certain point." She narrowed her eyes. "If you're trying to hint that you want us to get back together—"

"I'm not the devious one here," Ramsey interrupted. "If I had anything to say along those lines, I'd just come out and say it." He met her gaze, his own eyes dark. "I know what Alma hoped for, but as far as I'm concerned, she's trying to warm up cold soup. I'm agreeing to the renovation because her house really needs it, not for any other reason." His face relaxed a little. "It's just a bonus that you get to cope with the living conditions here."

"Some bonus." Mary Ellen tried to look offended, but she was too relieved to muster up much ire. It was just like Ramsey to get things out in the open; subtlety was indeed beyond him. She was glad to realize that she wouldn't have to spend her energy fighting him off, or looking for hidden meanings in anything he said. "I might have to rent myself a little apartment or something."

"Can't take it, hmm? You can smash the plaster, but you don't want to live in the dust. I see." Ramsey's smirk, she noticed, was just as annoying as ever. "And you get to design everything, after all, but I have to carry it out. That new bathroom is going to be a real pain the way you've got the fixtures laid out. If you'd put it over here instead of where you did, the plumbing would go in much easier. And—"

"All right," Mary Ellen interrupted. "We can put it where you want it. Tell you what—you can be in complete charge of that bathroom. Just don't interfere with the rest of it."

"Even if I find a flaw in your oh-so-perfect plans?" Ramsey's gaze challenged her.

"You won't find any," Mary Ellen said, glaring back at him. "But we will, of course, discuss things like adults." She rolled up the plans and handed them to him. "I've got another set in the truck."

"Thanks," he said warily.

"Now, if you'll excuse me." Mary Ellen got to her feet, moving casually toward the door. "It's a long drive back—"

"Back?" Ramsey strode toward her, reaching one long arm across the living room doorway. "Where are you going?"

"Back to Berkeley." She mustered some surprise, as if he was being dense. "You're the construction chief. Obviously, you don't need me right now. I'll be checking in—"

"You'll be here this afternoon so we can write up the work schedule and talk about hiring subs and grunts." He gave her a tight smile. "And when we start work, you'll be here every day. I need crew, remember? The client is paying us both, and believe me, Mary Ellen, you'll earn your pay."

"Crocodile," she muttered, glancing through the open front door. Her truck stood there, pointed down the semicircular driveway as if raring for freedom.

"What did you call me?"

"I said, you're a crocodile." She put her hands on her hips. "Standing there showing all your teeth, just waiting for me to make a mistake. Well, I'm not going to make one. You want me to stay here, fine! I stay! But I'm not taking any lip from you, Ramsey MacIver. If I have to work on your crew, you'll have to work on mine." She matched his stare with one of her own. "Every scut job you give me, every tongue-lashing you dish out, will come right back when I'm in charge. So put that in your concrete mixer and churn it up, buddy!"

Ramsey didn't answer. He was laughing.

"Damn it, Ramsey! I don't know what you find about this situation that's so damned amusing!"

"I don't, either." He shook his head a couple of times. "Probably this is just the beginning of a full-scale mental breakdown." The words were light, but there was something behind them. Mary Ellen met his eyes before turning away.

"Well, we'll both be crazy by the end of it," she predicted. "I am going to have to make periodic trips back to Berkeley. I'm in the middle of a couple of jobs, and I can't just drop everything."

"Don't you have a foreman?" Ramsey straightened, moving away from the door.

Mary Ellen read criticism into the words. "I don't need one," she said loftily. "My crew is capable of working without direct supervision. But I don't load them down with making all the decisions."

"Okay." Ramsey picked up the roll of plans. "I have work going on, too. We can each take the same amount of time every week to keep things moving." For a moment, he looked abashed. "Thing is, all my crew are busy. I can pull them off as they finish various tasks, but for the day-to-day stuff, there's just you and me. Unless your crew—"

"Busy as well," Mary Ellen said, thinking about the kitchen job in Berkeley, and the Piedmont master-bath addition. "Guess there'll be enough scut work to go around."

"Guess so." Ramsey gestured to her to lead the way out of the living room. "That being so, shall we adjourn for lunch? We can work out a schedule this afternoon."

"Fine," Mary Ellen said, heading once more for the front door. "I'll meet you here in an hour."

She walked as fast as she could toward her truck, glancing back to the house when she reached it.

Ramsey stood in the front door, his hands in his pockets. There was something almost lonely in the slump of his shoulders. When she started the engine, he turned and disappeared into the house. She felt a little guilty, and tried to stifle it. After all, he wasn't holding out any olive branches.

All the same, she wondered what he'd find to eat. The refrigerator, when she'd peeked into it earlier, had looked uncommonly bare.

RAMSEY THOUGHT SO, TOO, when he opened the door on the old white Frigidaire that had been new when he'd been a baby. It was perfectly capable, however, of keeping a couple of limp carrots and a tub of cottage cheese cold. He shut the door again, thinking, and went out to his own truck. Over the years, he'd eaten in plenty of restaurants, and the restaurant food in Dusty Springs didn't get far from the basic burger-and-fries concept. He hadn't expected anything different when Mary Ellen had lived with him; she was no kitchen queen. But after she'd left, he'd finally started cooking, and found to his surprise that he enjoyed it. He wasn't gourmet class or anything, but at least he could put fresh vegetables and a simple entrée together.

Mary Ellen still didn't know an omelet pan from a skillet, judging by the way she'd scampered out. Or maybe she just didn't want to share meals with him. The thought hardened Ramsey's jaw, and then he began to smile. If she could eat burgers forever, he'd be surprised. And when she saw the leftovers from home he planned to bring back for lunch, she'd be made of steel if she didn't crave some decent cooking. And maybe, if she asked nicely, he'd let her join him once in a while.

He scowled at the mess in the cab of his truck—piles of bids, copies of contracts, folded and rolled blueprints, and a few empty soda cans. This afternoon, he decided, he'd tidy up. He'd have a word with Wally, the foreman on both the spec house and the contract house he was building across town. But for now, he'd go to his place and throw some lunch together, bring a few things over to Alma's house. That piece of left-over flank steak would taste pretty good rolled up in a tortilla with some of his spicy homemade salsa on top.

His place was two miles out of town, less than a ten-minute drive from Alma's house. He stopped the truck in front of the radio-controlled gate, feeling a little sheepish at the probable overkill of his security. But there had been those two incidents, and anyway, he'd wanted to find out more about home security systems in case his clients asked. Since he'd installed the elab-orate system, there'd been no more threatening notes taped to his front door.

The flag was down on his mailbox, and he reached a long arm through the truck window, but he couldn't open the box from where he sat. Most of his mail was delivered to a postal box in town—the important stuff, anyway. He thought about just letting the mail wait. It was bound to be junk. But his newfound resolve to get rid of the excess paper in his life got him out of the truck.

He yanked the front of the mailbox down, but be-fore he could reach into it there was a sudden twisty, uncoiling movement. His first thought was of joke cans stuffed with coiled springs—the kind kids caused so much consternation with. But this was no practical joke. He jumped back. The seething mass in the dark depths of the mailbox resolved itself into a real snake, pouring out the front opening. Its small head, fangs flickering, quested desperately for a landing place. Its sleek diamond-patterned scales scraped across the metal, a sound almost submerged in the rattle that reverberated tinnily inside the mailbox until the snake fell, sprawling, onto the dusty gravel beside the road.

The rattling sound was louder, then, and he jumped back again, but the snake paid no attention to him. In a looping slither, it was across the road and out of sight among tall weeds before he could still his racing heart.

There was a bundle of batten boards and construction stakes in the back of his truck. He took one of the stakes and approached the mailbox cautiously.

At first he though it was empty, but then the breeze fluttered one corner of a folded piece of paper, far to the back. Using the stick, he brought the paper forward until it rested at the edge of the mailbox opening. He flicked it open without touching it, already knowing what he would find.

The crudely printed block letters, the cheap white typing paper, were the same as before. The message, too, didn't deviate much:

A FRIENDLY WARNING, MACIVER. DON'T TRY TO STOP THE SPRING HILL DEVELOPMENT AGAIN.

The message was very similar to the one he'd ignored twice before. But this time, Ramsey had to admit, the warning had really gotten his attention.

He pushed the note back into the mailbox, touching it only with the construction stake, and got into his truck. The electronically controlled gates opened when he beeped his private code from the little key-chain activator the security expert had given him. After his truck went through, the gates slid shut again.

Thoughtfully, he drove up to the house, trying to summon the rush of pride he felt whenever he saw it again. This house was his sanctum, the place he'd made only for himself after Mary Ellen left. It was a calm, quiet oasis that kept him from ever getting too stressed out. The real reason for all the security was his sense of outrage when it had been violated by the first two notes. It was like finding graffiti on a work of art. He'd protected it as best he could, trying to hold on to the serenity, but now it had been breached again.

This time he saw it with the eyes of a stranger, and was shaken by doubt. The spare arrangement of cubes and rectangles, sheathed with stone-colored stucco, with only a few shadowy window recesses facing the road, harked back, despite its modern, stripped-down design, to the Spanish style that had been the first European architectural influence in California. But now he wondered if it was too stark. It had seemed sensible to surround the place with a drought-resistant swath of river stones, but with the lushness of Alma's Victorian garden fresh in his mind, the landscaping seemed less austere than barren. In this critical mood, even the front door of massive, iron-studded wood seemed heavy and out of scale.

Irritably he shrugged off his apprehensions. He had promised himself that the notes wouldn't affect him, that he would certainly follow his conscience. One scared rattler in his mailbox wouldn't stop him from opposing a development that was at best irresponsible, probably illegal, and at worst criminally greedy. But it had shaken him. That was all that was the matter. He was disturbed, and he didn't like it. Whoever was sending those letters—and he had a couple of good ideas about who it was—wouldn't get any satisfaction out of it.

"I'm just hungry," he told himself, inspecting his own refrigerator without really seeing anything. Finally he registered the cold air on his midsection and took out the ingredients for his lunch. Munching flank steak and salsa without really tasting it, he filled a grocery bag with mineral water, fruit, cheeses and crackers, and a few of his homemade fudge bars. Then he rummaged in his desk for a fresh manila envelope and a pair of tongs.

He wouldn't back off. But he wasn't stupid.

FRANK ALVEREZ GREETED Ramsey with his usual beaming smile, standing up behind the chief of police's desk in Dusty Springs' ancient city hall building. "Ramsey, good to see you! You come to drool over the trophy? Sponsor another team next year, amigo. Maybe you'll get to keep it for a while."

Ramsey gave a perfunctory glance at the extravagant trophy in the corner, topped with a silvered baseball mitt that cupped an actual ball. "I wanted to show you something, Frank."

"Oh, official visit. I see." Frank sat back down, waving Ramsey into a chair beside the desk. "Someone been stealing from the construction sites again?"

"No." Ramsey produced the tongs that had mystified the dispatcher in the outer office, and opened the manila envelope. "I haven't touched this at all." He used the tongs to pull out the note and put it on the desk in front of Frank, who looked at him quizzically before bending to read the letter.

Ramsey put the tongs down, feeling a little silly. Frank looked at the letter for a moment, then at him.

"You've gotten others?"

"Two others." Ramsey told him about the other notes. "This one was in the mailbox, underneath a rattler."

Frank raised his eyebrows. "Exciting for you." He looked closer. "Were you bitten?"

"No. The snake was more afraid of me than I was of it." Ramsey didn't want to think about that one moment of total terror....

Frank looked back down at the note. "Everybody knows how to write an anonymous letter these days, thanks to movies and mystery novels," he said sadly. "Everybody knows to wear gloves, too. Even the snake—I think the idea probably came out of a book. But I'll send it through, anyway."

"Thanks, Frank." Ramsey got up, and Frank scowled at him.

"Is that all you're going to say? This counts as attempted murder, if you want to swear out a complaint. Don't you want some protection?"

"Could you give it to me?"

Frank thought for a minute. "No," he said, finally. "Not unless you want to spend your time in a nice cozy cell. That's pretty safe."

"No, thanks." Ramsey tried to stuff the tongs into his pocket, but the handles stuck out. "I just wanted you to know about it—in case anything happens."

Frank jumped up. "Do you know who's responsible for this?" The words came out rather reluctantly, and Ramsey cocked an eyebrow at him.

"I can make a couple of guesses. How about you, Frank?"

Frank shrugged. "I don't want to guess," he said in a burst of candor. "It could all be very awkward."

"You're damned tooting." Ramsey paused, his hand on the doorway. "Maybe I shouldn't have told you, gotten you into it."

Frank looked shocked. "It's my job," he said with offended dignity. "Naturally, if the choice is between doing my job and losing it, I'll do it." He smiled at Ramsey. "Then, of course, I'll lose it. So please, try to keep a low profile, amigo. For all of us."

"Right." Ramsey left the building, absently pulling the tongs out of his pocket and clicking them together as he walked down the steps. Had it done any good at all to go to Frank? What could he do, after all? There was no evidence of wrongdoing, with only his word about the snake. In fact, it hadn't been an effective attack, if an attack it was. What could anyone do to him here in Dusty Springs, where he knew everyone? He glanced around the sleepy main street before climbing into his truck, and saw a couple who'd been clients of his the year before, when he'd rebuilt their garage. They looked at the tongs in his hand with interest. He tossed them into the grocery bag, returned the couple's friendly waves and started the engine.

Driving down the main street, he counted the little businesses that were healthy. He wanted them to stay that way. One reason why he was making a pest of himself about the Spring Hill development was precisely because he loved Dusty Springs, and didn't want to see its commercial vitality drained. He didn't want it to turn into another faceless commuter village, like so many of the little towns around Sacramento.

Since it was on his mind, he drove straight through the downtown and out a couple of miles toward the interstate highway that cut a line through the farming land east of town. There were a lot of pretty spots around Dusty Springs, but one of the prettiest was Spring Hill, famous to all the kids in town as the place where you waded in the sparkling creek when you were little, hunting for crawdads, and returned to drive up to the top and park in the overlook when you were old enough.

The old oaks that grew in dignified clusters shaded the ground; the grass stayed green here longer in the spring than anywhere else, thanks to the water and the groves of trees. It was a lovely place, still wild despite encroaching civilization. Once he'd seen a fox, right at dusk, as he'd pedaled home on his bike. Once he'd camped with Jon, just the two of them, scaring themselves silly with ghost stories and then being scared in turn by mysterious noises, until they'd realized the whispers originated with a high school couple looking for privacy.

Ramsey drove to the top, along the twisty road, and parked the truck. He walked over to one of the picnic tables that had been there so long its top was a mass of carved names and dates. From this vantage point he could see the whole eastern side of the town, the feed store at one end of main street, the hardware store at the other. He could also see Alma's house, on a lower hill to the north. There was a tiny red dot in the driveway; Mary Ellen was back from lunch.

Ramsey drove down the hill, frowning to himself while he carefully negotiated the winding road. It wasn't just for his memories of youthful adventure that he wanted to save Spring Hill from the threatened development. It was for the whole town of Dusty Springs, still intact despite a recent infusion of commuter residents. The commuters worked and shopped in Sacramento, instead of spending their money in the local stores. They were a welcome addition to the tax base, but didn't make much more of a contribution to the town. He had ideas himself about how development could be handled, and it didn't include chewing up the special places around town so that outsiders could benefit.

He thought about his possible adversaries all the way back to Aunt Alma's house. But his thoughts changed when he pulled up behind Mary Ellen's truck.

He sat there, looking at the house as he had that morning, and this time he admitted that it was a pretty nice old place. He didn't relish the idea of digging out a new foundation under it, or knocking off all that rotten plaster, or coping with new wiring and plumbing. But Mary Ellen had a point about it. Like Spring Hill, it was a part of Dusty Springs—had been since being built by a prosperous lumber-mill owner in the last decade of the previous century. It had been the town showpiece then—the most modern, up-to-date place in Dusty Springs.

Indeed, the old MacIver house still retained a sense of benevolent dignity. He wouldn't want it despoiled, any more than he'd want his aunt trundled off to a studio apartment at some retirement home.

Ramsey picked up his paper bag of leftovers and started up the front walk. There wasn't much point in bellyaching about it. He was stuck with the kind of work he'd sworn never to do again. He and Mary Ellen had broken up after tackling a fixer-upper, but this time, at least, things could never be as bad as they had been. In fact, they were speaking to each other for the first time in five years. That was an improvement, he guessed. Of course, so far Mary Ellen wasn't saying anything he wanted to hear.

But wasn't that just a matter of time? Ramsey had an uneasy feeling, as he crossed the front porch, that to further improve relations between them, much more would be involved than time. He himself, for instance, might be required to contribute something— a willingness to listen, for instance—something which he hadn't bothered to do in their previous relationship. In the old days, he'd paid more attention to their compatibility in the sack than he had to building a permanent relationship.

That much had changed, anyway. He took a deep breath, standing in front of the screen door, and hoped he wouldn't totally alienate her, or make a jackass of himself. Not that he didn't wonder if they still could make that sexy magic between them. He remembered wistfully how it had felt to wake up next to her in bed, the way her eyelids had seemed so fragile, closed over those big green-blue eyes, the feeling it had given him in the pit of his stomach when her hand had tightened on his.

"MacIver, you're a sap," he told himself ruthlessly. He was working with Mary Ellen, not mooning over her. Best get on with it.

It wasn't until his hand was on the door that one particular problem occurred to him.

Mary Ellen had nothing to do with his vendetta against the developers of Spring Hill. But to many in town, it might look as though he and Mary Ellen were getting back together. Would someone who wanted to get at him try to strike through her? Was he putting Mary Ellen in danger?

He froze, his hand on the screen door, letting that horrible idea percolate through him. Then he relaxed. So far the jokers who were trying to scare him were playing softball. The snake in his mailbox was a bit of an escalation, he had to admit, but it wasn't likely to have killed him.

"I wish I was living here," he thought, and was surprised at the thought. He had no desire to leave his comfortable home, where everything worked perfectly, and live in a place that was scheduled for partial demolition in the next few weeks. But if his actions were going to put Mary Ellen in danger, there was no point in urging her to move in with him. So far, the trouble, what there was of it, had been at his place. He would have to move into Aunt Alma's place.

"She wouldn't come to my place, anyway," he muttered. She'd made her feelings clear. No one would dare harm her, he told himself decisively, still bothered by a lingering doubt. But if anything threatened, he would be sleeping down the hall from the tower bedroom, no matter what she said.

Shrugging, he tried to put the snake incident behind him. He'd done what he could, and he couldn't in good conscience obey his anonymous correspondents. Anyway, there was no point in stopping his efforts now.

In the meantime, there was work to be done. He opened the screen door and went into Aunt Alma's house.

CHAPTER THREE

HE COULD HEAR Mary Ellen laughing before he got down the hall. Someone was with her.

Ramsey strode to the kitchen, his body tight with apprehension. He wanted to believe that whoever was with Mary Ellen was no threat to her safety, or she wouldn't be laughing. But it didn't really follow. She might not realize who the enemy was until it was too late.

The swing door screeched when he pushed it open, and Mary Ellen looked around, a smile still lingering in her eyes. Ramsey was struck by how much she resembled the girl he'd fallen so heavily for years ago. She hadn't been smiling much this morning.

"Hi," she said, gesturing amiably across the table. "Your buddy dropped in to condole with me."

Ramsey glared at his best friend, Jon Hsui, who lounged on the hard kitchen chair as if he planned to stay there the rest of the afternoon.

"Howdy," Jon said, grinning. "You bringing home the bacon, Ramsey?"

"More or less," Ramsey grunted, feeling ridiculously domestic carrying his bag of snacks and drinks. He stood the sack on the kitchen table where it would blot out Jon's view of Mary Ellen. "I don't plan to wreck my stomach lining at the Blue Willow every lunch hour."

Mary Ellen made a face. "I was just there. It hasn't changed, has it?"

"No, not much." Jon moved the sack and re-adjusted his chair, winking at Ramsey as he did so. "I think they're still serving off the same side of beef they had before you moved to Berkeley."

"They're the same vegetables, anyway," Mary Ellen declared. "The salad greens had to be at least five years old."

Ramsey threw a plastic container of carefully washed lettuce into the refrigerator, and arranged bags of carrots and radishes next to it. He added milk, butter, eggs and the tub of leftover cream of spinach soup he'd made a couple of nights ago.

"This is good stuff," Jon told Mary Ellen, grabbing the soup container from him. "Ramsey makes it with his own fair hands. Hidden depths to our boy."

Ramsey gave him a murderous look. "Next time you want some of my special oyster-sauce beef, you can go—whistle," he said meaningfully. "Ditto the fudge bars."

"I take it all back." Jon handed Ramsey the container of soup and grinned. "Just because you've turned into the Chef of the West doesn't mean you've lost your manly vigor. I won't tease you anymore."

"The fudge bars are that good?" Mary Ellen still smiled, but there was a tinge of sarcasm in her voice. "I don't remember Ramsey making sweet things for me."

Folding the grocery bag, Ramsey stared at her, letting his eyes feast on her thick, fine, shiny hair, her big, frosty eyes. "I was just learning then, babe. Now I really know how."

Mary Ellen's eyes darkened with anger, and Jon applauded lightly. "This will be better than a tennis match," he crowed. "Too bad I can't stay and watch."

"You're actually going to get some work done?" Ramsey glanced over Jon's immaculate business suit, his dark red tie and discreetly striped white shirt. "Your dad will die of shock."

"He sent me on business." Jon shook his head reprovingly at Ramsey. "Why else would I be here, bandying words with my former co-worker and my best buddy?" He swept both of them with his ironical gaze, and Ramsey knew his friend was subtly suggesting that Ramsey get on the stick and grab Mary Ellen before she could get away again.

"Aunt Alma told me you were vice president now, Jon," Mary Ellen said with genuine enthusiasm. "That's wonderful." She shot a look at Ramsey. "I know you worked hard for it, too."

"You'll never get Ramsey to believe that." Jon reached out for the bottle of mineral water Ramsey had just taken from the refrigerator, and with a show of reluctance Ramsey gave it to him. "He thinks no one's really working unless they're covered with sawdust and caulk."

"So what did the golden boy of the Springview Bank come to say?" Ramsey got out two more bottles of mineral water, handing one to Mary Ellen. She raised her eyebrows in surprise, but accepted the drink. Ramsey wanted to keep looking at her, but he turned away to smile in spite of himself at Jon. Any other time he would have been glad to see his friend, if only to bring him up to date on the trouble that had been waiting in his mailbox. But he didn't want to talk about that in front of Mary Ellen.

"I'm here to fill you both in about your construction account." Jon lifted a briefcase from the floor and opened it, bringing out a sheaf of papers and a file folder. "Mrs. Mac arranged it in the form of a loan, mainly for tax purposes, I understand."

"Did you talk to her?" Ramsey sat at the table, too, giving Jon a puzzled look. "You knew what she was planning, and didn't say anything to me?"

"It could have happened that way." For once Jon wasn't laughing. "I wouldn't have told you if she'd asked me not to. But I just assumed you knew all about it. You always said you wanted to bring the place up to code, and I figured she'd finally agreed."

Ramsey nodded. "Okay, you're excused."

Jon's smile came back, and he turned to Mary Ellen. "Your aunt requested both of your names on the account. Does that mean you and Ramsey have patched things up?"

Mary Ellen snorted, and Ramsey broke in before she could broadcast her true feelings about him. "We're just working together, Jon," he said. "Like cousins."

"Kissing cousins?" Jon caught Ramsey's eye and cleared his throat. "Well," he went on, "I can just leave all this stuff with you. It's pretty obvious, and Mary Ellen will be able to explain anything you don't grasp, Ramsey."

It was Ramsey's turn to snort. "A bunch of gobbledygook," he said, flipping through the pages of the loan documents. "Why you can't say things in plain English—"

"It's very clear," Mary Ellen said with a patronizing smile. "Thanks, Jon. How are things at the bank?"

"Flora's still there. She had a baby."

"Really? And what about that one teller—the shy guy—"

They were off into a flood of reminiscence, and Ramsey sipped his drink and watched them. The animation on Mary Ellen's face when she talked to Jon was a far cry from the tight, controlled expression she wore around him. How he wanted to bring that glow to her face, to have her look at him the way she used to, when he would come to pick her up and she'd run down the stairs as if she couldn't wait to be in his arms. But then she'd been infatuated with him. He'd figured it all out after she'd gone; her infatuation had not been very deep, or she wouldn't have gone so soon.

He came out of his reverie to find Jon on his feet, briefcase in hand, regarding him quizzically. "You all right, Ramsey?" Mary Ellen was looking at him, too.

"I'm fine." He thumped his bottle down onto the table and stood. "I'll walk you to your car."

"I didn't drive over." Jon studied his expression. "You can give me a ride back if you want."

Mary Ellen looked from one of them to the other, and Ramsey could read the suspicion on her face. "Nothing to do with the house," he said, wanting to stroke that soft, bright hair. "Guy talk, that's all."

Mary Ellen relaxed a little. "Have a nice talk, then," she said, smiling mostly at Jon, but Ramsey got the tail end of it. "And get back soon, Ramsey. We've got quite a few lists to make."

"Right." He followed Jon down the hall, surprised to find in himself a little core of warmth at knowing that she was going to be waiting for him, even if it was just to go over plans.

Jon pushed the piles of paper into the center of the truck's big bench seat and sat down, looking as much at his ease as he had in the kitchen. "So what is it? Did you get another one of those letters?"

Ramsey stared at him. "How did you know?"

Jon shrugged. "You looked kind of shook up. It takes a lot to spook you. What did it say this time?"

"It wasn't what it said." Ramsey spoke slowly. "It was the way it was delivered." While driving to the bank he told Jon about the snake, and for once his friend was jolted out of his usual self-possession.

"You might have been hurt!" He stared at Ramsey. "This has gone beyond a joke."

"I took the note to Frank Alverez." Ramsey pulled up in front of the bank, the most imposing building on Main Street. "He wasn't really hopeful about tracking anyone down."

"What will you do?"

"I don't know." Ramsey shrugged. "Jon, do you think it's dangerous for Mary Ellen to be staying alone at the big house? What if they decide to get at me through her? I worry that I should make her go back to Berkeley."

Jon thought about it and shook his head. "The snake probably wouldn't have killed you—rattler bites respond to antivenin. I think they just mean to frighten you. Why don't you tell Mary Ellen about it and let her make up her own mind?"

"Because she might decide to stay, which I don't want if there's any danger." Ramsey shrugged. "She doesn't want to move in with me but I've got enough security to withstand an army." And if Mary Ellen returned to Berkeley, they wouldn't be able to explain to Aunt Alma why she was breaking her part of the bar-

gain; no old lady with a dickey heart needed to hear
that her nephew was being threatened with rattlers.

"I think you're borrowing trouble, pal, but why
don't you install some security at Mrs. Mac's?" Jon
opened the truck door and sprang onto the pavement
in front of the bank. His mischievous smile was back
in place. "You don't need to worry about Mary Ellen.
It'll be all over town in no time that you two are just
working together. Won't be long before there's a ver-
itable parade of us lust-crazed bachelors heading up
Mrs. Mac's sidewalk."

Ramsey gave his best buddy a sharp look. "You'd
try to make time with Mary Ellen? Behind my back?"

"Believe me, if I thought it would do any good I'd
do it right in front of your face." Jon stared back at
Ramsey, serious again. "She's posted the Not Available signs, you know. Friendly, nice, but not interested."

"I suppose you could tell all that from one little
conversation," Ramsey growled. "I didn't see those
hypothetical signs of yours."

"You wouldn't." Jon grinned again. "Maybe
they're not there for you. Or maybe those No Tres-
passing signs you've staked out around her hide
them."

"Mary Ellen is free to see anyone she wants,"
Ramsey said, trying to sound as if he meant it. He'd
always assumed she was dating in Berkeley—maybe
even finding her soul mate, though she'd never
brought anyone to Dusty Springs for Aunt Alma to
inspect. But now that she was here, he realized he
wouldn't relish the idea of her dating—not even Jon,
presumably a friend of both of them.

"Right. Sure." Jon slammed the truck door. "If I thought you really meant that, I'd enroll you in Marisa Connell's psychotherapy group." He leaned in through the window, staring at Ramsey. "This is your chance, man. If you blow it this time, there won't be another."

"I know that," Ramsey growled. "So get out of here and let me get on with it, already."

Jon stepped up onto the sidewalk and waved him away. "Go to it, Young Lochinvar," he shouted, much to the amusement of several passersby. With an unwilling smile, Ramsey drove away.

He stopped briefly at the spec house his crew was working on to check on their progress and see how soon he could pull some of the crew away. Wally Hurtado, the foreman, met him with a lugubrious face and a long list of problems, and Ramsey resigned himself to sticking around for a little while. He knew Mary Ellen was expecting him back. But this sort of thing took precedence. She would understand.

MARY ELLEN HAD ALREADY started the materials list when the front doorbell rang. She glanced at the clock, surprised Ramsey wasn't back yet, and went down the hall. Against the oval-shaped panel of beveled glass at the front door, she saw the looming outline of a man's head and shoulders, and the caution born of living in a city for the past five years had her stepping out onto the front porch, pulling the door shut behind her.

The man who waited on the porch appeared harmless, though. He looked vaguely familiar. His navy suit was a little rumpled, and the collar on his crisp pink shirt was open beneath a tie pulled askew. There was a folder tucked under his arm. She wrote him off as a salesman, by the practiced way he shook her hand.

"Good afternoon," he said, his voice soft and pleasant. "Is Mrs. MacIver at home?"

"She's not available just now." Mary Ellen scrutinized the man carefully. "Aren't you Arnold Hengeman?"

"Yes, I am." Arnold looked at her closely. "It's Mary Ellen Saunderson, isn't it? I didn't recognize you at first. Quite some time since you were here."

"Yes, it is. Aunt Alma told me you'd been elected to the county board of supervisors." Mary Ellen ignored Arnold's glance past her to the closed front door. It was a warm day, and though her aunt might have offered a local politician a glass of iced tea, Mary Ellen had been at a party with Arnold Hengeman once, just after she'd started working at the bank, and she still remembered having to fend him off outside the bathroom. She and her friend Lenore had christened him Amorous Arnold after that.

"It was quite an honor, having the well-being of Dusty Springs entrusted to me," Arnold assured her.

He wasn't bad-looking, Mary Ellen reflected, though his pale hair had receded a little more from his perspiration-dappled forehead. He now wore aviator glasses, and they became him, she thought; they shielded his rather beady eyes from immediate notice. He was a little wider in the waist, although not by any means running to fat.

"There's an election coming up soon, and I'm just out assuring my constituents that I'd be glad to keep representing their interests on a county level," he said, patting his forehead with a crumpled handkerchief.

"You're not going to run for the state Assembly?" Mary Ellen wasn't quite sure what to say. She wasn't registered to vote in Dusty Springs; in fact, it had been the furthest thing from her mind.

Arnold preened a little. "Certainly when I've gained a little more experience, made a few more contacts—I like to think that I could be of service to a wider audience." He looked at the front door again. "Is Mrs. MacIver in? I'd like to give her one of my brochures."

"I'll see that she gets it," Mary Ellen said, reluctant to let Amorous Arnold know that she was alone in the house. "She's a little under the weather these days."

"Nothing serious, I hope?" Arnold's words were polite, although she could see the avid interest in his eyes. Wanting gossip to spread around, she surmised. Well, if he began talking about Aunt Alma in the neighborhood, he'd probably find out soon enough that she was temporarily away.

"Not really." Mary Ellen made her reply vague. "Do you think there'll be early rain?"

Arnold joined her at the top of the steps, scrutinizing the clouds that massed slowly in the west. "I hope not," he muttered. "Got to cover the rest of this block today."

"We need the rain," Mary Ellen said. "Thanks for stopping by, Arnold."

"Nice to see you again," he said, squeezing her hand with far more warmth than he'd shown before. "Are you spending some time in town now?"

"A little while." She extricated her hand, barely restraining herself from wiping it on her jeans.

"You'll have to come to a little gathering I've planned," he said importantly, fishing another paper out of his folder and pressing it into her hand. "Very important matters for the future of Dusty Springs."

"We'll see." Nothing, she thought darkly, would get her to any occasion where she'd have to watch Amorous Arnold work the crowd.

He took himself off at last, and she gazed down the street for a minute to see if Ramsey would show up. He was nowhere in sight, though. Sitting on the porch steps, she thought idly about Arnold. He and Ramsey had been friends, or at least fellow roisterers, during their high school years. She'd heard that from Aunt Alma, who hadn't approved of Ramsey hanging around with "that Hengeman boy." Then there'd been some trouble, right before graduation, and although Arnold Hengeman had slithered out of it somehow, Ramsey MacIver had ended up threatened with reform school. It had taken all her aunt's clout and persuasion to get him the alternative sentence of the Youth Conservation Corps. It had all happened after Mary Ellen's mother had remarried and relocated them to Seattle, so she didn't have the rights of it. But she knew that Aunt Alma would never have voted Arnold Hengeman into office, no matter what he thought.

She started to get up, and realized that she still held the brochure Arnold had pressed into her hand. She would have crumpled it up, but the bold type on the front held her attention. "Luxurious Spring Hill will put Dusty Springs on the map!" it proclaimed, with a drawing of a big house, evidently designed by someone who was enamored of several different architectural styles and couldn't decide which to use:

medieval, Tudor, or ranch. In the background was a distinctive silhouette, and she stared at it in shock. Houses on Spring Hill? Surely that couldn't be!

Ramsey's pickup truck rattled up, parking behind hers, but she paid no attention. She was deep into the brochure's ecstatic descriptions of the benefits of development when Ramsey came up the steps.

"Where did you get that?" He snatched the brochure from her hands unceremoniously.

"Arnold Hengeman was by." Mary Ellen stared at him. "He's running for office or something. What is this about, Ramsey? How can they develop Spring Hill? I thought it was going to be donated to the town as a park after old man Dalhousie dies."

"They won't develop it," he said, yanking the front door open. "Not if I've got anything to say about it." He scowled at her. "You should know better than to let Hengeman in."

"I didn't let him in," she protested, following him down the hall. "He wanted to see Aunt Alma."

"Thinks he can persuade a sick old woman to support him, I suppose." Ramsey threw the crumpled brochure on the kitchen table. "Don't have anything to do with him, Emmy. Promise me."

She drew back at the authority in his voice. "I make my own decisions, Ramsey."

He ran a hand through his hair and gave her a sheepish smile, but she could see the tension simmering in him, just below the surface. "I know you do," he admitted. "But good old Arnold—he's dangerous. I don't want you to get hurt."

She was amused. "I can take care of myself," she assured him. "I haven't lived in Berkeley for five years without learning how to deal with men like Amorous Arnold."

He laughed, shortly. "If it were only that," he said, with a searching look at her. "Mary Ellen—"

The telephone rang, and Mary Ellen went to answer it, not sorry to have the conversation cut short. If Ramsey was going to start acting like a—a lover or something, giving her orders about who to see and who not to see, working with him would be even more difficult than she'd anticipated.

Mr. Featherstone was on the line. "I just wanted to let you know," he said, in his precise voice, "that I've heard from your aunt. She's settled in well, and the first reports are favorable. She asked me to tell you that all systems might not be go, but at least they haven't went."

Mary Ellen chuckled appreciatively and gave Mr. Featherstone a message for her aunt. She turned back to Ramsey, ready to give him a piece of her mind, but the phone rang again.

"Lenore! I was just thinking about you. How did you know I'd be in town?"

Lenore's warm voice floated over the telephone wire. "Ramsey told me the other evening. He said you might be around for quite a spell, and I had a letter from Mrs. Mac asking me to look after the garden for her. Is it true? Are you going to stay this time?"

"For a while." Mary Ellen glanced at Ramsey, and was surprised to see an approving smile on his face. "Can you come up this evening? We can talk about it then."

"I'd love to. I'm just taking a short break right now from putting out an immense hedge of *pittasporum eugenioides,* and I want to work right up to dark on it. How about eight or nine tonight?''

"That's great." Mary Ellen hung up the phone, excited over the prospect of a really good talk with Lenore.

"So is Lenore coming over?" Ramsey smiled. "It'll be great to see her. She likes my fudge bars; maybe I'll whip up a fresh batch for her."

"That would be nice, but she's not coming until this evening. You'll be home by then." Mary Ellen felt deflated, suddenly. She told herself that it was just because Ramsey showed signs of hanging around when Lenore came that evening, and she wanted her friend to herself. "Now, what were you going to say about this Spring Hill trouble?"

Ramsey looked at her, stroking his chin. "Nothing, really," he said, turning away. "It'll keep, anyway. We'd better get on those lists."

"Right." Mary Ellen joined him at the kitchen table. There was enough work ahead of them without having to cope with local politics. Ramsey had always been more interested in that stuff than she was, and he didn't seem particularly alarmed about the possibility that Spring Hill would be developed. She loved it herself—there were many happy memories bound up in it—and she knew it had always been a special place for him. If he said the development wouldn't happen, it probably wouldn't.

She showed Ramsey the lists she'd already made, and they started reviewing the plans.

Ramsey was full of ideas and suggestions, and Mary Ellen needed to keep her wits about her to stay on top of the discussion. But when Ramsey began to draw up a rough materials list, she found an unwelcome thought intruding.

"So when did you make fudge bars for Lenore?" She hadn't meant to blurt out the question, but since it was out, she inspected her fingernails, trying to look casual.

Ramsey looked up from his paper. "We've done some stuff together. She's one of the few women in this town who doesn't talk everlastingly about what a good homemaker she'd be and how cute babies are."

"No, Lenore wouldn't do that." Mary Ellen tried to laugh, wondering what was wrong with her. She didn't want Ramsey herself—most definitely not. But she didn't want her best friend Lenore to be hoodwinked into a relationship with him. "She's always been different."

"You bet." Ramsey's voice was entirely too enthusiastic, Mary Ellen thought. "We got together when she landscaped a project of mine." He shook his head. "Wish I'd known to ask her about my place. It could use a little less austerity."

"Lenore's not really into austere," Mary Ellen agreed. Her friend was loving, expansive, generous to a fault—just the kind of woman to feel sorry for Ramsey and put up with his nonsense. "You and she must be pretty compatible."

Ramsey stared at her, and she had time to realize how inane her remark must have sounded.

"She's a nice woman," he said dismissively, turning back to his list. "Are we framing the knee wall with pressure-treated or redwood?"

"Redwood," Mary Ellen said promptly. "It'll be off the ground, and I don't like using PT if I can help it. Those chemicals are bad for the environment, you know.''

Ramsey ran a hand through his hair. "Maybe so, but there's nothing better for a mudsill. I take it we can use it there?''

"Fine," Mary Ellen conceded. "Shall I call the house movers, or will you?''

"House movers?" He shook his head. "We don't need movers for this little job. You and I can jack it up and trench out the new foundation without movers. Save a bundle, too.''

Mary Ellen stared at him. "Jack the house up by ourselves? You must be crazy.''

"It's easy." He smiled patronizingly. "I'll show you how. Don't worry. A little demo, a little digging, and we'll be ready to replace that foundation by the end of the week.''

He pushed back his chair as he spoke, getting up from the table and stretching. Mary Ellen, her mouth open to object, was silenced by the sheer physical grandeur of that stretch.

"Four-thirty," he observed. "I gotta go talk to some people at my job sites. What say we start that demo work bright and early tomorrow?''

Mary Ellen came to attention. "We'll start tomorrow," she agreed, "but we're not going to jack the house ourselves. That's a job for a qualified subcontractor, and I know just the people.''

Ramsey stared at her. "At least let me explain my ideas," he said at last. "Then, if you still want to call in the movers, I'll agree.''

"Fine." It was a good compromise, Mary Ellen knew, but part of her was miffed because it had come

from Ramsey and not from her, the well-known queen
of compromise and consensus.

"See you tomorrow." Ramsey gave her a long look,
then strode down the hall. She sat where she was, listening to the front door slam shut behind him, and
wondered at her let-down feeling. She was used to
having evenings alone in Berkeley. Of course, she
wasn't usually home until eight or so, and that meant
there was just time for her to have a shower and a
quick frozen dinner and do some paperwork before
falling into bed, exhausted.

She didn't feel exhausted. She felt keyed up, in need
of hard work. "I'll go to the market," she decided,
talking to herself to fill some of the echoing quiet of
the big old house. "Who needs homemade brownies?
Lenore will be glad enough for the ones Sara Lee
makes."

Thoughts of her friend were cheering. She would get
a good supply of frozen dinners, and that evening
Lenore would explain the status of her unlikely
friendship with Ramsey.

"Everything's going to be fine," she muttered,
grabbing her tote bag from the hall tree. "Smooth as
silk."

The floorboards creaked under her footsteps. It was
ridiculous to feel that an inanimate structure consist-
ing of wood and glass could communicate. But if it
could, Aunt Alma's house was surely radiating an ir-
ritating combination of smugness and satisfaction.

LENORE DIDN'T COMPLAIN about the store-bought
brownies. They sat on the veranda, on the ancient
porch swing, and ate the sticky things right out of their
foil container.

"So, how's the drought affecting your business?" Mary Ellen crunched a walnut and regarded her friend curiously. Lenore was tall and willowy, with thick, curly chestnut hair that lent her an ethereal look. Her fair skin owed its freshness to the liberal use of hats and sunblock. Her gray eyes, shadowed with dark lashes, could be reserved and inscrutable, and clients sometimes thought her quiet and standoffish. But with her friends she relaxed, revealing a pixielike sense of humor and a wry wit. She had spent several years in Los Angeles, moving back to Dusty Springs just before Mary Ellen had left five years ago. She never spoke of her experiences in the city.

"Not so bad." Lenore licked a little chocolate off her finger. "I couldn't afford to buy much equipment when I started my business, and that turned out to be a good thing. The landscaping firms with big inventory loans to pay off are really suffering. I just rent what I need, so I can make it from job to job."

"I guess there's not so much landscaping going on." Mary Ellen inhaled the scent of the late roses that swathed the veranda, feeling vaguely sorry for those without gardens.

Lenore shook her head. "A surprising number of people are tearing out their old yards for new, drought-tolerant plantings. I encourage that, of course." She grinned at Mary Ellen and took another brownie. "These are good."

"As good as Ramsey's fudge bars?" Mary Ellen hadn't meant to mention Ramsey, but his name had popped right out of her mouth.

Lenore raised her eyebrows, a smile edging up the corners of her wide mouth. "Ramsey's fudge bars," she said deliberately, "are out of this world."

Mary Ellen sniffed. "I don't remember him being any great shakes in the kitchen."

"He took it up after you moved out," Lenore said, running a finger around the edge of the container to scoop up some frosting. "I remember bumping into him at the Food Mart when he was badgering the meat guy about the best way to cook a roast."

"You've certainly gotten buddy-buddy," Mary Ellen said, eyeing her friend. "How did that happen?"

"We're friends," Lenore said quietly, after a moment. "Not lovers, no matter what you might have heard." The light that shone from the living room onto the veranda left her face in shadow. "He was hurt when you left, and although I totally sympathize with you, I discovered after talking to him a little that he wasn't such a bad guy, for a friend."

"He's hell as a lover," Mary Ellen said, trying to disguise her warning as mere comment.

"He was then, for you." Mary Ellen peered closely through the gloom, wondering if that was a smile she heard in Lenore's voice. "He's changed, Emmy. Why don't you give him a chance?"

"He doesn't want one," Mary Ellen said, and added quickly, "and neither do I. I don't need romantic complications in my life right now." She took a deep breath. "Why don't *you* give him a chance?"

Lenore laughed outright, a golden peal, and set the swing going with one slender foot. "He doesn't want a chance with me, any more than I do with him. Ramsey MacIver is only interested in one woman."

Mary Ellen snorted again. "It's academic, anyway, because we both agreed to work together only as colleagues," she said finally.

"Are you seeing someone in Berkeley?" Lenore put the question to her idly, scooping up yet another glob of excess frosting.

Mary Ellen wished she'd led a more active social life, so she could brag about it. But she had to answer her friend honestly. "Not really," she said, sighing. "I'm so tired when I get home from work, the last thing I want to do is go out. I have a shower, microwave dinner, and watch TV while I eat it. The last date I was on was—" she counted on her fingers "—three months ago. The guy sold windows. He seemed nice. His windows were top quality. I spent the whole evening listening to tales of his great salesmanship, how he could talk anyone into anything." She chuckled. "He was so pissed when he couldn't talk me into bed, you can't imagine. Never heard from him again, and our window order arrived late, in the bargain."

Lenore laughed, too. "There must be some great guys in that teeming urban environment," she insisted. "Why don't you meet a few?"

Mary Ellen shrugged. "I'm just not interested. If a marvelous man dropped into my lap, didn't get in my way while I was working, and never made any demands on me, I'd think about it."

"Some relationship that would be," Lenore grumbled.

"So if you're so expert about it, why don't you have a fellow on the string?" Mary Ellen took the last blob of icing. It was beginning to make her feel a little sick, but she couldn't stay away from it.

"You're right." Lenore sighed. "I should be thinking about the rest of my life. I've got seven or eight years on you, and I'd like to have a family before it's too late." She stared through the branches of the climbing rose bush that blanketed the veranda. "It's been pleasant having Ramsey for companionship because he's just what you described—no demands, no conflicts. I'm not willing to go looking for love, either. That's a good way to find real trouble."

Mary Ellen opened her mouth to probe, and then closed it again. Lenore valued her privacy highly. She wouldn't trespass, no matter how curious she was.

"Why don't you hogtie Ramsey, then?" She crumpled up the empty foil container. "Maybe he's ready to settle down."

"Maybe he is," Lenore murmured, "but not with me. You can relax, Mary Ellen. I'm not going to back Ramsey into a domestic corner."

"I never thought you would," Mary Ellen stammered. "I mean, he seems fond of you—"

Lenore stopped the swing and turned to face her. "How many times must I tell you? We're friends, that's all. Just like you and Jon are friends. Ramsey doesn't give the impression of a man looking for love," Lenore added, turning away again. "To me, it seems he's just waiting, waiting for something he's already decided is going to happen."

"You think he's waiting for me," Mary Ellen said pettishly. She got up from the swing so quickly that it bumped forward and hit the back of her legs. "But he's not. And I'm not interested in him romantically. Would you like some lemonade?"

"Sure," Lenore said. Mary Ellen got the impression she was laughing again, but when they entered the kitchen, her face was sober.

Jon Hsui found them there a few minutes later, sipping frosty glasses of lemonade. "That looks good. Made in the shade?"

Mary Ellen poured him a glass. "Made in the freezer compartment at the Food Mart, I'm afraid. What's happening?"

Jon stretched his legs out under the table and took a big gulp. "Not much," he said frankly. "This place is still dead as a doornail in the evenings. But there are a few lovely ladies around." He raised his lemonade glass to each of them in turn.

Lenore and Mary Ellen solemnly clinked glasses with him. "To small towns!" Mary Ellen smiled at her two friends. "Long may they roll up the sidewalks at night."

"Hear, hear." Ramsey's deep voice sounded from the back door. He strolled in, taking the last chair at the table and straddling it. "Heard you'd be over tonight," he said, smiling amiably at Lenore. "Did you miss my fudge bars?"

"Mary Ellen had brownies," Lenore said, wrinkling her nose at him. Jon looked around expectantly, and she slapped his hand. "We already ate them all."

"Tragic," Jon said, smiting his forehead. "I was all set for some chocolate."

"I've got some at my place. Come on out." Ramsey looked at them all as he issued his invitation.

"I just got here," Jon complained. "But maybe tomorrow, okay?"

"Sure," said Ramsey. "My place, tomorrow." He gazed the longest at Mary Ellen, she was sure.

The others murmured their agreement, but Mary Ellen was silent. She wouldn't go, she knew that already. She had told herself once that she would never set foot in a house owned by Ramsey MacIver again. And though she felt a certain amount of curiosity about his new place, she had no intention of breaking that vow.

He looked a little disappointed, as though he was waiting for her to accept his casual invitation. But Lenore mentioned something that had happened on her landscaping job that day, Jon topped it with an anecdote from the bank, and the moment was gone. Ramsey joined easily in the conversation; if he'd been disappointed, it hadn't been for long.

Mary Ellen looked around the old kitchen, its single ceiling light bathing everything in a golden glow. It was as if she'd never left, as if the intervening Berkeley years hadn't happened. She'd grown up with Jon and Ramsey; Lenore had changed from being her baby-sitter when she was little and into a friend when she grew older. Only her aunt was missing to make the circle complete.

Please, let her be all right. Let her be here in the kitchen next spring, making us all laugh at one of her jokes, Mary Ellen breathed, before rejoining the conversation.

CHAPTER FOUR

"I OUGHT TO have my head examined."

Mary Ellen let the words out with a grunt of effort, while balancing her half of the framed two-by-four wall on her shoulder. The woman at the other end of the wall nodded. Mary Ellen realized she probably hadn't paid a bit of attention to her boss's diatribe against aunts, men and fate.

"Up we go," Jeanine Wiley said, walking the wall the rest of the way from the floor with little apparent effort. Mary Ellen, pushing up her side, had to admire Jeanine's skill. She couldn't have weighed more than a hundred and twenty. But she knew how to lift when it was necessary. Mary Ellen hadn't worked with a better carpenter in the course of her construction experience.

Except, perhaps, one. One big, trouble-making, macho, condescending—

"Let's get it level," Jeanine said, a faint note of reproof in her voice. Mary Ellen pulled her mind back to the job at hand.

Jeanine used the big level, and when she decreed everything ready, Mary Ellen nailed the bottom plate with the nail gun, and moved the stepladder to nail the top plate against the ceiling. The new wall framed the doorway into what would soon be a palatial new bathroom for a client who had decided her life wouldn't be complete until she was surrounded by marble and gold faucets. To achieve that, she'd sacrificed a small room next to the master bedroom.

"Mrs. Hedstrom is going to have the world's biggest walk-in closet when we're finished," Jeanine said, hitching her tool belt higher on her slender hips.

"She needs it." Mary Ellen glanced around, making sure the client wasn't within earshot. "She's got a shoe collection that rivals Imelda Marcos's."

They enjoyed a comfortable snicker. "So, we can have the shower and the toilet cubicle framed in and maybe even the rough framing for the vanity before quitting time." Jeanine picked up the tape measure and began checking the chalk marks on the floor that delineated where future walls were to go.

Mary Ellen groaned. "I have to get back to Dusty Springs. We're putting the jacks under the house this afternoon so we can start work on the foundation tomorrow."

Jeanine sighed. "You really meant it when you said you wouldn't be much help on this job, didn't you? Oh, well." She managed to smile. "Say hello to Jake for me." Jake Murray ran the house-moving business that Mary Ellen normally used for lifting a house in the air preliminary to foundation work.

"I won't see Jake." Mary Ellen tried to sound jaunty. "We're doing it ourselves."

Jeanine pursed her lips. "You're jacking a big place like that in one afternoon?"

"Easy as pie, according to Ramsey." Mary Ellen had her doubts. Ramsey was inclined, she remembered, to suffer from the contractor's disease of amazing optimism, which meant deadlines were constantly being pushed back because one phase of a project took more time than had been allotted for it. In her opinion, it would take far longer to do the foundation his way than it would have in her way.

"Pie isn't so easy for you, as I recall." Jeanine smothered a laugh, and Mary Ellen had to smile, too, remembering that ill-fated group picnic for which she'd volunteered to make a pie, and the mess she'd ended up with.

"Pie probably is easy for Ramsey, and if he can do it, so can I." She lifted her chin determinedly.

"Okay, Annie Oakley." Jeanine's brown eyes were sympathetic. "You're really letting yourself in for it, aren't you? But while you're horsing around up there, what happens here?"

"I hired you a helper," Mary Ellen said.

"Hazel?" Jeanine looked up from the blueprints she was checking. "She's handy with a hammer."

"Hazel is busy—she won't be free for another month." Mary Ellen fidgeted with the compound square that stuck out from her tool belt. "I had to get someone else. He said he'd show up by noon at the latest."

"A man?" Jeanine's lip curled slightly. "Does this guy understand that I'm the head carpenter?"

"The guy is a grad student at Berkeley, majoring in Victorian literature," Mary Ellen assured her. "I hired him because he looked big and strong. He said he has no problem taking orders from a woman. He's had a couple of summer jobs in construction, done some rough framing."

"A hod carrier." Jeanine sounded pessimistic. "Oh well, at least he's better than no one." She ran her tape measure along one of the two-by-fours that were stacked against the wall. "In the meantime, I could use some help with the shower framing. If you're only going to be here for a little while, let's make the most of it.''

"Yes, boss," Mary Ellen said meekly.

They worked together with the ease born of long association, and a steady economy of movement that might have looked leisurely to an outsider. Jeanine marked the boards and Mary Ellen cut them. They tacked a framework together with the nail gun, making sure each stud was straight. Then they hoisted the wall into place along the chalk mark on the floor. The bathroom walls were nearly finished by the time Oscar Wharton arrived.

Mary Ellen heard his tentative knock and went to let him in. She trudged through Mrs. Hedstrom's elegant living room, staying on the plastic carpet protectors the client had put down between the job site and the front door. Mrs. Hedstrom didn't really like having a remodeling crew in her house. One reason she'd chosen Victorian Visions to do the work was their reputation for neatness.

Oscar stood at the front entrance, bending his head slightly as tall men are inclined to do when confronted with doors. He smiled bashfully at Mary Ellen. "Found it without any trouble, Ms. Saunderson.''

"Call me Mary Ellen," she said briskly, leading the way inside. "Listen, Oscar, stay on these plastic mats when you walk around inside. The client has white carpets.''

"I see." He looked around appreciatively. Mrs. Hedstrom had very nice furniture, Mary Ellen had to admit, even if it seemed a little anemic to her. Pale walls, pale floors, neutral upholstery—the place was so pale it barely existed. She preferred a bit more color, although she was no decorator, as the hodge-podge nature of her apartment in Berkeley testified.

She introduced Oscar to Jeanine and explained the scope of the project. He listened intently, and scrutinized the blueprints as if they actually meant something to him. His manner toward Jeanine was just right, too, an irresistible blend of deference and helpfulness. He raised the framing for the last wall, dividing the newly delineated bathroom from the expanded closet area, with one hand. Jeanine blinked, but her approval was really won when he reached up easily and nailed it into place.

"I guess it's handy to be tall sometimes." Her voice was just a little huffy. Her height—or rather lack of it—was an occasional sore point.

"It has advantages," Oscar admitted cautiously. "But there are times when my size works against me. The last construction job I worked on was in an attic." He rubbed his head. "My skull was sore for days afterward."

Jeanine gave a grudging smile. Mary Ellen was relieved. Harmony among the crew members was important to her. The group of women she called on as subcontractors usually had no problems. She liked working with women; they were neat, conscientious, and they tended to show up when they were supposed to. She hadn't purposefully set out to assemble a female crew, but opportunities for women in the construction business were not exactly limitless, and it had been a pleasure to give work to the competent female subcontractors she'd happened across.

However, Mary Ellen was no chauvinist, and if a man seemed right for any job she had, she hired him.

Oscar, she trusted, would work out well. It was unfortunate she had to throw him in with Jeanine, who'd just undergone a painful separation from her husband and was still taking it out on every man she met.

Mary Ellen could only trust that Jeanine would retain her usual good manners. She brushed some of the sawdust off her jeans. "Betsy and Sue will start tomorrow," she said, referring to the plumber and electrician. "Will you be ready, Jeanine?"

"We'll be finished here by five," Jeanine promised. "All that's left is framing the vanity. You want me to come over tomorrow morning and let them in?"

"That would be great." Mary Ellen smiled at her. "I henceforth decree that you be my foreperson, in charge in my absence."

"I hereby accept, with a commensurate raise in pay." Jeanine bowed, sweeping off her baseball cap, letting loose a long ponytail of shiny brown hair that cascaded down her back.

"Call me if there's any problem," Mary Ellen said, picking up her fanny pack and briefcase. "But I'm sure things will go smoothly. The dry wall guys want to get in next week, and we need to have the plumbing and electrical in place."

"We will." Jeanine shot a look at Oscar. "Little John, here, can help out with the plumbing under the house, since he's good in small places."

Oscar grinned again. "I didn't know women had arcane initiation rites. Thought that was just the macho side of the population."

Mary Ellen hid her own smile. "Well, see you in a few days. Don't kill each other."

Jeanine was staring with measuring eyes at her giant helper. "I'll try not to," she said.

The drive to Dusty Springs took over two hours. Mary Ellen had been up at five that morning to escape the traffic heading into Berkeley, and now she sipped a cola and forced herself to concentrate on the road. There was so much to think about; with one hand she flipped open her briefcase and took out the little voice-activated tape recorder she used for making notes. "On schedule with the Hedstrom job," she spoke into it, giving the date and time. "Materials okay. Plumbing and electrical going in tomorrow."

She'd spent a couple of hours that morning getting in touch with her future clients, putting them off when possible, revising completion dates, and now she gave that information to the tape. "Cancellation on the Shotmeyer project. They took a cheaper bid." Ordinarily this would have caused Mary Ellen some grief, but this once she'd simply breathed a sigh of relief. The Shotmeyers were to have started next week, and they shouldn't have backed out of their agreement, but they hadn't signed their contract yet and Mary Ellen wasn't of a mind to take them to court. They'd probably be sorry in the long run; her bid had been fair. Anyone coming in cheaper was planning to skimp somewhere.

"Postponed the Evanses till after the first of the year." They hadn't minded. Margo Evans had mentioned that they were still saving for their new family room addition, and this would give them more time. And they hadn't really liked the idea of construction going on during Thanksgiving and Christmas.

"Revised the start dates of the Koegel bathroom, the Warner bathroom, and the Montori kitchen over the next three months, so I should be able to keep track of them easier." She didn't want to cancel all her

Berkeley jobs. She'd spent the past four years building her business, but it would only take a few months for it to go down the tubes if she wasn't careful.

She put the tape recorder away. For some reason, she couldn't tape her thoughts about Aunt Alma's house. It wasn't as if she was in charge, anyway. Though her aunt had nominated her chief of design, the structural stuff came first, as Ramsey had pointed out. And he had insisted on making the decision to do the foundation work themselves.

It was his habit, she knew, to forgo subcontractors and handle things like concrete work and stuccoing himself. She figured he did it to give himself a financial edge. Perhaps he needed that edge if his bidding hadn't gotten better. When she'd lived with him, one of his greatest problems as a contractor had been underbidding, cutting his eventual profit to the bone. Another problem was his habit of taking on too much work and trying to juggle clients and completion dates.

Maybe he'd changed. She considered that, taking the Dusty Springs exit, and dismissed it. Some people might change, but not Ramsey. He had that same Scots stubbornness that was bred into the MacIvers. How often had she listened to tales of her uncle, Ramsey's namesake? Alma had deplored his stubbornness, but she'd accepted it as part of him. Ramsey was no different.

Mary Ellen drove the last two miles deep in thought, sparing barely a glance for Spring Hill on her left. It felt amazingly good to be returning to Dusty Springs as an inhabitant, not a visitor. She waved to Ned Purcell, standing in the open door of his hardware store, and to Jon Hsui, returning to the bank after lunch. It was good to see people she knew, even if they were gossiping about her and Ramsey as fast as their tongues could wag.

There was no sign of Ramsey's truck in the driveway. He would be late, of course; he always was. Mary Ellen felt a bit smug at having gotten her business out of the way with such efficiency. She lugged her briefcase and fanny pack into the front hall and dropped them, taking a moment to look around. In another few days, construction would overwhelm the house; things would be taken ruthlessly apart, and not put back together until much work had been accomplished. She didn't really blame Aunt Alma for wanting no part of it.

The gracious, shabby rooms were silent, waiting for the assault. She ran one hand along the mahogany railing of the stairs, thinking how best to protect it from what was to come. The wood was smooth and cool under her hand, and she saw herself at four, watching from the top stair as her devil-may-care cousin slid all the way to the bottom, fast as lightning. She had climbed up on the railing somehow, and then hugged it tightly, paralyzed at seeing the floor of the hall so far below her. "Scaredy cat, scaredy cat," Ramsey had chanted. "Better get down, baby." She'd loosened her grip, little by little, inching down the railing until she bumped the newel post and fell off. She still remembered the pride she felt when Ramsey had helped her up and wiped her nose with the tail of his shirt. "Guess you're not a baby after all," he'd said gruffly.

She tossed her head to dispel the memory, but she knew there was little point to that. The whole house was saturated with memories, and a good portion of them had to do with Ramsey. One of the earliest had been when she was three, at a gathering of grown-ups whose legs formed an impenetrable forest, keeping her away from her mother, whom she could just glimpse reclining on the sofa and sobbing softly into a hand-kerchief. Ramsey, she supposed, had been told to look after her. He'd taken her arm and hustled her into the kitchen, climbing up on the counter to rummage in the cookie tin. She'd tried to kiss him for giving her a vanilla wafer, and he'd recoiled in disgust. "You're not really my cousin," he'd said, gobbling his own cookie.

It had hurt at the time, and even more so when she was old enough to understand it was her father's fu-neral that had made for the crowd of grown-ups and her mother's tears. Later, when she'd been ten and Ramsey fourteen, she'd been glad they weren't first cousins, that he was Aunt Alma's husband's nephew, and her father had been Aunt Alma's brother. She'd twined some moonstruck dreams around his adoles-cent person until Donny Osmond had taken first place in her fantasies.

But getting Ramsey out of her head was difficult when she was in this house. He had alternately teased her and stuck up for her during her childhood. Both of them had done a good bit of their growing up un-der Aunt Alma's benevolent eye.

She carried her things up to her room, and then used the bathroom, already seeing it in her mind's eye as it would be when she was finished with it. She would re-place the old galvanized pipes with copper, keep the old claw-foot tub but add a brass shower assembly, keep the old pedestal lavatory, but put in a modern, water-saving toilet. She would add some wainscot-ting, some fresh black-and-white wall tile to match the little hexagonal tiles on the floor, new paint and another light fixture. The finished bathroom would be charming, and completely in keeping with the era of the house.

Somehow she knew that the new second bathroom, the one she'd given to Ramsey, wouldn't look anything like what she'd planned for this one. He would take the opportunity to demonstrate how much better and more efficient modern fixtures were. She wished now she'd never let him have carte blanche, but he wouldn't give it up. He was sure to be getting too much charge out of the idea of showing her once and for all that she was wrong.

RAMSEY TURNED his baseball cap around so the bill shaded his neck, and listened to Wally Hurtado's lugubrious complaints.

"*She* wants to change the whole layout here," Wally told him, indicating the spot on the blueprints with a grubby finger. "Wants to put a wet bar in the dining room now. We've already roughed in the plumbing, Mac, including the copper. If they have to come back and mess around after we've closed the walls, it'll cost you."

Ramsey tried to tamp down his irritation. "Yeah, I know, Wally." *She* was Gloria Gruenwald, the client whose dream house was being constructed on a big lot north of town. He hadn't cared all that much for the plans she'd shown him, drawn by some Sacramento architect too busy to have a hand in the construction. Gloria had accepted some of the changes he'd suggested, but she kept coming up with loopy ideas, depending on which home decorating magazine she'd read that week. "I explained to Gloria that the changes would start costing her since they weren't in the contract."

"That's good." Wally's long, dark face lightened a little. "About time you started counting the cost."

"Yeah, well, she didn't agree." Ramsey pulled out a bandanna and rubbed his sweaty face. It was hot in the sun, October though it was. Wally didn't seem to notice. He'd picked the middle of the driveway for this conference, spreading the blueprints out on an improvised work bench that consisted of plywood laid across two sawhorses. It held an assortment of tools and paper.

"Whaddya mean, she didn't agree? She can't go changing everything and upgrading the floor coverings and expect you to eat the cost, can she?"

"Evidently." He stared at Wally through narrowed eyes. "What's this about the floor coverings?"

"*She* wants hardwood floors in the kitchen, now," Wally told him, his face falling back into its habitual mournful expression. "Said linoleum is dee-class-ay, whatever that means."

Ramsey's lips twitched. "I'm going to have to sit down with Gloria and get this cleared away," he decided, reluctantly.

"Yeah, well, it ain't sittin' down she's got in mind," Wally muttered.

"What's that?" Ramsey glared at his foreman.

"Nothin', boss. You go right ahead and talk to her—try to, anyway." Wally's wrinkles realigned themselves into a smile. "Meanwhile, what should I do about this here wet bar? We need to close the walls—can't wait around for the plumber."

"Go ahead and close in the bedrooms," Ramsey said. A bright turquoise convertible pulled up in the driveway, and he hitched up his belt at the sight. "Here's Gloria now. We'll have it figured out before you get to the dining room."

Gloria Gruenwald climbed out of the car and leaned against it, waiting for him to get there. Every strand of her dark hair was perfectly in place, despite the open car. Her makeup was exotic and striking, her scent strong enough to reach him when he was within five feet of her.

She was a beautiful woman, he supposed. But her flamboyant style didn't really appeal to him. Wally was right; Gloria had made it plain on previous occasions that she was ready to take his comments on her house lying down. Ramsey, not a tactful man, had found it difficult to avoid her advances without a showdown that might mean even more trouble for this already mixed-up project.

"Afternoon, Gloria," he said easily, stopping a few feet away. Her sleekly casual pants and shirt displayed her ripe charms. Behind him, he knew, the crew members were taking in every voluptuous curve.

"Ramsey." Her voice was a stagy, throaty purr. "How is it coming?"

"Fine," he said heartily. She moved a step nearer, her scent billowing out to envelop him. He felt like a mouse caught in a bulldozer's headlights. She had turned up the firepower from their last encounter. He cleared his throat and resisted the urge to back away. "Except for these changes you keep making. I thought we'd agreed, Gloria. If you want to stick to the bid, you'll have to forgo the changes. Otherwise, I'll have to charge you for them."

Her face hardened a little. "Must we talk about money? I thought everything was settled between us." She came closer yet.

"So did I, but now Wally tells me you want plumbing in the dining room and hardwood floors in the kitchen." He shook his head, ignoring the scowl that flitted across her face. "Offhand, I'd say that's an extra five thou, depending on how elaborate you want this wet bar. More, if the cabinetry is custom."

"Our bid covers plumbing," she said, abandoning some of the throatiness. "And the hardwood floors."

Ramsey held her eyes steadily. "Plumbing in the bathrooms and kitchen, number of fixtures noted in the contract," he said. "Hardwood floors in the living and dining room. Vinyl flooring in the kitchen. There's a big price difference between vinyl and hardwood. And you, Gloria, will have to pay for it if you want it."

"I don't have any extra money," Gloria admitted sulkily. "This house is taking my whole divorce settlement the way it is. I thought housing was supposed to be so much cheaper up here than in the Bay Area."

"It is," Ramsey said patiently. "A house like you've planned would cost you plenty more in the city, if you could find a place to build it. Making changes is expensive, too. Why don't you let us finish it, and you live in it? If it's not fancy enough, you can always sell it later."

"Or you can." Gloria shot a look at him. "My lawyer thinks I should never have signed that contract with you. I could break it, you know." She lowered her long, mascaraed lashes. "That might leave you in a bit of a hole, Ramsey dear."

"It would certainly be profitable for our lawyers," he agreed, forcing a smile.

She moved closer, until there was very little space between them, and slid her hand up his arm. "There's got to be a better way to resolve our little difficulties," she breathed. "I'm renting a place on Willow Grove. Come by tonight for a drink. We'll talk about it."

"There's not that much to talk about," Ramsey said with deliberation. He stepped back and turned. "Wally?"

His foreman popped out from behind the house with an alacrity that suggested he'd had his ears stretched. "Yeah, boss?"

"Mrs. Gruenwald can't decide whether she wants those changes or not," Ramsey told him, aware of Gloria's baffled fury behind him. "Move the crew over to the spec house for the time being. We'll finish up here when she decides."

"Right." Wally bustled away, and Ramsey could hear him talking to Jeff and Donald.

"Just give me a call when you've figured out what to do." Ramsey gave Gloria a bland smile. "I've got a lot of work around here—no need to worry that you're holding me up." He shrugged. "Of course you've got a construction loan. You'll have to be paying on that. But it's worth it to take some time, figure out what you really want. I just hope we can get back here before the weather makes working difficult. Once we get into that spec house, it could be hard to leave."

Gloria abandoned all sultry pretense. "You son of a bitch," she spat out. "You can't walk off my job."

"Watch me," he said gently, and turned to his own truck, parked at the curb. It gave him great pleasure to drive it away, leaving her there. If he'd thrown a pail of water on her, she would have steamed.

He glanced at his watch and took the quickest route to Alma's house. He was late, and Mary Ellen would have been on time, of course. She was always irritatingly punctual. They had agreed to take half days twice a week to check their crews and keep their own projects going, though as she'd pointed out, she'd have hours of commuting time tacked onto that. He could have cut her some slack, but he'd insisted on the letter of the law.

Now he squirmed a little, thinking about it. The encounter with Gloria Gruenwald had underlined the dicey nature of contracting, the need to be on top of the work as well as the client relations. He wasn't leaving Mary Ellen much time to do all that. Hell, he was having trouble keeping things running, and he was within ten minutes of most of his jobs.

He pulled his pickup behind hers, and found her in the dirt-floored cellar under the house, scowling at the massive redwood twelve-by-twelves that supported the floor joists. The cellar was a small, six-foot-deep pit dug in the middle of the crawl space, which stretched around it like a dark, grubby plain, ending at the old foundation walls.

"We're going to get very dirty," she said in a voice of gloom. "Three feet of headroom everywhere, if you can call it that, except this little spot. That means working on our knees."

"Stomachs, too," he said, grinning at her. "Why do you think they call it a crawl space?"

"I like to hire this part out," she said with dignity. He could believe that. Mary Ellen was so neat for a contractor. Her hands were clean, her jeans had just a couple of crumbs of sawdust on them and her T-shirt was immaculate. Her hair was hidden under a baseball cap, much like the one he wore, except hers was made of some flowery fabric and didn't mention the Oakland As.

"It's a dirty job," he said cheerfully.

"Yeah, I know the rest," she growled. "Well, let's get down to it, MacIver. You've left it late enough already."

"I've got the jacks in my truck." He turned, pointing to the strategic spots under the house. "See those old twelve-by-twelve timbers? They go all the way from one side to the other." He eyed the big timbers admiringly. "They really knew how to build them, I'll say that for the old days. We'll put the jacks under them and level everything, and put a few more jacks close to the perimeter. Then we demolish the old knee wall. We don't even have to cut the other supports, since we're not raising the house. Just use the jacks and beams to take the place of the knee wall until we get the old foundation dug out, the new one poured, and the new knee wall built."

"Yeah, that's all." Mary Ellen followed him to his truck, drawing on a pair of leather work gloves. She hoisted two of the jacks as easily as he did, and carried them back beside him. "How long have you allowed for all this, Ramsey, taking into account that just the two of us are working on it?"

He began to feel a little defensive. She knew about his little failing, of being a bit too optimistic when setting schedules. He tried to correct for that, now, but even his padded time estimates came in short now and then. "I've scheduled two weeks," he muttered. "Six days to demolish and excavate, two days to form for the concrete, one day to pour and set up, two days to frame the new wall, and one day to tie it all together again. Leaves two days over for slop."

Mary Ellen snorted. "We'll be lucky to make that schedule, but you won't be able to blame it on me. And you've forgotten that I get two of those days to go down to Berkeley. I don't want to do half days. It doesn't make sense when the commute takes so long."

He agreed, grudgingly, but maintained that the half days would be more convenient for him.

"So take them," Mary Ellen said, setting the jacks down where he had indicated and starting back out for more. "I can work without you breathing down my neck."

He grabbed her arm as she went by. "Yes, but will you follow directions? I get the feeling, Emmy, that you don't see any reason to do what I say here."

"In this phase," Mary Ellen said, her eyes flashing in the dimness, "I will consider you the supervisor. I expect the same consideration from you when I supervise."

"Yeah, sure." Ramsey watched her head for the truck, and pondered how different she was from Gloria. Mary Ellen wore no perceptible makeup, and her scent was barely noticeable, a light floral fragrance that reminded him of his aunt's potpourri. She looked cute, stalking to the truck ahead of him, her firm little rear swaying from side to side with a femininity that was all the more entrancing for its very lack of consciousness. She would never use her body to bargain with—more's the pity. He tried to swallow that thought as she reached the truck and turned to frown at him.

"You gonna help carry these, or is that too much like peon work for you?" She hefted a couple more of the jacks from the truck bed, and he hastened to help out.

"Why don't we at least try to be civil to each other," he said plaintively, following her back to the cellar door. "I don't enjoy being raked over the coals all the time. Whatever happened to the Golden Rule?"

"It's probably buried somewhere under all this dirt," Mary Ellen grumbled, and then smiled. "Sorry. I know I sound grouchy—" His snort of disbelief made her roll her eyes. "All right, I *am* grouchy, but it's hard to keep up with working in two different places." She dumped the jacks on the dirt and looked around. "Let's make some progress here, and I'll feel better."

THE SUN WAS GETTING low by the time they finished placing the jacks to Ramsey's satisfaction. "That's the last one," he said, adding another shim and tightening the jack into place. "We'd better wait until tomorrow to start the demo."

Mary Ellen stretched. "Our first day, and we're already behind schedule." She looked at Ramsey, and color flooded her face. "Sorry," she said gruffly. "I didn't mean to criticize."

"Yes you did," he growled. "Let's just say it'll take as long as it does, and leave it at that."

"You've got to have a schedule," Mary Ellen began.

"Usually, yes," Ramsey said, brushing his hands together. He was filthy from wallowing on the dirt floor. His back ached from crouching. And yet Mary Ellen could stand there, draw the gloves off her clean hands, brush a little dust off, and look almost as fresh as she had when they'd started. And she hadn't slacked off, either. It was exasperating. "This time," he told her, heading for the steps that led outside, "we're doing the work. We don't have to worry about scheduling the subs."

"But—the plumbers, the electricians, the dry-wall—"

"I can do all those things," he shot back.

She stood in the setting sun beside him, chewing thoughtfully on her lip. "I don't know, Ramsey," she said, stuffing the gloves in her hip pocket. "I like to work with licensed subs. You know where you are. And doesn't the permit require it?"

He grinned at her. "Honey, you're not in the big city anymore. Permits are more a matter of form here. Sure, the inspector's going to sign it off. But she doesn't care who does the work, as long as it's up to code."

"Don't you have better things to do with your time than mess with the plumbing?" She brushed at the spiderwebs on her shirt, and he reached to get one on her back. Beneath the thin cotton, her skin was warm and alive, her muscles smooth. She stood very still for a moment, and then moved away. "I'll just take a shower," she said, and he thought there was a hint of breathlessness in her voice.

"Me, too," he murmured, for one heated moment picturing them together in the shower.

"I don't think it's a good idea," Mary Ellen said, and he started, staring at her, wondering if she'd read his mind. "If you make a mistake, it'll be time-consuming to fix it. And I'll probably need you somewhere else." He kept his eyes fixed on her face, and a slow tide of red washed over her cheeks. "When it's time for the plumbing to go in," she stammered, backing away. "Gosh, it's late. I'm starved. Guess we can finish this discussion tomorrow."

He opened his mouth to invite her to dinner, then closed it with a snap. She wouldn't come, he knew. "Lenore and Jon are dropping in tonight," he said instead. "You coming?"

"No, I have a lot to do." She moved toward the back porch, her words coming out in nervous bursts. "Lots of projects—no time to socialize—say hello for me. Bright and early tomorrow, Ramsey!"

"Right." He watched her disappear into the house, and then stalked down the driveway to his truck. It galled him that she wouldn't even drop by for a friendly evening of conversation, but he supposed it was a bit much to ask. After all, they'd spent the last five years not talking to each other. Now, at least, they were doing that.

"If you can call it talking," he grumbled, getting into his truck. More like arguing, like the arguments they used to have all the time before she'd moved out in a huff. She'd said then that he never listened to her side.

Okay, so this time he'd try listening. If she was still willing to talk. And maybe they could rewind their relationship—go from the arguments back to the beginning, when the day hadn't been long enough to hold their love.

"In your dreams, MacIver," he told himself, and gunned the truck down the drive.

CHAPTER FIVE

"TERMITES."

Mary Ellen rubbed the sweat out of her eyes and laid her crowbar down. "Where?"

Ramsey put down his crowbar, too. So far that day, they had worked in silence, with only an occasional comment or request for tools. Mary Ellen was used to a job site where the conversation was cheerful, even if sporadic, and the atmosphere much lighter than it was here at Aunt Alma's house. Today they were tearing the siding off the knee wall that went between the floor joists and the inadequate brick foundation.

Now she walked over to Ramsey, who'd been tackling the back northwest corner. He was staring at the old redwood framing members he'd exposed after taking off the clapboard siding. Mary Ellen stared at them, too. Unmistakable grooves tunneled into the surface of the timbers.

"Termites," she agreed gloomily. "Guess we'll have to tent the whole house."

"I expected it," Ramsey said. She glanced at him, but he didn't seem smug. His expression when he turned to her, however, was definitely exasperated. "We've spent a couple of hours treating that old siding like gold, instead of just smashing through it, and now we'll have to throw it away, anyway."

"We could salvage some of it," Mary Ellen said weakly. It had been her idea to try and save the siding for reuse. Ramsey had been against it from the first. Siding, he'd pointed out, was not hard to find, and not that expensive, even if she insisted on redwood clapboards to match the old stuff. But Mary Ellen had wanted to prove a point.

"What's the use?" Ramsey yanked at the siding he'd levered partly away from the wall, and it splintered off. "This stuff is dry and hard to work with. We're throwing it into the debris box, and we're going to get all new stuff when we put in the new wall. I don't want to mess around with termites."

"Neither do I," Mary Ellen agreed. "You're absolutely right."

"I am?" Ramsey stared at her. "I mean, of course I am." He tried to suppress it, but Mary Ellen could see he was gratified. "Glad you admit it. Now, let's just tear this stuff off and get rid of this wall. We've wasted enough time today."

Mary Ellen marched back to her own corner of the house. The man didn't know when to shut up, she fumed, levering recklessly at the siding. She didn't mind admitting when she'd made a mistake, but he shouldn't gloat like that, either. The shoe was bound to be on the other foot as they went on, and he'd be sorry he'd been so graceless.

The work did go faster after that. They labored on opposite sides of the house, tearing off siding and carting it in wheelbarrows to the debris box that had been delivered that morning and parked in the middle of the curving driveway. Mary Ellen hadn't done this kind of demolition for a while; she preferred to hire relatively unskilled workers to start demolition while she finished up the previous job. But there was something satisfying in wielding crowbar and hammer, in seeing destruction as progress. She delivered her last load to the debris box before lunch, closely followed by Ramsey. He stopped to gaze back at the house. It rose proudly as usual, but its denuded foundation looked like a smile full of missing teeth.

"That went fast." He turned to her, and she managed a pleasant, noncommittal expression.

"After lunch, we take out the knee wall, right?"

"Yeah." He frowned, removing his baseball cap to rub a sleeve over his forehead. "Tenting the house— that's going to throw off our schedule. We should have it done before we pour, don't you think?"

"I think the termite people are going to want the house closed in before they tent," Mary Ellen said. "Guess we'd better ask them. Who do you use here?"

Ramsey told her, adding, "I'll call, I know Hal Gershen—he runs the place. Right after lunch."

"Great." Mary Ellen watched him walk over to his truck and take out a small cooler. "Whatever happened to the brown bag?"

"Couldn't get enough into one." Ramsey gave her an unreadable look. "Mind if I use your kitchen? I know you'll be going out, anyway."

"You can use the kitchen if you don't get in my way," Mary Ellen said loftily. "I'm fixing my own lunch. Once a month at the Blue Willow is about all I can stand."

She led the way inside, not really wanting Ramsey to watch an exhibition of her meager skills in the kitchen. But he wouldn't care; he had his own food, and it would probably absorb all his attention.

She put the old teakettle on, watching out of the corner of her eye as Ramsey washed his hands and opened his cooler. He took out a good-sized plastic container full of romaine lettuce, which he tore into small pieces. Another plastic container held sliced tomatoes and cucumbers. When he took the lid off a third container, her nostrils twitched. A wonderful, pungent aroma spread through the kitchen.

He glanced up and she turned hastily away, rummaging in the cupboard for one of the cups of instant soup she'd bought at the market the day before. Pouring boiling water into it, she promised herself that one day she would learn to cook. It was too humiliating to be making packaged soup when Ramsey was crafting a marvelous Caesar salad.

When she took her cup of soup to the table, Ramsey was adding croutons to his salad from a paper sack. The scent of Parmesan cheese wafted across the table. Mary Ellen's nosed twitched again, and she buried it in her soup. It tasted fine, she told herself, a familiar standby that she lived on for days at a time. Nevertheless, she couldn't help but watch Ramsey take his first bite.

He was exaggerating the bliss, she knew, but his closed eyes, his indrawn breath, all served to point up the wonderfulness of his lunch. After one quick look to see what she was eating, he didn't pay any attention to her soup. She should have been glad.

"Want a bite?" He offered her his fork, with a glistening mound of romaine on it. She had meant to say no, but somehow her mouth opened and the salad was inside before she knew what had happened. It *was* good.

"Very tasty," she said, forcing the words out. "Salad is all you're having?"

"Oh, no." He reached into his cooler again. "I'm always ravenous at lunchtime. I made a turkey-and-avocado sandwich, too."

The sandwich would have to be on sourdough, she reflected crossly. Alfalfa sprouts made a delicate froth along the edge of the avocado.

"Soup all you're having?" He looked once more at the foam cup and frowned a little. "How can you do a lot of hard work on that little dab of food?"

"I have yogurt, too." She got a carton of it out of the fridge, disposing of the remains of her soup while she was up.

"Wouldn't keep me alive," he said, chomping into his sandwich with gusto. "Of course, I don't eat much dinner. A little vichyssoise, a few sautéed vegetables, some rice.... I have my main meal at lunchtime."

His teeth tore into the sandwich again, and she watched, fascinated in spite of herself. He would eat like this every day, in front of her, unless she figured out some way out of it. "I don't like hanging around in the kitchen that much," she said, trying for a tone of polite disinterest. It was true, as far as it went. She wouldn't mind eating like he did, though.

"It's a hobby," he said, shrugging as he finished off the salad. When his hand went down to the cooler again, she closed her eyes, dreading what was to come. "I made these for Lenore and Jon last night. Brought a couple for you." She opened her eyes to find him holding out a plastic bag full of dark, chocolaty bars. "Thought you might like one, since you didn't come over."

"Thank you, Ramsey." She was touched. "You didn't need to do that." She took the bars, anyway. They looked fabulous. The first one was gone in no time.

"They're pretty good," he said complacently. "My own recipe. Kind of a combination of brownies and candy bars. Have another."

"No, thanks." Belatedly, Mary Ellen realized that she was sitting at a table with Ramsey, the hated one, sharing civilized conversation about cooking while scarfing a rich dessert. In her wildest dreams a week ago, she wouldn't have envisioned anything this bizarre. "I'm stuffed. I'll just get back to work."

"Fine," he said amiably. "I like to digest a little while, so I'll be out in half an hour."

"You do that," she muttered, stalking to the back door. She couldn't resist a backward look. Ramsey was reaching for the fudge bar she'd turned down. He looked as though there was nothing more weighty on his mind than the total enjoyment of its decadent pleasure. She found that infuriating.

She went down into the cellar and inspected the jacks that supported the edges of the house. Ramsey had figured they wouldn't need to lift the house off its central supporting piers, but she wondered about fitting the new knee wall in snugly. In fact, she had a lot of questions about this kind of work since this was the first foundation job she'd been intimately involved with.

"I don't doubt his expertise," she grumbled, pulling a crumbling flake of mortar out from between the old bricks. "I just wonder about his methods. He's too used to working without inspectors. You can get sloppy."

She forgot to duck on the way up the steep cellar stairs, and bumped her head. Rubbing it, she examined the termite damage on the old mudsill. It wasn't everywhere, but in a couple of places it was extensive. The termite people would probably want to spray while they had it dug out to form the new footing.

She picked up her sledgehammer and swung it experimentally. Ramsey would probably just start whamming away at the old framing, but she felt it was better to cut the studs off beneath the rim joist. That, at least, was untouched by termites. They wouldn't have to replace it. They could just pry off the old top plate and nail up a new one when they got around to framing the knee wall. Whenever that was. She felt she'd already worked weeks on this foundation, and it was barely started.

Ramsey came out when she was getting the case containing her reciprocating saw out of her truck. "Going to saw the studs off? Good idea. I will, too." He heaved his own saw out of a cluttered toolbox and they walked up the front path together. Suddenly Mary Ellen giggled.

"Something's funny?" Ramsey looked at her. "Let me in on the joke."

"I was just thinking that we look like a couple of gangsters with our guns," Mary Ellen said, indicating the nearly identical cases they carried.

"You're right. They could be tommy guns," Ramsey said judiciously.

"Where have you been for the past few years? It's AK 47s now," Mary Ellen told him, setting her case down on the front porch steps and opening it.

"Well, you would know, working down in the city and all."

"The Bay Area is a great place, mostly," Mary Ellen said, fitting a blade into the saw. "There's a few spots to avoid, but it's that way in most cities."

Ramsey looked over her saw with the unabashed interest a contractor feels for tools. "Is that new? How do you like it?" He pulled his own battered saw out of its case.

"It's three years old. Works fine." Mary Ellen was remembering a day soon after she'd moved in with Ramsey, when he was off on a job site and she'd come home from her own job at the bank feeling restless. They'd been in the middle of fixing the bathroom; they'd started with a new floor to replace the old, rotten one. She'd picked up the saws-all he'd left behind and begun cutting through the old sub-floor when Ramsey found her there. He'd given her hell for using his tools without permission.

"Jeez, it's clean. Looks like you never did a day's work with it," he grumbled. "How do you keep everything so clean?"

"I just do." Mary Ellen was a little defensive about her care of her tools. Even in her crew of neat women, it was considered excessive. "I pay a lot of money for my tools. It just makes sense to keep them in good shape."

"Sure." Ramsey glanced from her saw to his own. "Well, I never have that many problems." He heaved the coils of an orange extension cord over his shoulder and eyed her in challenge. "We'll just see who gets done first, shall we?"

Mary Ellen shouldered her own cord. "There's no point in competition," she said loftily. "Safety and speed don't go together." Nevertheless, she shoved her safety glasses up on the bridge of her nose and marched away without a backward look. She would keep up with him at the least, and beat him if she could. The man needed to be taken down a few pegs.

Ramsey's saw roared into life, and the sound of her own followed it. She moved steadily along the outside of the foundation, cutting through each stud in the knee wall. There were complications in the form of sewer pipes and vents, but she soon found a rhythm for the procedure. The old redwood cut easily. She was turning the corner at the back of the house when she realized that Ramsey's saw was silent.

He couldn't be finished already; the whole back of the house stretched, untouched, in front of her. She turned off her own saw. In the sudden quiet that followed she could hear Ramsey cursing, low and steady.

She put down the saw and ran around the far corner. Ramsey stood a couple of feet from the end. His saw was at his feet, its blade snapped off. He was holding one hand with the other, and blood dripped out from between his fingers.

Mary Ellen had bandaged her share of accidental cuts, but the sight of blood never ceased to make her stomach feel shaky. "Come inside," she urged, whipping a clean bandanna out of her back pocket. She handed him the bandanna, and he wrapped it around his first finger. "How bad is it?"

"I didn't cut the finger all the way off," he growled. "But damn near."

Mary Ellen followed him up the back stairs, her eyes glued to the bright drops of blood that splattered on the kitchen floor. At the sink, Ramsey gingerly unwound the bandanna. There was a deep, ragged gash in his first finger, running along the side between the knuckles.

Mary Ellen caught her breath at the sight of it. "That should be seen by a doctor. It probably needs stitches."

"I'm not going to a doctor." Ramsey stuck his finger under the water, and winced as it washed away the blood. "It's not as bad as it looks, and stitches are the devil."

"Well, at least put some pressure on it and stop the bleeding," Mary Ellen snapped. She rummaged in a drawer and pulled out a clean dish towel. "Here, use this. I'll get my first-aid kit."

She ran for her truck, where she always carried a big first-aid kit. There were plenty of accidents on construction sites, although she did her best to make everyone in her crews safety-conscious. Often, all that was required was extracting splinters or putting bandages on blisters. Ramsey's cut would be more of a challenge, especially if he refused to let a doctor stitch it.

She lugged in the big plastic case. Ramsey was sitting at the kitchen table, his hand sticking up in the air, the towel already soaked in blood. "Another AK 47?" He eyed her first-aid kit.

"I believe in being prepared, that's all." Mary Ellen opened the case, revealing an array of bandages and unguents. "But if you'd rather go to a doctor, say the word. Or you can take care of it yourself, get an infection, bow out of the project...." She shrugged and half closed the lid of the case.

"Okay, okay." Ramsey glared at her. "You've made your point, Nurse. Just get on with it."

"Doctor," Mary Ellen said firmly, unwrapping the blood-stained towel. "I get an honorary MD when I do this kind of work." The cut had stopped bleeding, and she could glimpse muscle tissue inside it, under the flaps of skin. Ramsey's lips were tightly gripped together. She knew it must hurt. To distract both of them, she babbled on. "Got my degree in the School of Hard Knocks and Scrapes." She took out some butterfly bandages and a tube of antibiotic ointment. "Guess I won't have to use the distress flares, but I might need the smelling salts."

"I'm not going to faint." Ramsey perused the contents of her kit with fascination while she pulled the edges of the cut together with the butterfly bandages. "Scissors, pliers, tweezers—you've got as much hardware in here as any tool kit. Do you ever use this stuff?"

"I am using it," Mary Ellen pointed out, snatching the scissors to cut an adhesive bandage down to size. "And the smelling salts are for the doctor."

"Does this upset you?" He watched her while she used waterproof tape to secure a rigid finger cot. "You seem so good at it."

"I took a course," Mary Ellen mumbled, putting on the last piece of tape. "Somebody on a site has to know what to do."

"Guess I'm backward," Ramsey said, inspecting the finished bandage with a sardonic lift of his eyebrow. "We just stick on a bandage and get back to work."

"People get infections that way, lose time, and next thing you know you're facing a worker's comp claim." Mary Ellen tidied up her kit and picked up Ramsey's hand, turning it to make sure her work was adequate all around. "I've given you the best protection I can against dirt and stuff, but I'd advise you to wear gloves or lay off for a couple of days. A doctor would have definitely stitched that cut, and it still might have to be done."

"I heal fast," Ramsey said, shrugging off her concern. "This is a pretty good setup here. Won't slow me down at all." He gave her a long, unreadable look. "Thanks—Doc."

Mary Ellen turned away, picking up her case before she realized there wasn't much point in putting it back in the truck. She didn't mention the ridiculous competition again, and neither did Ramsey. For the rest of the afternoon they worked in silence, but this time it had a different quality. The unvoiced hostility had lessened.

Just before six, Ramsey threw his tools back into his truck and drove off. Mary Ellen was left to her frozen dinner, another evening of paperwork and yet another night in the virginal bed that had been hers until six years ago.

THE MORNING WAS BRIGHT and crisp, another perfect fall day. Mary Ellen swung the sledgehammer and a section of brick foundation toppled. "Ramsey was right," she told Lenore, who stood beside her, peering interestedly at the hole Mary Ellen had just created. "There's hardly any footing here. It should be pretty easy to demolish."

"Well, don't throw the bricks away." Lenore picked up one of them. "This is good old clay brick, hard to find and expensive. It's great for patios and walkways. A brickyard might be interested in salvaging them. Or you could use them here— I know Mrs. Mac wanted to terrace the back garden."

Mary Ellen knocked over another section of the foundation. "I don't know where we'd store them," she said, dodging the dust. "The whole place will be covered with construction materials pretty soon."

"I've got some spare time. Let me get the wheelbarrow," Lenore suggested. "I can haul them into the backyard and stack them behind the garden shed where they won't be in the way. Then Mrs. Mac can decide how she wants to use them."

"That would be great." Mary Ellen moved along the wall as she spoke. "I'll hire you as a helper, if you want. Aunt Alma wouldn't want you working for free."

"I can't afford to work for free," Lenore admitted. "But I won't overrun your budget, either. Let me start the sprinklers in the rose garden, and I'll be right with you."

Mary Ellen gave her sledgehammer a rest, and took a deep breath of the cool morning air. Her muscles felt a little stiff, after the previous day's work. Ramsey hadn't shown up yet, but Lenore had come right after breakfast to work on Aunt Alma's beloved flower beds and rose bushes.

Lenore came back trundling a wheelbarrow, and started picking up bricks. Mary Ellen adjusted her safety glasses and used the sledgehammer again. It was gratifying how fast this part of the job was going, but she couldn't fool herself. This was the easy part. The hard part would be digging for the new foundation. Given Ramsey's stubborn refusal to hire grunt labor, she was bound to get a real workout.

She was halfway around the house when Ramsey's pickup chugged up the driveway and parked behind the debris box. He came charging around the house, his sharp black eyes taking in everything. Lenore, on her hands and knees grubbing bricks out from under the house, got a casual greeting, but Ramsey didn't stop until he got to Mary Ellen, who had pushed her safety glasses atop her head and stood, braced for what was clearly going to be an attack.

"Just what does this mean?" Ramsey was flourishing a newspaper—the Dusty Springs weekly *Wellhead*.

"Good morning to you, too," Mary Ellen said coolly. "You seem a little feverish, Ramsey. Is your cut bothering you?"

Ramsey spared a baffled glance at the bandage that graced his finger. "It's fine," he spat. "I just want to know what this means." He shoved the newspaper at her.

Mary Ellen took it. "'Cow wanders onto train tracks,'" she read, puzzled. "'Threatened derailment prevented at last minute.' What does this have to do with me?"

"Not that one," Ramsey said impatiently. He pointed to the next article, his bandage already looking grubby. Intrigued, Lenore drew closer, her wheelbarrow filled with bricks.

"'Local politician to hold fund-raiser,'" Mary Ellen read aloud. "'County Supervisor Arnold Hengeman, a Dusty Springs resident, will hold a fund-raiser at his luxurious Eastridge home this Friday. The reception is open to all. Rumor has it that a very attractive newcomer to Dusty Springs will be acting as his hostess.'" She lowered the paper and stared at Ramsey. "I don't know anything about it."

"You mean—" Ramsey let his breath out and took the newspaper back. "I thought it was you, the attractive newcomer who's acting as that slimeoid's hostess."

Mary Ellen shook her head, torn between exasperation and a secret gratification. "You got the wrong end of the stick, buddy. I'm here to work, not to hostess. Not," she added truthfully, "that I would know how to hostess, or even if that word can be a verb."

"Huh?" Ramsey looked crestfallen. "Sorry," he mumbled. "Guess I went off half-cocked."

"Technically speaking," Lenore put in, her eyes dancing, "Mary Ellen couldn't be called a newcomer. She's a returnee, or something like that."

"Sounds like a fun bash, anyway," Mary Ellen said, winking at her friend. "What say you and me go, Lenore? Can't have too many attractive women at a party like that, whether they're newcomers, returnees or transplants."

"Right." Lenore looked solemn. "It's our duty to go. Friday, is it?" She wrinkled her eyebrows. "Shoot, I was going to go to the tractor pull, but I guess I can pass it up this time."

"Sure you can," said Mary Ellen, getting into the spirit of it all. "It means a run-in with Amorous Arnold. But I can face that if there's going to be hors d'oeuvres."

"Even for pork rinds, if they're free," Lenore said frankly. "A meal on Arnold is not to be missed."

"It's not a joke," Ramsey insisted, although his expression had lost its sternness. "He's looking for support for his damned development, and if you go, you'll be seen as a supporter."

"Nonsense," Mary Ellen said, picking up her sledgehammer. "It's a community thing. I look forward to seeing all the people I grew up with. I'm not going to give Arnold a cent, you can bet on it, but I don't see why I should miss a party."

Ramsey glowered again. "You won't go," he said with certainty. "It's no place for a decent person."

"Right," Lenore chimed in, grinning at him. "I take it you're going, then. You could ask him all sorts of embarrassing questions."

Ramsey was struck with this idea. "Now that you mention it," he said slowly, "I do have a few things to confront Arnold about. And if I take you, Emmy, no one will think you're in Arnold's camp."

The women exchanged thoughtful glances. "I'm going with Lenore," Mary Ellen said firmly, moving closer to her friend. "You and I know, Ramsey, that there's nothing between us now but business. But if you take me to that party, the whole town will start asking when we're setting the date. It would drive me around the bend. I refuse to consider it."

"You're exaggerating," Ramsey said, after a moment of judicious silence. "It wouldn't be that bad." He didn't sound convinced.

"And where do you get off laying down the law to me, Ramsey MacIver?" Mary Ellen began to get hot under the collar. "Telling me where I can go and what I can do! You have absolutely nothing to say about my free time."

Ramsey's brows drew together in a brief frown. "Right," he said again, after another pause. "I should have kept my big mouth shut, obviously. Don't worry. I won't step out of line again." He ran a hand through his hair. "What was I thinking of? You can take care of yourself. You just forget what I said, Emmy. Enjoy yourself, have a good time. Just keep your brass knuckles handy." He held up one hand, although

Mary Ellen, thunderstruck by this capitulation, hadn't even the breath to speak with. "That wasn't telling you what to do—just a neighborly little hint." He turned away, calling over his shoulder, "I'll get my sledgehammer."

Once again Mary Ellen's gaze met Lenore's. Her friend looked as puzzled as she felt. Ramsey was not acting true to form. "I don't know," Lenore said, grasping the handles of the wheelbarrow. "He's up to something. That was the strangest little speech I've ever heard."

"He's just being honest," Mary Ellen said, dismayed by the hollowness Ramsey's friendly advice had created inside her. "You see? I was right. He doesn't have romantic feelings for me at all anymore."

"That's why he came up here with that newspaper, so hot he could have burned a hole in the ground," Lenore said. "There's something going on in his weird male brain. Just watch out."

Mary Ellen didn't know what else to do, so she picked up her sledgehammer. "Men may come and men may go," she muttered under her breath, "but work goes on forever."

IT WAS LUNCHTIME before Lenore finished moving the bricks. Mary Ellen wiped her face with her bandanna. The foundation was demolished, and they were setting the course for the excavation. The sun had gotten very hot, though there were big clouds building in the west.

"Let's go out to lunch," she said impulsively when Lenore came to report her task finished. "It's too hot to cook anything, and anyway, there's nothing to cook."

Ramsey, on his belly underneath the house, poked his head out. "I brought a lot of stuff in my cooler," he offered. "We could have a picnic."

"Enough for three?" Lenore fanned her flushed face. "That was foresight."

"Well, you dainty ladies don't eat much, right?" Ramsey pulled himself out from under the house and stood, dusting off his front. Idly, Mary Ellen's gaze followed the path of his hand. Those muscular contours, visible beneath the sweat-darkened T-shirt, seemed very familiar all at once. She pulled her eyes away just before he looked up.

"I could eat—a pony, certainly," she said brightly. "And we don't want to deprive Ramsey of his lunch, right, Lenore? We can just go downtown—"

"Uh-uh." Lenore shook her head firmly. "When I get the choice between Ramsey's cooking and the Blue Willow's, I always take Ramsey's. You don't know what you're saying, girl. This man, during his vacation last winter, he took one of those cooking courses over in Napa Valley. The whole town drools over his food."

"Maybe you should chuck construction and open a restaurant," Mary Ellen said sourly.

"Hear, hear." It was Jon's voice. He joined them from around the corner, looking immaculate in his charcoal slacks and tweedy sport coat. His tie, though, a wild floral number, was loose at the throat of his banker's white shirt. He stepped neatly through the piles of old mortar and bits of wood that littered the ground around the house. "You're really tearing it up, aren't you? Came around to eat lunch with the proles." He flourished a paper bag. "Mom's Chinese chicken salad, enough for an army."

A babble of voices answered him, Ramsey reiterating the capacity of his cooler, Lenore chiming in eagerly, Mary Ellen protesting. Jon held up one hand. "Whoa," he said. "I've got to get it straight, here. Ramsey has sandwiches, Lenore brought some pears, Mary Ellen made iced tea this morning, and we're going to take it all to Spring Hill? Is that what I hear?"

"Good idea." Ramsey clapped Jon on the back. "Let's get going."

Mary Ellen found herself swept along by the others. She wanted to protest more, but had the sense to know that it would just make her feel like a wet blanket. She found herself sitting by Lenore in the back seat of Jon's Audi, holding her jug of tea, while he and Ramsey bickered amiably in the front about whether Jon's mom used sesame oil or peanut oil in the Chinese chicken salad.

Jon's car purred around the curves that led to the top of Spring Hill. He pulled into the parking lot, and they piled out. Mary Ellen went to the edge of the cliff, where a low railing marked the drop-off. Looking down, she had to admit that it made a great break from demolition. She could see the red dot of her pickup in the drive of Aunt Alma's house, and the white dot of the debris box, with Ramsey's white truck behind it. The whole town was like a perspective map at her feet. She swept the horizon, from the interstate highway two miles south, with its cluster of gas stations and fast-food restaurants, to the vast expanse westward of Horton Dalhousie's estate.

"Come and get it," Lenore called, and Mary Ellen turned back to the picnic table, which Lenore had covered with a faded tablecloth Mary Ellen recognized as one of Aunt Alma's. Ramsey kept pulling little containers and packets from his seemingly bottomless cooler, and Jon stuck a spoon into the plastic tub of salad.

Mary Ellen was careful not to sit beside Ramsey, but that just meant she had to look across the table at him. An uncomfortable silence lasted just a brief second, before Jon began discussing the various salads and sandwich spreads Ramsey had brought. "This one is made from chick-peas? No kidding?" He dipped a wedge of pita bread into it, and sampled it judiciously. "A little bland, but good."

"Try it with some of this," Ramsey suggested, passing him a small container filled with bright red, chunky salsa.

Jon dipped again, adding salsa generously. They all watched while he chewed. "It's great," he said afterward, but his voice sounded strangled. He drank half a bottle of mineral water. "Really great. What is it, straight Tabasco?"

"My secret recipe." Ramsey sounded smug.

Mary Ellen munched her own piece of pita, topped with a little of everything. "Say, what's old Horton Dalhousie up to these days?" She gestured across the valley, where amid a cluster of tall pines and eucalyptus was a glimpse of white walls. "Still hiding out on his estate?"

Lenore waved a slice of cantaloupe. "He's into hybridizing roses these days. I was talking to a guy who works for his maintenance service last week. He's had some successes, too—one of his first roses might be selected by the AARS—the national rose association," she explained, seeing the blank looks on everyone's faces.

"Seems like a funny hobby for a guy who used to be such a business shark," Jon commented. "They still tell a few shady stories about how he made his money during World War II."

"Really? I hadn't heard that." Lenore looked thoughtful. "Maybe they just talk about him because he's turned into such a recluse since his wife died."

"I heard he's given up business entirely to devote himself to his hobby," Jon added. "It's all in his son's hands, now. Clive Dalhousie is very smart. He was in business school when I was an undergrad at Berkeley, and could do the coursework with one hand tied behind his back. But reclusive, like his dad. No clubs or anything."

Ramsey took a thoughtful swallow of his iced tea. "Dalhousie should have deeded this place over to the county years ago. Then it would really be a park and couldn't be threatened."

Lenore looked surprised. "It isn't a park already? Everybody comes up here for picnics and such." She grinned at Ramsey. "Certainly the kids treat it that way, just like we did."

"If it truly was dedicated parkland," Jon said, reaching for a pear, "there wouldn't be a housing development planned for it."

Lenore was shocked. "I hadn't heard about a development. And how could they build here, anyway? I'd think it was too steep for housing."

"Probably they mean to build on the lower slopes and leave the upper part as open space," Mary Ellen said, trying for optimism.

"Is that so?" Ramsey was looking back at the parking lot, an immense frown gathering on his face. "Is that why there are surveyors up here?"

He pointed across the top of the hill, and they all looked. Moving along one of the trails was a man carrying a surveyor's tripod and a supply of little red flags.

Mary Ellen knew what those little red flags meant. They were used to mark off building lots. Someone was definitely trying to make a subdivision atop Dusty Springs's favorite park.

CHAPTER SIX

THE READY-MIX TRUCK alone was loud enough to make speech nearly impossible. When the concrete pump kicked in, any semblance of verbal communication ceased entirely. Watching for George Olsen's signal to start, Ramsey grabbed the thick hose that snaked out of the pump and braced himself. The concrete came pouring out of the hose, and like a fireman Ramsey had to struggle to aim the heavy sucker where he wanted it to go. As he filled the wooden forms with porridgy gray concrete, Wally Hurtado scooted from form to form, poking each one with a big stick and stirring the concrete down into the forms, to get rid of the air pockets.

On his knees beside the trench that held the forms, Ramsey crawled slowly along the wall, watching the forms fill, trying not to slop the concrete over the tops and trying not to make a mess when one of Aunt Alma's many foundation shrubs got in the way. He knew that both Mary Ellen and Lenore would give him hell if he destroyed one treasured forsythia or bridal wreath. He didn't need any more trouble from women. At least, no more than he'd already be in when Mary Ellen discovered he'd gone ahead with the pour without her. But she would be in the Bay Area all morning, and the concrete people had wanted to get the pour over with.

The steady stream of concrete began to falter; the pump shut down. The emptied concrete truck roared away, and suddenly there was quiet. Ramsey got to his feet, stretching. Crawling around, wrestling with a hose as difficult to manage as a boa constrictor hadn't done much for his back.

He walked over to the pump, where George was puttering around while waiting for another truck to pull up. The pump was about the size of a small tractor, made to be pulled behind George's pickup. The concrete trucks poured their product into the pump's open hopper, and the pump sent it surging through the long hose, to be directed with precision into the forms.

"How's it goin'?" George stopped hosing out the pump and looked up at Ramsey. "This ain't your usual thing, this restoration, is it? I usually see you at the new construction."

"Favor for my aunt," Ramsey told him, watching him assemble the grids he'd been cleaning. "How are you doing, George?"

"Can't complain." George spat judiciously into the driveway. "I get my share, though there's not so much new construction around these days."

"You make out like a bandit, and you know it," Ramsey said, clapping the older man on the shoulder. "When my back finally goes out for good, I'm gonna get me a pump. Money for nothing."

George smiled placidly. "It don't take a rocket scientist," he agreed, "but there's a few tricks in it. Here comes the next truck, boy. You better get back on the hose."

Ramsey took a little time to do more stretching as the big ready-mix truck lumbered into position in front of the pump. The weather had finally turned cooler, which was better for concrete, anyway. He'd pulled a couple of guys away from other jobs to help dig out the footing for the new foundation, and he and Mary Ellen had nailed up the forms in just the two days he'd scheduled. It seemed they could work well together, as long as neither of them spoke.

While he waited for the pump to start, he joined Wally in troweling off the forms; together they managed to scrape the excess concrete onto a piece of plywood for disposal elsewhere. At a new job, he didn't have to be so neat; the landscape contractor always sent in a crew to clean up the site before planting. But now that it was in his own backyard, so to speak, he knew it was up to him to keep it tidy.

"She yell at you much?" Wally Hurtado watched him maneuver a big glop of wet concrete onto the plywood. Despite Ramsey's pains, some of it fell off, right into the middle of an elderly forsythia.

"Yell at me?" Ramsey held his dripping trowel over the plywood and stared at Wally. "What are you talking about?"

"You know. Ms. Saunderson. You gettin' so neat and all. I just wondered if she was yellin' at you for bein' messy on the job."

"She doesn't yell at me." *At least, not for that,* Ramsey told himself. *At least, not yet.* Because he'd gone out of his way to keep it clean. "It's my aunt I'm afraid of." He grinned at Wally. "She might be far away, but she'd still have my head if I trampled her bushes."

"Sure." Wally looked unconvinced. "This Ms. Saunderson, she's a contractor, too?"

"That's right." Ramsey set his piece of plywood aside and picked up the concrete hose. Any minute the pump would kick in, and Wally's inquisition would be over.

"One of the boys heard you and her was a hot number a while ago."

"The boys have ears like Dumbo's," Ramsey muttered. To his relief George turned on the pump, and its roar blasted the conversation away. He didn't want to give Wally any more information. Wally loved gossip. Probably his wife would pick up everything he wanted to know in the village, and Wally would tell the rest of the crew all about his and Emmy's former relationship. Although hotter love affairs had occurred in the past five years, old news was always treasured in Dusty Springs, where some of the citizens knew the peccadilloes of families back for generations, and were not hesitant to air the sins of fathers and grandfathers.

By the time they made it all the way around the foundation, Ramsey's knees were aching, even though he'd strapped on knee pads that morning. Whistling to himself, George washed up his grids and hoses before towing the pump away. Wally drove off to supervise at the spec house, and Ramsey settled down to finishing the top of the foundation wall.

He was putting yellow safety caps on the sharp ends of the rebar when Gloria Gruenwald drove up. Her white convertible had the top up on this brisk day. She wore white, too—a white jumpsuit that covered her sleek body but was in no way demure.

"Ramsey," she said, smiling brilliantly at him. "I've tracked you down at last."

"So I see." Silently he cursed whichever member of his crew had given him away. "How are you, Mrs. Gruenwald?"

"Gloria," she told him, coming closer. Her nose wrinkled a little, and he glanced down at his T-shirt, stained with gray cement dust and black dirt. "I'm fine. Disappointed, but fine."

He gazed at her stolidly, refusing to rise to the bait, and she was forced to continue. "I thought you'd be working on my place by now, Ramsey. How am I going to move in if it never gets finished?"

"You haven't let me know what you decided," he said, refusing to brush off the dirt that she kept looking at. "As I recall, you were going to go with the contract or pay for upgrades. Which is it to be?"

"I can't afford the upgrades," she said plaintively, coming a little closer. Her scent, heavy and erotic, filled his head. He had to fight the urge to step back out of its range.

"We'll go ahead with what the contract specifies, then."

Her eyes narrowed. "But that wouldn't satisfy me, Ramsey. I like satisfaction." She laid one hand on his arm. He looked down at the perfectly manicured nails, the many rings.

"Legally," he said, keeping his voice even, "you already owe me a milestone payment for getting the house closed up. I can't proceed until I get that. Then we can go ahead with the finish work, as specified. That's all the satisfaction I can give you."

"I don't think so." Her voice was husky. "There's another kind of satisfaction. It doesn't cost anything, and it gives so much. You could provide me with that, Ramsey, if you wanted to."

He saw confirmation of what she wanted in her eyes, and was sorry. He'd seen it before in woman clients, once in a while, although none had been so blatant as Gloria. There had been one time when he'd come in to a house, expecting to find it empty so he could tear out the old kitchen, and instead discovered the owner still asleep—or so she said. The memory of her nearly transparent nightie never failed to bring an appreciative smile to his face. But the offering there had been tacit, and his own retreat unharassed.

He'd seen what happened when contractors canoodled with clients. It nearly always ended in disaster. He'd had a few lovers, before and after Mary Ellen, but he was choosy, and he wasn't looking for short-term relationships, anyway. He couldn't give Gloria what she wanted—he didn't even feel the urge to. What he wanted was for her to leave him alone, let him do what the contract said and get away from her.

She must have seen the rejection in his eyes. "You'd like it, Ramsey," she purred, crowding him. Even the dirt on his T-shirt didn't stop her from pressing against him. "I can be very—satisfying. Especially for a man like you. I've heard about you in the village, you know. They say you're a loner."

Ramsey looked down at her dark, glossy hair and prayed for deliverance.

JEANINE HELD THE LEDGER board against the kitchen wall and watched critically while Oscar nailed it in. Mary Ellen, waiting to hoist the first cabinet into place, had to appreciate the meek way Oscar took Jeanine's strictures. It was like watching a kitten chide a tiger.

"Not so hard," Jeanine grumbled. "We're not trying to bring down the temple walls here, Samson. Just get it to the wall and don't make rubble while you do it."

"Right," Oscar said, darting Jeanine a glance she didn't see. Exasperation and humor were contained in it, and Mary Ellen decided that Oscar would soon be giving back as good as he got.

As soon as the ledger was up, Jeanine turned to help Mary Ellen lift the cabinet. Her hands were very gentle on the beautiful wood. Mary Ellen didn't blame her. The cabinets were made of butterwood to fit into the Shaker-style kitchen the Montoris had designed. There weren't many carpenters who also made cabinets; Jeanine was one of the few.

Oscar, too, was impressed as they unwrapped the cabinets and hung them. "These are something. You must have an incredible woodshop."

"It's okay," Jeanine said. She guarded her shop fiercely, Mary Ellen knew, after her ex-husband had absconded with a router and several of her most cherished chisels. Jeanine had gotten the chisels back by merely marching into Derek's new apartment and demanding them, but he'd sold the router. Now she didn't let anyone in without doing a security clearance. Mary Ellen felt sorry for Oscar. Simply by expressing interest in her tools, he'd encouraged Jeanine to be even more hostile.

"Better than Norm Abrams's, huh?" Oscar winked at Mary Ellen, and Jeanine took the bait.

"I make do with quite a bit less wattage than he does." Jeanine scowled at them. "I suggest we stop discussing my tools, such as they are, and get these cabinets hung."

"Right. Absolutely." Mary Ellen helped Oscar screw the cabinets to the ledger board while Jeanine fussed around with the base cabinets, dodging past them to mark a level line on the wall.

"So, are the tilers about done in Mrs. Hedstrom's bathroom?" Jeanine pulled the paper off the sink cabinet.

"They'll be over here in a couple of days. You should be able to rough in the counter by then, right?" Mary Ellen braced one of the cabinets while Oscar drove the screws home.

"No sweat." Jeanine marked the location of the plumbing studs on the sink cabinet's back. "We'll have the center island in by tomorrow."

Oscar drilled the holes for the plumbing, proving himself as handy with the big spade bit as with the screwdriver attachment. Mary Ellen drew Jeanine into the hall while he worked. "Oscar seems to be doing fine," she said.

"He's not bad," Jeanine admitted grudgingly. "If only I didn't keep tripping over him all the time."

"He's certainly big enough to avoid," Mary Ellen said, watching Oscar brace the cabinet back with one hand while he pushed the drill effortlessly through the wood.

"He's okay. I take it you want to keep him on the crew."

"Well, he's going back to school in January. But until then, yes, if he works out well, I thought we could use him." Mary Ellen looked at Jeanine carefully, noticing the lines of strain on her face. "Is this too much for you, Jeanine? Filling in for me, I mean. The responsibility—"

"It's not that." Jeanine cut her off. "You're handling the paperwork, and the jobs are running quite smoothly."

"Is Oscar bothering you?" Mary Ellen glanced at him again. He had picked up the sink cabinet to move against the wall, needing no help from them.

"Oh, no." Jeanine looked shocked. "He has a girlfriend, a very nice woman who came by one day with lunch. She's doing women's studies at Berkeley. No, it's nothing to do with work."

"Derek," Mary Ellen guessed, and knew by the increased misery on Jeanine's face that she'd hit it right. "What's he done now?"

"He wants alimony!" Jeanine threw her hands in the air. "He claims I owe him alimony because he always did the housework and stuff and couldn't establish himself in a career." Her voice rose, and Oscar turned to look at her, concern evident in his expression. "Alimony! I ask you. How am I supposed to keep supporting the bum? He didn't do jack while we were married, and now he wants to keep living off me. Why did I ever marry him? How could an intelligent woman make such a mistake?"

"Have you got a good lawyer?" It was the only thing Mary Ellen could think to offer her friend, besides a shoulder to cry on, and Jeanine wasn't the crying kind. She was the yelling, cursing, getting-even kind.

"I've got a lawyer." Jeanine took a deep breath, and seemed to regain some composure. "She says he hasn't got a chance in hell of being awarded alimony. But she warned me that there would probably be a lot of publicity, and that the costs would be larger than the no-fault divorce I'd planned." She shook her head. "I can't believe this is happening. I made the kind of mistake a lot of women make—marrying a guy who turns out to be a no-account loser. It just blows me away that I'm getting the shaft like this. I'll never let another man make a fool out of me.''

Mary Ellen could believe it. She said whatever comforting things she could, helped with the rest of the cabinets, and then left for Dusty Springs. But she couldn't concentrate on making notes for her projects; thoughts of Jeanine's miserable face kept intruding.

Why did love have to keep making fools of them all? Here she was, literally rubbing shoulders with Ramsey, and remembering all too well the chemical combustion that had made them lovers six years ago. Just thinking about the way he looked in his sweat-stained T-shirt, his broad shoulders and lean hips, the way the black hair tumbled down his forehead, made her catch her breath.

''Hormones,'' she told herself. Instead of Ramsey, she forced herself to conjure Jeanine, complete with hurt voice and wounded eyes. Jeanine and Derek had been hot for each other less than two years ago. He would show up at the construction sites around noon, and sometimes they'd vanish for a couple of hours, before Jeanine would sheepishly reappear and work late to make up for it. Everyone on the crew had taken a sisterly interest in the blazing romance and smiled knowingly at the long lunch hours. And now it had gone sour for her, too.

Could love last longer than a year? Mary Ellen considered this problem instead of thinking about tile wholesalers, appliances and floor coverings. Her love and Ramsey's had seemed to burn out in that time; Jeanine and Derek had broken up a year and a half after their hasty marriage.

"You're wrong, Aunt Alma," she murmured, making the turnoff for Dusty Springs. "A piece of paper, a legal commitment, don't mean anything when the chips are down. It just makes the whole situation more difficult to get out of." At least she and Ramsey had parted, if not amicably, without overt hostility. She'd simply left, taking with her the few things she'd brought—"only that and nothing more," she muttered to herself, passing Spring Hill. The sight of it reminded her of those ominous little red flags they'd seen on their picnic a few days earlier. No more than Ramsey or Lenore did she want to see tract houses all over Spring Hill. She would have to find out what was happening there.

Of course, if there was a way to stop development on Spring Hill, Ramsey would figure it out. She had to grant him a stubborn will verging on bullheadedness when it came to something he really wanted.

Too bad he hadn't really wanted her.

There was a dangerous thought. She pushed it hurriedly away, swinging her truck into Aunt Alma's driveway. She had nothing to regret about her year with Ramsey. Their mutual passion had made it inevitable that they would live together. And during that time she'd learned valuable skills. She'd gotten a start in work that she loved. They'd been unable to stay together, but that didn't mean the whole affair had been a mistake—just that it was over. Over. She didn't want Ramsey anymore. He didn't want her. They were both free—

Her truck screeched to a halt, a few feet in front of the spot where she'd meant to park. She didn't even realize she'd stepped on the brakes. Her eyes were riveted to the scene in front of her.

Ramsey MacIver was in the throes of a passionate embrace, right there in public view on Aunt Alma's side lawn, with some voluptuous, dark-haired woman Mary Ellen had never seen before.

She came to herself immediately, carefully shutting off the truck and putting on the hand brake. For an instant she wondered if she should wait for a few minutes for the entwined ones to come up for air.

Then she noticed that Ramsey was up for air. His eyes were fixed on her in a desperate plea. The woman, it was true, had her arms around him, but Mary Ellen saw that Ramsey was trying, gently but ineffectually, to release himself.

Stomping across the lawn, Mary Ellen told herself that her only reaction was one of tolerant amusement. But it wasn't true. She knew that, as surely as she knew that she would never admit it. Some primitive part of her wanted to yank at the woman's thick, glossy hair until it left her scalp.

Instead, Mary Ellen summoned a smile and said sweetly, "Can't you do this on your own time, Ramsey?"

The woman released her hold on Ramsey, and Mary Ellen was glad to see that the front of her elegant white linen jumpsuit was smeared with concrete dust and dirt. The stranger inspected Mary Ellen and dismissed her as a threat with one comprehensive stare. "Who is this, Ramsey?" Her voice was throaty and breathless. "Another disgruntled client?"

"Not exactly." Mary Ellen noticed for the first time the blobs of hardening concrete all around the house. The forms that had been empty when she'd left early that morning were now full of glistening gray matter. "You poured without me!" She glared at Ramsey, who'd lost no time in putting space between himself and his glamorous lady friend. "I thought we agreed—"

"Mary Ellen," he interrupted, "this is Gloria Gruenwald, who's building a new house over in the Cherry Lane area. Gloria, Mary Ellen Saunderson, my cousin and partner in renovation here."

Gloria's eyes narrowed. "Your cousin? I've heard something about you and a cousin—"

"That's a small town for you." Ramsey turned to Mary Ellen. "I didn't see any reason to waste time waiting for you. Now you're here, you can help finish."

"I know what that means—clean up the mess," Mary Ellen grumbled.

"He is messy, isn't he?" Gloria's voice was a possessive purr. "While your cousin cleans up here, Ramsey, why don't you get the guys back to my place?"

Ramsey took yet another step back when Gloria reached for his arm. "Sorry," he said. "I can't work there until we get the bugs out of the contract, and you meet the milestone payment. If you want to write me a check..."

Mary Ellen watched interestedly, as if it was a play. Gloria Gruenwald brought a theatrical quality to every movement, every sentence. Mary Ellen wouldn't have been surprised to learn that she was an actress. Certainly she was beautiful. That made Ramsey's obvious distaste for her even more astounding.

"I didn't bring my checkbook," Gloria muttered at last. The look she directed at Ramsey was less amorous than angry. "I want to get that house finished, quickly. I can't meet my social obligations in that little dump I'm renting.''

"I can't meet my financial obligations if clients don't pay up," Ramsey said reasonably. "The lumberyard, the crew, everyone wants to be paid. I'm no different.''

"There's more than one way to pay," Gloria said, and now the sultry overtones were completely gone from her deep voice, leaving it harsh. "You may pay more than you expect, Ramsey MacIver. I've offered you an opportunity few men get. I don't like being turned down.''

She turned and strode away, as fast as her chic white sandals would go. Mary Ellen raised her eyebrows.

"Pretty scary, huh? What's she going to do, poison her fingernails and then scratch you?''

Ramsey glanced at her. "That hadn't occurred to me," he admitted. "I thought the worst she could do was default and leave me with a half-built house on my hands.''

Mary Ellen dismissed Gloria. "What I want to know is why you went ahead with the pour after we agreed that you'd wait for me.''

Ramsey scowled. "We didn't agree. You announced that there'd be no pour until you were here. The pump was only available this morning, not this afternoon." He looked at her closer. "Why was it so important, anyway? I know how to get concrete poured. Were you afraid I'd ruin everything?''

"Not exactly," Mary Ellen mumbled. "I just wanted—well, you might as well know, Ramsey. I've never helped in a pour. I've seen it done a couple of times, but I wanted to work with the stuff so I could learn how to do it.''

Ramsey stared at her, open-mouthed. "You mean, for all that experience you keep throwing in my face, you've never slopped around in the concrete before?" He threw back his head and laughed. "I'll be. I never would have guessed it."

"I've formed several times," Mary Ellen retorted. "For your information, Mr. Know-it-all, many people learn by doing, and even from their mistakes. You, of course, were born knowing everything."

"Sorry." Ramsey looked genuinely abashed. "That was out of line." He hesitated a moment. "Actually, I've got to say I admire you for coming right out with it. If it had been me doing something unfamiliar, I probably never would have let on."

"Well," Mary Ellen said, clearing her throat. "Thanks."

"Don't mention it." He started to turn away. "And thank you," he said, turning back, "for rescuing me from Gloria. She sees herself as some kind of femme fatale—comes from being a two-bit TV reporter before she married this rich guy and divorced him. She keeps trying to seduce me into putting all these expensive extras into her house."

"Looks like she doesn't take no for an answer," Mary Ellen said, uneasily reminded of her visceral reaction to the sight of Gloria's arms wrapped around Ramsey. It was nothing more than cousinly protectiveness, she rationalized. She wouldn't think about it again.

"She's persistent," Ramsey agreed. "Well, shall we get to it?"

They worked on opposite sides of the house for a while. Mary Ellen's thoughts were rambling and chaotic. She would start a mental checklist of what had to be done, and find herself thinking of how brown Ramsey's hand had looked against that white linen.

It was a relief when Lenore showed up around three. She scolded Ramsey for the damage to the old foundation shrubs, and then cut them back to provide easier access to the sides of the house. Her cheerful conversation filled the silences that seemed so fraught with unspoken messages between Ramsey and Mary Ellen.

"So what are you going to wear tonight?" Lenore had to repeat the question before Mary Ellen came out of her fog enough to pay attention.

"Tonight? What's tonight?" She heaved a last blob of cement onto her wheelbarrow. "I planned to wear my pj's and bunny slippers, if you must know."

Lenore laughed. "That would create quite a sensation." She tossed an armload of forsythia branches into the wheelbarrow. "Do you mind if I put these branches in there?"

"Not at all," Mary Ellen told her. "It all goes to the debris box in the end."

Lenore added some more clippings. "Don't you remember? Tonight's the reception Arnold Hengeman is sponsoring. We're going to snoop around and find out what he's up to on Spring Hill."

"Oh, right." Mary Ellen remembered those little red flags. "Good idea. But it requires dressing up, you say?"

"Oh, yes." Lenore struck a pose, ruffling up her hair. "We like an excuse to don our fine feathers out here in the sticks, you know."

"Fine feathers. I don't think I have any."

Ramsey had come up during this last exchange, his eyebrows lowered over fierce black eyes. "You aren't seriously planning to prop up Arnold's walls tonight? That's tantamount to saying you approve of his scheming."

"Not at all." Lenore made her voice sound patient. "We'll be subversives. Not only can we find out what's happening, we can whisper our doubts into the ears of our good citizens."

"You're nuts," Ramsey said flatly. "Actions speak louder than words, and your actions will be the seal of approval."

Mary Ellen wavered a little, but Lenore simply smiled at Ramsey. "You just don't want your females to wander into another alpha male's herd," she said tolerantly.

"Huh?"

"I was reading about it in a magazine last night," Lenore explained. " 'Monkeys on our Backs,' the article was called. Said our hormonal cues are very similar to those of certain animals, like monkeys and wild horses—"

"Wild horses couldn't drag me to read that kind of drivel," Ramsey interrupted.

"It does sound weird," Mary Ellen said. "And we, of course, are not Ramsey's females. We can wander into any place we want to tie on the feed bag." She turned to Lenore, ignoring Ramsey's groan. "What time shall we go? Do you want me to come pick you up?"

"That would be good," Lenore agreed. She grabbed the wheelbarrow's handles. "I'll dump this stuff and see you around seven—late enough to be just one of the crowd, but before the food runs out."

"You sound like a regular social butterfly," Ramsey said, smiling in spite of himself. "Where did you learn all this?"

A shadow crossed Lenore's face. "It was awhile ago," she said evasively. "Maybe things have changed. But then, in Dusty Springs, hardly anything changes, right? That's why we love it." She trundled the wheelbarrow away.

Mary Ellen looked after her, troubled. "Has Lenore ever talked about that time she spent in L.A. to you?"

Ramsey took a moment to answer. "Not directly, no. She rarely refers to it, and I haven't pried."

"I'm not going to pry!" His words had sounded critical, and Mary Ellen's defenses kicked in. "I'm her friend, and I want to help. Maybe it would help her to talk about it. Obviously something bad happened."

"I'd let well enough alone if I were you." Ramsey scowled at her. "If she wants you to know, she'll tell you."

"Thank you for the advice," Mary Ellen snapped. "You, who are so great at interpersonal relationships, must of course be right."

Ramsey raised his voice. "I only meant—"

"When I want your advice—"

"Excuse me." The voice was quiet, but both combatants heard it anyway. They turned to face Mr. Featherstone, standing on the walk. He regarded them gravely, although his eyes were twinkling.

Mary Ellen was the first to recover. "Mr. Featherstone! Sorry not to see you sooner. We were having a—a conference."

"We were arguing, as usual," Ramsey said, shooting her a glaring look. "How are you, Featherstone? Any word yet from Aunt Alma?"

"I brought you each a letter." Mr. Featherstone reached into his suit coat and pulled out two small envelopes. "She sent me some forms and asked that I forward anything I have from you. So if you'd like to write, I'll be glad to send your letters on."

Mary Ellen took her envelope wordlessly. On the outside, her aunt's handwriting was familiar, but shaky. She blinked.

"Thank you so much, Mr. Featherstone. I'll just take mine upstairs to read, and drop off an answer to you tomorrow, if that would be all right."

"That's fine," the old lawyer said. Clutching her letter, Mary Ellen walked briskly around to the back of the house. She could feel Ramsey's gaze on her, but she didn't look back.

MARY ELLEN SANK DEEPER into the bathwater and deciphered the spidery writing for the second time.

Dear Emmy,
I was delighted to get your note, and so happy that you could forgive me for my rather imperious maneuverings. I wish I could have taken you into my confidence before leaving, but I knew you would find many objections with my idea, and so I'm afraid I just went ahead on my own.

I am sure you and Ramsey will do a wonderful job of fixing up the old place. Already I miss that cracked plaster and those uneven floors. It is silly of me, I know, but the very shabbiness of the house was so familiar. However, I want it to be strong and endure, if possible, far longer than I myself will.

As for my health, I find it quite peaceful here, with no housekeeping or gardening cares, although we are encouraged to get a great deal of exercise. I swim daily, and take long walks. Luckily there is not much smog right now. We eat delicious fruits and vegetables and rather terrible baked goods and cereals. There's no butter anywhere, or eggs, and of course no cream. I am told by the end of the six months I will no longer wish for these bad things. Right now I find myself thinking how much better the raspberries would be on top of some ice cream!

I am very proud of you for being so understanding to your nutty old aunt. The work is going well, I'm sure. Perhaps you could send me news of the old place once in a while. The roses must be putting out their final blooms. Lenore will be mulching the beds for winter soon. I shall be enjoying the hot tub while you are getting your fingers nipped with frost! Somehow it doesn't seem possible.

It gives me a wonderful feeling of peace to know I can leave my house cares in your hands, my dear. Please accept my deepest thanks, and let me know about your progress.

Mary Ellen reached up to set the letter on the window ledge, and soaked for a few more thoughtful moments. If Ramsey and Mary Ellen quarreled irrevocably, would Alma return too soon, undoing the good of her rest cure?

That couldn't happen. Mary Ellen let out the bathwater and dried off with brisk movements. She would put up with Ramsey, no matter how obnoxious he was, because she loved her aunt and didn't want to worry her.

"All the same," she muttered rebelliously, stalking back to her room to dress, "it would be easier if Ramsey had to go away, too."

CHAPTER SEVEN

ARNOLD HENGEMAN'S living room was big. But not big enough to accommodate all the people it was stuffed with. "Everybody in town must be here," Lenore yelled at Mary Ellen. They were huddled against a wall, eyeing the crowd around the buffet table. Lenore's voice was barely audible in the uproar.

"Mary Ellen! How nice to see you." The middle-aged woman who paused in front of them held a heaping plate of hors d'oeuvres in one hand, and a glass of champagne in the other.

"Nice to see you too, Mrs. Fordice." Mary Ellen smiled warmly at her eighth-grade teacher. "Are you still trying to beat *The Red Badge of Courage* into adolescent brains?"

"Actually, the Civil War is quite popular now," Mrs. Fordice confided, munching on a bacon-wrapped water chestnut. Lenore watched her hungrily. "We do a whole unit on it. Hello, Lenore. Have you visited the buffet yet?"

"Not yet," Lenore admitted. "We were waiting for the crowd to die down."

"Don't wait too long, or all the goodies will be gone." Mrs. Fordice waved a toothpick-impaled smoked oyster. "Dusty Springs loves free food." She turned back to Mary Ellen. "I was sorry to hear that

Alma has health problems. She said you'd be staying in her house while she's gone?''

"We're doing a little renovating for her," Mary Ellen said. Lenore murmured something and slithered away through the crowd.

"You and your cousin, is that right?" Mrs. Fordice's eyes were bright with interest. "We heard he was working there, too. Are you two patching it up?"

"We're just helping out Aunt Alma." Mary Ellen wished she, too, could escape. Perhaps Ramsey had been right for all the wrong reasons. It wasn't politics that would make this party uncomfortable for her, but simply meeting her former friends and neighbors, all of them full of questions.

"So you don't have any plans?" Mrs. Fordice looked a little disappointed.

"Just to fix up the house. We're not romantically involved, if that's what you mean," Mary Ellen said bluntly, and changed the subject. "Are you in favor of this Spring Hill development Arnold's promoting?"

Mrs. Fordice's face clouded. "Well," she said hesitantly, "I don't really know. I'm all for new families moving in and keeping the schools full, you understand. But Spring Hill has always been a recreational area for us. I had some idea that it actually was a park, or going to be a park. I thought maybe Arnold would explain how a housing development could go there."

Lenore returned, with two plates. "The oysters are gone, just like you said," she told Mrs. Fordice. "But they've got some prawns n .''

"Oh, how lovely." Fordice backed away. "Nice chatting with yo ave fun, now.''

Mary Ellen dabbled a prawn in the pool of cocktail sauce Lenore had spooned onto her plate. "Thanks," she said gratefully. "I was starving."

"Me, too." Lenore savored one of the salmon canapés. "Great spread. This must have cost Arnold a pretty penny. Oh, look." She stopped a passing waiter and they each helped themselves to a glass of champagne. "To having fun." Lenore lifted her glass to Mary Ellen.

"Ditto." They drank, and Mary Ellen began to relax. Despite the noise and the anticipation of more questions about Ramsey, she was glad she'd come. For one thing, the food beat her usual frozen dinner.

"That's a nice outfit." Lenore lifted an eyebrow. "Did you go shopping?"

"This is from Aunt Alma's archives," Mary Ellen said grandly. "She's never thrown anything out. There were trunks full of clothes in the attic." She lifted the hem of the embroidered peasant skirt. "But I couldn't find shoes to fit, and I hadn't brought good ones."

"I see." Lenore contemplated her feet. "High-top tennies—purple ones. They certainly add a unique touch."

"They go with the shawl." Mary Ellen touched the long, tasseled fringe on the violet silk shawl. "I can vaguely remember my mother wearing this outfit to a party in the sixties." She pulled the elastic neckline of the creamy lace blouse down on her shoulders. It had been white all those years ago when her mother had dressed in it. She remembered sitting on the bed, watching her mother's pretty, discontented face as she turned this way and that in front of the mirror. Cheryl Saunderson had found Dusty Springs dull, especially having to live with her much-older sister-in-law. When

Mary Ellen was thirteen, her mother had married again, to a prosperous Seattle businessman. The children she'd had since with her second husband absorbed most of her attention. There was little left for her oldest daughter, who'd left Seattle right after college graduation to return to the place she really considered home.

Mary Ellen took another sip of champagne, pushing the memories away. "A Halloween party, I think it was."

"It's fashionable again," Lenore said practically. "Gee, maybe there are some valuable vintage items in that attic."

"There are," Mary Ellen told her. "But Aunt Alma wouldn't want to get rid of them. She has every last artifact of her life with Scottie put away up there, and some of his mother's stuff, too. It's even clean, if you can believe it. She must get someone to sweep out the cobwebs regularly."

"She would." Lenore smiled fondly. "You know, what this party needs is Alma MacIver to come sweeping in, demanding to know what Arnold's up to."

"I can tell you that." The voice came from beside them. Mary Ellen turned, sloshing champagne onto her blouse. Propping up a nearby piece of wall was Ramsey, his arms crossed over his chest.

"What are you doing here?" Mary Ellen glanced nervously around. Already several of the people to whom she'd politely said that she and Ramsey were merely working together were watching avidly. "I thought wild horses couldn't drag you here!"

"Maybe they couldn't," Ramsey said, biting off the words, "but worrying about you and Lenore certainly could."

Mary Ellen scowled at him. "Just what harm do you think we can come to, surrounded by ninety-five percent of the adult residents of this town?"

"You can make Arnold think you're on his side." Ramsey looked deep into Mary Ellen's eyes. "That could be very dangerous."

For whom, she wanted to ask, but something in his eyes stopped her. Ramsey didn't like explaining.

Lenore shook her head tolerantly. "You've got conspiracy theory on the brain, guy. Old Arnold just sees a chance to make a bundle and is pursuing it. Don't underestimate your fellow citizens. They don't plan to roll over and play dead for him."

Jon pushed his way through the crowd and handed Ramsey a plate. "At least the food's good," he said plaintively. "But the crowd is getting rowdy. Can't give us small-town folks too much champagne without asking for trouble."

Ramsey declined the champagne. "I won't drink with Arnold Hengeman," he said, frowning at the rest of them. "I wouldn't eat with him, either, but I skipped dinner to ride herd on you two fractious women."

Lenore poked Mary Ellen. "See," she said in a loud whisper. "Just like that article I read. Next thing you know, he'll be beating a drum and wearing animal skins."

A smile struggled onto Ramsey's face, but it disappeared almost immediately when Arnold Hengeman stepped up to them.

"Great to see you folks," he said, beaming at them. "Ramsey! Nice of you to bury the hatchet, finally. I really appreciate your coming."

"Do you?" Ramsey pointedly didn't take the hand Arnold stretched out to him. "I didn't come here to lick your money-grubbing boots, Hengeman." The crowd's noise quieted and a circle formed around the group as the party-goers sensed drama. "I came to ask you some questions."

"Well, this is really just a kickoff celebration for my campaign, you know," Arnold said, his eyes narrowing. He pulled a little at the collar of the crisp white shirt he wore. "Have you met—oh, there you are, my dear. Gloria has graciously consented to act as my hostess tonight. You must remember her from her television days on the Channel 17 news team."

Mary Ellen blinked, taking in Gloria Gruenwald's white lace jumpsuit, its plunging neckline displaying a tanned expanse of well-toned flesh. She was every inch the affable TV celebrity, though Mary Ellen couldn't remember her from the few occasions she'd watched Channel 17, a small Sacramento station that mainly broadcast syndicated sitcoms and old movies.

Now Gloria was smiling and nodding at Lenore and Jon. Her smile didn't change when she faced Ramsey and Mary Ellen but her eyes were very cold. "We've met." Her voice was slow and husky.

Ramsey nodded, but absently. His attention was fixed on Arnold. "This development you've planned on Spring Hill—"

Arnold forced a laugh. "Now, Ramsey. That's not really on the table tonight—"

"If you're running for reelection, Arnold, everything about you is on the table," Ramsey said evenly.

There was a slight murmur of agreement from the crowd. Mary Ellen saw Mrs. Fordice in the front row, listening intently while she dipped raw vegetables into a mustard-colored sauce.

Mary Ellen didn't want to be encircled by the whole town; she felt like an actor with no idea what the play was or why she was even on the stage. She glanced at Lenore, who looked stern. Mary Ellen recognized that look; she'd seen it before when Lenore was uncomfortable. Only Jon seemed at ease, leaning against the wall, watching like a spectator at a volleyball game.

"Well, Ramsey, I suggest you come by tomorrow sometime and I'll be glad to discuss it with you. I have more information at my office," Arnold said. He would have edged away, but the crowd surrounding him didn't part.

"You can tell me right now just what the extent of the development is to be, and how you've gotten permission to build it on land that's supposed to be designated as a park in the future." Ramsey's voice was implacable.

Arnold fingered his collar again. "Now look here, Ramsey," he started, but Mrs. Fordice spoke up.

"I've been wondering that myself," she said, and around her many heads nodded. "Just how can anyone build houses on Spring Hill?"

"Not exactly on the hill," Arnold said, his gaze seeking through the crowd. "Of course we wouldn't build there."

"But if you build all around," said a man whom Mary Ellen recognized as Jim Crouch, manager of the Food Mart, "how will that affect our use of the hill? My family has a big reunion there every year."

"There would be easements—rights of way. The public would still be free to use the top of the hill." Arnold's voice began to take on the smooth, practiced locution of the politician. "By the terms of the development contract—"

"Just a minute." Bradley Hess pushed his way to the front of the circle. He owned the feedstore and was an outspoken opponent, Mary Ellen knew, of building houses on what had formerly been family farms. "Doesn't Spring Hill belong to the Dalhousie family? It was my understanding that old man Dalhousie had promised to put it in his will as parkland. Has he changed his mind?"

Arnold looked over the crowd again and smiled. "That question would be better put to Bob Markham, who I see back there. Bob, as you know, manages Mr. Dalhousie's property concerns."

People craned their heads and cleared a path to Bob Markham. He looked vaguely familiar to Mary Ellen. He was short and stocky, with receding hair that had once been red and was now mostly gray. Unlike Arnold, he appeared at ease.

"Well, Arnold," he drawled. "Thanks for putting me on the spot here." There was a ripple of laughter, and Bob Markham's eyes crinkled. "To tell the truth, folks, I'm rather in the dark about all this. As far as I know, Mr. Dalhousie has not changed his plans. He's made provisions for Spring Hill and some of the surrounding land to be donated to the county as parkland, along with a small trust fund for its upkeep. A very generous gift, I might remind you all, given land prices these days."

There was a murmur of agreement from the crowd. Now that attention had shifted away from them,

Lenore relaxed enough to whisper to Mary Ellen, "Looks like Mr. Markham should be running for public office. He knows how to handle them."

"But—" Mary Ellen began, and then Mrs. Fordice's voice cut through.

"That's very interesting, Bob," she said easily. "But if it's the case, what's all this development talk about? I got the brochure, same as everyone else. If Spring Hill is protected from development, how can they develop it?"

Bob Markham smiled again. "My guess is that they plan to buy some land around the hill, stick some of those big fancy houses out there, like the commuters buy, and call it Spring Hill Estates just because there's a view of the hill. Isn't that the way it really is, Arnold?"

Arnold's smile was tight. "Well, Bob, it pretty much comes down to that." He turned to Ramsey. "That satisfy you, MacIver?"

"Not really," Ramsey said. "Of course we all want to know if you have the proper permits and environmental impact reports. Some of us want to know why our elected representative is involved so heavily in this commercial venture—"

Arnold held up a hand. "Why, you make it sound morally questionable, Ramsey," he said, resuming his smooth persona. "I assure you, *I* would never be involved in anything illegal." His emphasis was slight, but Mary Ellen caught it, and she saw by the contraction of Ramsey's eyebrows that he'd noticed it, too. So, for that matter, had some of the old-timers in the crowd. They poked each other and broke into whispers.

Mrs. Fordice spoke, her teaching experience making her easily heard over the whispering. "No one suggested that," she said briskly. "However, Arnold, we are concerned about your motivation for pushing this development."

"I'm not pushing development per se," Arnold said earnestly. "However, as you know, new houses increase our tax base, and taxes fund our schools, pave our roads and help our poor. It's the only way to make it in today's world, friends. You've got to move ahead or get buried."

Some people nodded; others shook their heads doubtfully. Ramsey, his arms folded across his chest, was unconvinced, Mary Ellen could tell.

"I welcome inquiries such as my friend Ramsey MacIver has made," Arnold continued, aiming a big smile at Ramsey. "Believe me, my public life is an open book. And now, let's finish up all this great food. The caterers have done a swell job, haven't they?"

There was wholehearted agreement to this statement, and once again the conversation became general, and deafening. People drifted toward the buffet tables.

Ramsey looked at Mary Ellen, Jon and Lenore, and shrugged. "It was worth a try, anyway."

"You stirred 'em up, Ramsey." Jon straightened. "People will remember. Arnold managed to weasel out of it tonight, but we'll all be more alert now. If he tries to put one over on us, we'll know what to do."

"Will we?" Lenore twisted her hands together. "I keep remembering those surveyors, right on top of the hill. What were they doing there if all the development's going to be at the bottom? Arnold's tricky. Once they start bulldozing, it'll be too late."

"It won't come to that—at least not for a while," Ramsey promised. "There's no subdivision map on file yet in the county office—I checked yesterday. If necessary, we'll go to court and get an injunction."

Mary Ellen didn't say anything. She felt like an outsider. Spring Hill was important to her, but she hadn't lived in town for years. She wouldn't be staying after Aunt Alma's house was done. How could she add her voice to the argument?

She couldn't help watching Ramsey, though. That passionate defense of the right thing had attracted her to him in the first place. He'd been crusading then about the need for stricter building standards, and had made some enemies among the trades people, who considered him a troublemaker. But she had admired his concern for the consumer, and when the county had agreed to oversee construction, he'd felt vindicated.

There was something so attractive in that kind of integrity, Mary Ellen thought, staring at Ramsey, and then looking away quickly before he could catch her at it. Something that stirred her deeply, even though she didn't want to be stirred.

"Come on," Lenore said, poking her. "Didn't you hear? We're going to get a pizza. Too loud to talk in this room."

"Right," Mary Ellen said, feeling dazed. "Okay."

They piled into Jon's car. Lenore teased him about his car phone, and he chaffed her about composting everything, even pizza boxes. Mary Ellen listened without really hearing what they were saying. She sat in the back seat beside Ramsey, and his brooding presence seemed to fill the space between them.

Spiro's was crowded, mostly with high school students. Jon ordered the pizza to go, and they squashed themselves into a small booth to wait for it. Alexis Kapopolis, Spiro's son, came over to talk to Jon and Ramsey, with whom he'd gone to high school.

"You at the big doin's?" He eyed the women's elegant clothes with interest. "Mary Ellen, good to see you again." He shook his head. "Time passes fast, doesn't it? We had some fine parties a few years ago. And even before. Remember that time—oh, must have been twenty years ago, you wanted to come swimming with us? Ramsey got really steamed because your mom said he had to take you."

"I remember." Mary Ellen glanced sideways at Ramsey. "You wouldn't let me use the tire swing, or dive off the low-water bridge, or play water tag with you."

"Yeah, ol' Ramsey was pretty hostile, wasn't he?" Alex punched his buddy in the arm. "He did a hundred-and-eighty later, though, didn't he? Guess you got your revenge then. Heard you two were back together."

"You heard wrong," Ramsey growled. "We're doing a family favor, that's all."

"So you went to Arnold's." Alex shook his head. "Never thought you'd even speak to that guy again, let alone go to his party."

"He wasn't exactly your ideal guest." Jon grinned at Ramsey. "Gave old Arnold the regular Spanish inquisition."

Alex laughed. "Well, watch out then. We all know what Arnold is capable of."

"No, we don't." Lenore looked at Mary Ellen. "Let us in on it."

"It's ancient history," Ramsey growled. "Isn't that pizza ready yet?"

"Maybe." Alex went off and came back soon with a large box. "So is our place not good enough for you? Have to take it somewhere else?"

"Too noisy," Ramsey said, and Jon added, "too full of young kids. Makes us feel old, you know."

"You're telling me." Alex shook his head. "They treat me with such respect." He handed Jon the box. "Where are you going?"

Jon looked at them all. "Spring Hill, probably. Thanks, Alex."

It was only fitting, Mary Ellen thought. She managed to maneuver Lenore into the back seat with her. The pizza filled the small car with its spicy scent. As Jon drove, he and Ramsey chatted idly about their other high school friends. Lenore and Mary Ellen were silent.

The winding road to the top of the hill was punctuated with turnouts, each occupied by a parked car whose taillights flashed as Jon drove past. He and Ramsey glanced at each other, snickering.

"Yep," Jon said, pulling into the small parking lot at the top of the hill, "there sure would be a problem around here if Spring Hill weren't available. Where else could the hot-blooded youth go?"

"Disgraceful," Lenore said, smiling. "I'm starved. That little handful of hors d'oeuvres didn't amount to anything. Let me at that pizza."

Jon put the box on one of the picnic tables when they got out. There were no other cars parked in the lot, although Mary Ellen could glimpse a couple more pulled off the road.

"Thank goodness there aren't any neckers here," she said, biting into a slice. "Takes away your appetite." Her words came out muffled.

Lenore laughed. "I know what you mean. They'd be sitting there waiting for us to leave."

"Or not waiting, an even more horrifying idea," Jon said.

Ramsey deliberated for a moment. "What's on this? Looks like there are more toppings than crust."

"Everything," Jon said simply. "It's loaded."

"Anchovies," Mary Ellen said, pleased.

"You still eat anchovies? Thought your taste would have improved by now." There was a smile in Ramsey's voice, though his face was in shadow.

Lenore drew away with Jon, arguing over the merits of garlic. Ramsey sat at the table next to Mary Ellen, his jaws moving contentedly. "This is good," he said finally. "I was starting to get faint from hunger."

"You should have tried the prawns." Mary Ellen licked tomato sauce off her fingers. "They were excellent."

"Couldn't break bread with Arnold." Ramsey sounded more relaxed about it.

"What did happen between you and him?" Mary Ellen was curious. She took another slice of pizza. "Aunt Alma told me a little about it—said Arnold got you into trouble and weaseled out of it or something. What was it all about?"

"You make me sound like a pregnant teenager," Ramsey complained. "There isn't much of a story, really. Arnold was ripe for mischief in those days, and I was a bit rebellious myself. Did you say something?"

"Not at all. Just clearing my throat. Ahem."

"Well, anyway, we had wasted a six-pack one night and were looking for trouble. Arnold wanted to steal all the street signs downtown, but I talked him out of that. So he just took down the stop signs instead."

"Not a very civic thing to do," Mary Ellen observed.

"No, not at all." Ramsey's voice was grim. "I was going to put them back up, but I passed out. Next morning there was an accident because of the missing signs. No one was killed, but there was a big outcry about Arnold's little prank. Only he said he wasn't in on it. All the stop signs were in my car because I was going to put them back. Arnold said I must have done it, he couldn't believe it of me, but there was the evidence, and a lot more crap like that. I nearly got hauled off to jail. If I'd been eighteen, I probably would have been."

"But didn't you tell the truth?" Mary Ellen's blood boiled at the story of this ancient outrage. "Didn't you say that Arnold did it?"

"I told the cop who came around." The rising moon threw light on Ramsey's face. Mary Ellen could see his bitter smile. "He didn't believe me. Gave me a lecture about putting the blame on someone else. Reminded me I had quite a rep as a hellion." He shrugged and reached for more pizza. "After that, I kept my mouth shut. Aunt Alma, bless her, arranged for me to get into the Youth Conservation Corps. Arnold became a model citizen, and I still carry that baggage around."

Mary Ellen was quiet for a minute. "I wonder that you want to live here," she said finally.

"I didn't, for a while. But after college, I decided that I had been guilty, if not of the actual event, of the circumstances that made it possible. I said I'd pay Dusty Springs back. Since then, I've tried to do some good where I could."

"You've succeeded," Mary Ellen murmured. "Those building standards you helped get—that was worthwhile."

Ramsey stood and stretched. "Just enhanced my reputation as a troublemaker, among the trades," he said. "But I've discovered that I don't really give a damn what people say about me. I know the truth about myself." He picked up the empty pizza box. "Shouldn't we be getting out of here?"

Mary Ellen reached out and then dropped her hand, glad the darkness had hidden her impulsive gesture. "Why didn't you tell me this before?"

"No reason to." Ramsey folded the box into a smaller square. "We had other things to talk about then."

"Right." She could feel his eyes on her, even if she couldn't read his expression. It made her uncomfortable, as if he was actually touching her. "You're right, we should get going."

Jon and Lenore came back to the table. "Fourteen cars, just on top of the hill," Jon said breezily. "We counted. Too bad these kids aren't old enough to vote. You could get a petition going."

"Isn't the view beautiful." Lenore walked over to the railing at the drop-off. "The moon over the valley, the lights of town—" Her voice sharpened. "Wait a minute—is that a bonfire?"

They joined her, and Ramsey stiffened. "That's near my house," he said hoarsely. "Maybe—" He turned, running for the car.

They followed him, Jon starting the car before all the doors were shut. "It's probably okay," he said, gunning down the twisting road. "But why don't you call the fire department, just in case?"

Ramsey picked up the car phone. "Never thought these things would be useful," he admitted, his voice sounding cool. But Mary Ellen could hear the urgency behind the casual words. His terse conversation with the emergency dispatcher was over in seconds. "Hasn't been reported yet," he said, replacing the phone. "It must not be as big as it looked from up there or someone would have seen it."

Mary Ellen heard sirens start. Jon reached the highway and opened his BMW up. They flew along the back roads, avoiding the slower town streets.

The fire truck had pulled up outside Ramsey's house. He groaned. "The gate! I forgot. They couldn't get in." He pulled his keys out of his pocket and punched some buttons on the calculator-type gizmo that dangled from the chain. Mary Ellen was fascinated, but there was no time to ask questions. The gates opened and the fire truck charged up the driveway. Jon followed them, as fast as he dared. Already a couple of neighbors had gathered at the fence.

There was a red glow flickering through the windows of Ramsey's house. Mary Ellen had never been there before, and she took in the spare, stark lines, the huge front door. Ramsey ran to unlock it before the fire fighters could batter it down. One group had gone around to the side, where the glow seemed to originate. Another group disappeared cautiously into the house.

Jon pulled his car around to the side of the driveway, out of the way of any more emergency vehicles that might arrive. Ramsey joined them there, his face tense. "They wouldn't let me go in," he said.

"Well," Jon said after a minute, "it doesn't look too bad. Wonder how they got in to set it with your alarm in place."

"I was wondering that myself." Ramsey's voice was a low growl. Mary Ellen realized he was very angry.

"Why do you think someone set the fire?" She, too, was mesmerized by the red flicker that was visible at the rear corner. "Maybe it was the wiring or something."

"The wiring is fine," Ramsey said, snapping off the words. "I did it myself."

"That's what I mean."

Lenore tried to disguise her slightly hysterical laugh as a cough, and Jon said quietly, "Ramsey's had some threats before. There's little chance that this is accidental."

A coldness started inside Mary Ellen. "What kind of threats?" Her throat was very dry.

"Not death threats, so don't get melodramatic on me," Ramsey said irritably. "Just warnings to back off."

"Back off of what? This Spring Hill thing?"

Ramsey didn't answer. After a moment Jon said, "It seems so."

"What if you'd been there when the fire started?" Mary Ellen clenched her hands. "What if you'd been overcome by smoke—"

"Look, whoever did this probably made damned sure I wasn't there. They don't mean to hurt me, just scare me." Ramsey took Mary Ellen's shoulders between his hands. She just stared at him, feeling her teeth begin to chatter. "You'd better go home. Jon, can you—"

"I'm all right." She wrenched herself away, and suddenly hot, welcome anger poured through her. "Don't order me around, you stubborn, stupid...*man!* You couldn't open your mouth to tell anyone what was going on, but you couldn't keep it shut to save your life! What kind of—"

"Emmy. I told Jon." Ramsey reached toward her again, his face intent. She avoided his hand. "I told Frank Alverez."

"But you couldn't be bothered to tell me." She tried to keep the bitterness out of her voice; it betrayed something she didn't even want to think about. "Sure, turn up dead one day and let me get stuck with pouring your dumb foundation. Thanks a lot. Fine way to treat a co-worker."

"Emmy—"

The fire chief approached, and they all turned to face him. The orange glare was gone now, Mary Ellen noticed dully. Adrenaline could no longer keep her anger alive. All she wanted was to get away from the smell of smoke.

"Well, Ramsey, you were sure lucky," the fire chief said. Mary Ellen tried to remember his name—Harry or Henry, or something like that, she thought.

"Thanks, Herb." Ramsey clapped the chief on the back. "What happened, do you know?"

Herb held up a Ziploc bag with something black inside. "Found this. Looks like some kind of detonator. We'll send it to the specialists in Sacramento." He pointed up the road. "Your alarm didn't keep them out because they'd cut the phone lines, and it reports over the lines. Guess they cut the lines and then just climbed over the gate. One of your neighbors saw the fire a few minutes before you did and couldn't get through to report it.''

"Good thing Jon has a car phone.'' Ramsey looked back at his house, his face grim. ''What's the damage?''

"Not so bad.'' Herb took off his hat and wiped his forehead. ''Kitchen's gutted. A little structural damage—nothing much. Your house is well-built—shear wall and Sheetrock kept the fire from spreading.'' He clapped his hat back on. ''You can get in now to get your things, if you want. We'll leave someone out here tonight to make sure it's truly out. I'd advise you to board it up tomorrow, if you want to hold on to your valuables. Be best if you find somewhere else to stay while we're conducting the investigation.''

They watched Herb walk back to the house. ''You can stay with me,'' Jon offered.

"Your place is tiny,'' Ramsey said absently. ''Who knows how long this investigation will drag out? I need someplace where I won't be in the way.''

His eyes were fixed, speculatively, on Mary Ellen. She glanced around at the circle of faces, and saw they were all looking at her with that considering expression.

"The Sta-More is supposed to be good,'' she said helplessly.

"Can't hack a motel for more than a night or two,'' Ramsey said.

"Well—rent a house, then.''

"Why bother?'' He stepped toward her. ''There's a whole house available, very convenient for my work, that happens to belong to a close relative of mine. I'll move into Alma's with you, Emmy.''

CHAPTER EIGHT

MARY ELLEN SAT on the front porch swing, her knees drawn up to support the pad of paper she held. Though it was getting dark, there was still enough light to write by. The air was crisp and very clear, one of the reasons she'd chosen the porch. Inside, it was getting pretty thick, both literally and emotionally.

"Dear Aunt Alma," she wrote, conscious of the faint sound of water running in the bathroom. Her own hair was still damp from an evening shower. They wouldn't have the bathroom much longer; soon it would be sponge baths in the sink.

"You'll be glad to know that your fondest dream has come true. Due to a mishap at Ramsey's place, he's moved in here."

Mary Ellen stopped for a minute, considering. Could her aunt possibly have— No, no. It didn't bear thinking of. Aunt Alma could be ruthless when she wanted to accomplish something, but she'd never go so far as to bomb Ramsey's house.

The faint sound of water ceased, and Mary Ellen hurried with her letter. She wanted it finished and sealed before Ramsey came downstairs.

"Since he's going to be living here while his place is put right, it would be better if I stayed in Berkeley and came here daily. It's quite a commute, but I don't mind, really. And although I have some projects there that need attention, I would spend the majority of my time here. Please let me know if this arrangement is acceptable to you.''

Mary Ellen was not at all confident that her aunt would let her off the hook. After all, fate had conspired to hand Alma just what she'd been angling for. But Mary Ellen had to make the gesture. If she didn't try to get free, she would be signaling that the situation was fine with her. And that just wasn't true. Already she was finding it hard to live side by side with Ramsey.

Her pen poised just off the paper, she thought about the previous week. Ramsey had spent a couple of days clearing away the debris in his house, and she'd gotten things pretty well organized in Berkeley while he was busy. She would not have even known he was in the house except for his shaving kit next to her flowered toiletries bag in the bathroom. That had lent an unmistakably male aura to a house long used to feminine rule.

Now, with his crew busy replacing the damaged wiring and drywall in his kitchen, Ramsey had turned his attention back to Alma's house. They'd spent three long days demolishing plaster and tearing out walls. The Dumpster at the curb was overflowing.

But the main difference was that he didn't leave at the end of the day. Instead, he stayed around, taking showers, commandeering the kitchen, getting in her hair. Arguing with her constantly about her renovation choices.

"We have started demolition on the downstairs to make the powder room where the old butler's pantry used to be," she wrote, "and to convert the maid's bedroom and bath into an efficiency apartment, as you requested. The kitchen goes next, and then we'll go upstairs to put in another bathroom and walk-in closet where the small bedroom was, next to your room. At that point it will be incredibly uncomfortable here. I hope Ramsey's place is ready for him by then.''

She reread that paragraph, uneasily aware that she was whining. But she needed to, and no one else was willing to listen to her. When she'd voiced a complaint to Lenore, her friend had merely indicated that anyone who objected to a first-class cook moving in with her had a hole where her brain ought to be. So she was reduced to making a written moan of it to her aunt, who would doubtless simply enjoy the idea of all this forced proximity.

Besides, Mary Ellen told herself, when the kitchen went, there went Ramsey's usefulness. They'd be reduced to a microwave and a hot plate; she defied even the world's best cook to do any better with those tools than she could.

But she was ashamed of complaining to her aunt about these petty details. ''Never mind my grouchiness,'' she wrote quickly, hearing the stairs creak under Ramsey's feet. ''I love you lots and want you to get completely well. Ignore all this and just concentrate on your oat bran, or whatever.''

She stuffed the letter into an envelope ready to hand to Mr. Featherstone, and then put the swing lazily in motion. The sky was cobalt blue with violet streaks of leftover sunset, and the faint spangles of early stars. She wrapped her elbows in her hands against the increasing coolness, and told herself she'd go in when Ramsey came out.

From Aunt Alma's front porch she could see down
the hill to practically the whole of Dusty Springs: the
few streets of the downtown area with its central
square, the storefronts with their awnings, the library
in the old elementary school, the new elementary
school to the east of town, and to the west, the middle and high schools.

If she followed that road farther west, she'd come
to Ramsey's house. She remembered when there'd
been nothing out there except pastureland and scrub
pine. Now there were several large houses, the owners'
privacy carefully preserved with surrounding trees and
shrubs. From something Jon had let slip, she understood that Ramsey had been responsible for the subdivision map, and had built many of the houses. If so,
his work was a credit to him. She had driven out there
the day before yesterday and been quite impressed with
the area. In her mind, it represented a vast improvement from its undeveloped state.

A cold breeze came along, lifting the hairs on her
arms, and she jumped to her feet. It was getting later,
and Ramsey hadn't bothered to try to find her. That
was encouraging, she told herself. It meant he'd accepted that they were nothing more than unwilling
roommates. It was what she wanted.

With those hollow thoughts ringing in her head, she
went inside.

The living room was empty, and the hall was dark.
But the swing door at the end of it that led into the
kitchen was open, and a flood of light poured out of
it onto the black-and-white marble floor. She thought
about going on up to her room, but she was hungry
and a tantalizing aroma was wafting through the hall.
It pulled her toward the kitchen door.

Ramsey stood in front of the old Wedgewood stove, his hair still damp from the shower. He was barefoot, scowling in concentration at something in the big skillet on one of the burners. There were greens and tomatoes on the counter beside the sink. The domestic scene caused a strange, almost painful, sensation in Mary Ellen's chest. She put it down to heartburn, or hunger pangs.

Ramsey turned and saw her standing in the doorway. "There you are," he said, waving the wooden spoon at her. "I thought the smell of this jambalaya would fetch you."

"Is that what it is?" Suddenly Mary Ellen wasn't as interested in the food as she'd expected to be. She felt breathless, as if she'd been kicked in the stomach or was coming down with something. "I could help, I guess."

"You can throw a salad together if you like," Ramsey said magnanimously. "The dressing's in the bottle on the counter there."

Like an automaton, Mary Ellen tore greens and sliced tomatoes and cucumbers. Ramsey remained silent, stirring his concoction. She wanted to speak, wanted some light chatter to distract her, but with Ramsey, there would be none of that. If she opened her mouth, he would start talking about getting rid of the pantry she'd planned in favor of European-style cabinets, or arguing for vinyl flooring instead of hardwood in the kitchen. And just then she didn't think she could hold up her end of an argument.

When the salad was finished she set the table, adding napkins and, after she opened the refrigerator for the butter, wineglasses. There was a bottle of dry Sémillon cooling in there. Her uneasiness deepened.

"Done," said Ramsey, spooning the rice-and-shrimp mixture into a serving bowl. He brought it to the table, and then got the wine. "This goes well with spicy food," he commented. "Do you want some?"

Silently Mary Ellen indicated the two wineglasses. Ramsey's eyebrows rose briefly. She felt she'd crossed a line he'd drawn, and shivered.

It wasn't possible to sit at the table with him, eating the dinner he'd cooked, and not talk. She forced herself to make conversation.

"So what will you do for a kitchen after we tear this place apart? We're almost ready to do that," she said.

Ramsey helped himself to salad. "You know, we could finish the downstairs apartment before we do this kitchen."

"We could," Mary Ellen said, savoring a plump, pink shrimp. "But it's much more efficient to do it all at once. Otherwise we'll be calling the trades back every whipstitch."

Ramsey frowned, but didn't deny it. "My own kitchen won't be done for another month," he said, shooting a look at her. "The cabinets have to be special-ordered. Otherwise, we could move in there while this place is being torn up."

Mary Ellen laid down her fork. "Ramsey MacIver, you're out of your mind. I'm letting you live here, but it's not by choice. Even if your house was ready, I would never move in with you."

"Even when the bathrooms are gone?" He summoned a smile, but his eyes were tense. "I just felt I could return the favor, that's all. It's going to be awful here pretty soon, Emmy. Especially if you do what you just said, and rip out all the plumbing at once. What will you do then?"

"My plans are to have the plumbers run copper in the upstairs bathroom first," Mary Ellen said distantly. "I can use the toilet in the maid's room and the kitchen sink while that's going on. Then when they're ready to move down here, I'll be able to put the upstairs bathroom back together."

"You're going to sneak over to Lenore's for showers," Ramsey stated with certainty.

"Well..." Mary Ellen saw the smile he struggled to contain, and matched it with a rueful grin of her own. "How did you guess?"

"I'm going to Jon's for the same reason." He added a little more wine to both their glasses. "Good to have friends, eh?"

"It makes life worth living," Mary Ellen said fervently. She took a small second helping of the jambalaya. "This is very good, Ramsey. Too bad you lose the stove tomorrow."

His eyebrows snapped together. "We won't get to the kitchen until next week, if we're taking out all the plaster in the maid's room and reframing there."

"Demo first, then framing." Mary Ellen laid down her fork. "If I remember right, you taught me that, Ramsey. Don't you follow your own rules anymore?"

"I'm flexible, something you were always nagging me to be." Ramsey stared across the table at her. "What's the point of making a big mess in here before we need to? Let's get everything else done first."

What he said was reasonable enough, but his tone was the dictatorial one that always put Mary Ellen's back up. "We're doing it my way," she said coldly. "Remember? I'm in charge now."

"That's right," he said, his voice tight. "You're the boss. Well, I see your plan, Emmy. You want to make me so uncomfortable I'll leave." His eyes burned into hers. "It won't work. I'll stay as long as I feel like it—even after my house is done, if I want to. There's not a damned thing you can do about it. So think about that, boss lady."

He threw his napkin on the table and stalked out. Moments later she heard his truck roar down the driveway.

Mary Ellen stared around the kitchen, contemplating the unwashed dishes, the general air of festivity gone wrong. She cursed the stupidity that had led her to drink wine with the enemy. All that time he'd simply been working on her, trying to get his own way. Her chin rose. He wouldn't succeed. She would go on with her plan, no matter how hard he fought against it.

But in the meantime, there were a lot of dirty dishes. She thought about leaving them for Ramsey to find, but he had cooked dinner. It was only fair that she wash up. She would clean up the kitchen, and then she'd go over to Lenore's for a little tea and sympathy.

AFTER A PERFUNCTORY KNOCK on Lenore's door, Ramsey pushed it open. "It's me," he called gloomily.

"Be right there," Lenore's voice came from the kitchen. Ramsey prowled her compact living room, with its antique furniture smothered in hand-crocheted doilies and small tables brimming with plants and dried flowers. Lenore's little house was just right for her, somehow, he thought. Cozy and unexpected.

Beyond the living room was an even smaller dining room, with built-in, glass-paned cupboards and a sideboard. On the square oak table were packs of cards and some coasters.

He walked on through to the kitchen, which was really nothing more than a hallway with elderly appliances—a tiny stove and a refrigerator—along the walls. A small counter was topped with cupboards. Everything was scrupulously neat, and the window over the sink was screened with hanging vines. Lenore had a lot of little knickknacks and pictures around which gave the room a cozy air, even if it was a nightmare for cooking. He had to admit that Lenore did a credible job, but he suspected she mostly ate out of cans and boxes, like Mary Ellen.

"Where's Mary Ellen?" Lenore turned from making a pot of coffee and looked past him. "You did tell her, didn't you?"

"No." He shoved his hands in his pockets, unable to meet her clear gaze. "We had a big argument and I just left. I don't want to play cards with her."

"Well, that's a mature attitude," Lenore said, pushing past him to set the tray of coffee and cups on the dining room sideboard. "I was looking forward to having another woman at our monthly poker games."

"Why didn't you tell her, then?" He wandered after her, pouring himself a cup of coffee before he realized he didn't want to drink it. "Is this decaf?"

"I forgot," Lenore said frankly. "It's decaf, but you can have a beer if you'd rather. There's some in the fridge."

Ramsey poured the coffee down the kitchen sink and went to find a beer in the refrigerator. Jon arrived while he was looking for it. He waited a minute before going back out, so Lenore could tell Jon about his bad behavior and save him having to confess. He looked forward to these poker games. Usually it was just the three of them, although sometimes Jon brought another woman along, or Lenore invited someone to join them. They usually played at Ramsey's house, but this month Lenore had volunteered to host the group, given the state of his place.

He carried his beer to the dining room and chose a chair. Jon shook his head at him. "Fighting again." He disappeared to get himself a beer, then sat down opposite Ramsey. "Not the grown-up behavior I expect from you, MacIver."

"She wanted to get my goat," Ramsey muttered. "But the weird thing is, I thought we were going to have a nice dinner together for a change. Just for a few minutes, there was a feeling—" He shrugged and looked up, realizing that they were both staring at him eagerly. "It was nothing," he said, waving one hand. "What have you all been up to today?"

Lenore and Jon exchanged a significant look, ignoring his change of subject. "I should call her," Lenore said, chewing on her lower lip. "I meant for the four of us to play cards tonight, whether you have trouble getting along with your cousin or not."

"You can ask her over," Ramsey said, pushing his chair away from the table. "It's your privilege. And I can discover some important business I have to do elsewhere."

"Cut off your nose to spite your face, you would," Lenore grumbled. "You want to play poker and you know it. I know how you lust to win."

"It's not lust," Ramsey protested. "I just like to take home a big pile of winnings."

"I'm going to win tonight," Lenore said calmly. "You'll be leaving empty-handed. I feel lucky."

Jon rubbed his hands together. "I feel lucky too," he said gleefully. "I'll need a grocery bag to haul my take away. So deal, already."

"I'm calling Mary Ellen first," Lenore said, going over to the phone. "And you're not going anywhere," she added. Ramsey blinked at the sternness of her gaze. "You're going to sit there like a civilized person and behave yourself, or I'll bring out those pictures I took the time you buried your Bobcat to the axle in the gravel pit."

Jon clamored to see the pictures, but Lenore was busy dialing. Ramsey didn't leave. He wanted to play poker, he told himself, and that's what he'd do, Emmy or no Emmy. The notion of having Lenore and Jon broker a truce for them was compelling as well. He'd definitely sensed tender emotions in Mary Ellen that evening, before she'd dug her heels in. Before he'd tried pushing her around, which he was able to admit he'd done. It was his nature to push, to put himself in charge. And it seemed to be her nature to resist. How could two such people ever come to any accord?

"She's not there," Lenore announced, hanging up the phone. "Did she say she was going out?"

"No." Ramsey's mind switched onto another track. Maybe she'd been thinking about some other guy, and that was the reason for the expression he'd glimpsed on her face. Maybe she had a date—with that creep Arnold. If that was the case, he'd been crazy to spend even one minute imagining himself conceding to her judgment and direction. But then, he thought, gripping the beer bottle, he was crazy. Since Mary Ellen had been thrown back into his life, he'd lost the capacity to reason.

Lenore cocked her head, and a moment later Ramsey heard the footsteps on the front porch. Lenore threw open the door. "So you knew, after all! Great."

"Knew what?" Mary Ellen stood in the doorway, blinking. Ramsey stared hungrily at her wind-ruffled hair, her flushed cheeks. She wore a blanket-plaid fleece jacket and well-washed jeans. When her gaze met his, she frowned and looked away. "I just came over to shoot the breeze. I can leave if you're busy."

Lenore dragged her into the house. "Now, now," she admonished her friend. "You're supposed to be joining us for our monthly poker game. I told Ramsey to tell you, but he says he forgot. Luckily, you've got nothing better to do."

"I didn't say that." Mary Ellen hung back when Lenore tried to pull her over to the table.

"I said it, but it's true, isn't it? You wouldn't have come over if you'd had something else to do." Lenore was triumphant. "Now, you sit down there, next to Jon. Want a beer or some coffee?"

"A beer," Mary Ellen decided. "I'm not driving."

Ramsey scowled again. That was a rub at the way he'd peeled out of her driveway earlier, he knew. Well, he didn't usually let his temper get the better of him on the road. From now on he'd drive as though he were carting eggs.

Mary Ellen surveyed the packs of cards and coasters. "I didn't bring any money," she said, accepting the beer Lenore brought her. "What are the stakes?"

"We just play for peanuts," Lenore said reassuringly. "I'll stake you. My first deal. Five-card stud, double or nothing, jacks to open."

"SEE YOUR RAISE, and raise you two." Ramsey pushed three peanuts toward the pile in the center of the table. He was doing okay, but he couldn't afford to lose another pot. And his hand wasn't all that great. He would have folded, but it was just him and Mary Ellen. Jon and Lenore were watching, Jon absently ruffling the rest of the deck.

"Call." Mary Ellen tossed a couple of peanuts into the pile. "What do you have?"

Ramsey flipped up the down cards and arranged his hand, best five out of seven. "Two pair, jacks over sixes," he admitted. It wasn't much of a hand for seven-card stud.

"Full house, aces and tens." Triumphantly, Mary Ellen put her hand on the table, and raked in the pile of peanuts. She had a considerable mound already. His stash was definitely depleted.

"Pass the deal," Lenore said briskly. "Your turn, Ramsey. What game?"

He shuffled, and let the cards riffle back. "I hadn't thought. Spit in the ocean? Blackjack?"

"You don't have a very big stake for blackjack," Mary Ellen observed.

"Right. I'll leave that for your turn." He shuffled once more and began dealing. "Seven-card stud again. Jacks or better. High-low split the pot."

"Aces high or low?" Lenore looked at her hole cards.

"Yup." He glanced slyly at Mary Ellen. She had a good poker face on her, he had to admit. But she sometimes forgot to put it on first thing in the game. He might have an inkling about her hole cards if he could catch her expression.

Judging by the look on her face they were nothing special. But then, he had taught her that look when he'd taught her how to play poker one summer, when he was twelve and bored out of his skull, and she was an eager-to-please eight-year-old. She'd been very earnest about learning, and they'd whiled the hours away with many games: crazy eights, poker, canasta, war, kings-on-the-corner. He'd made his way through Hoyle's, and taken Mary Ellen with him. Playing cards together had been a feature of summer until she'd moved away at thirteen when her mother remarried. By then he'd been more interested in hell-raising than in playing with his little cousin.

But when she'd come back to Dusty Springs after she'd graduated from college, she'd bowled him over. After a month, they'd been lovers. In two months, they were living together. Things had happened fast, but not really fast enough for him.

He remembered a night when he'd picked her up at Alma's, and instead of the movie they'd meant to see, they ended up at his place, the run-down house he'd bought the year before and was slowly renovating in his spare time. He didn't remember which of them had spotted the deck of cards and suggested they play strip poker. He only remembered how he kept trying to win, and how Mary Ellen had looked when she'd finally unhooked her bra, and how he hadn't been able to wait any longer, and how the cards had ended up all over the floor, with the two of them on top of them—

"Are you going to bet, Ramsey?" The patient note in Lenore's voice got through to him. She must have already asked him once.

"Sure," he said, blindly shoving a peanut into the middle of the table. His eyes found Mary Ellen's, and he knew that she, too, was remembering that game. One searing look, and then she studied her cards, refusing to meet his eyes again. He tried to steady his hands as he dealt the next couple of rounds, but he kept seeing her discarding that little scrap of lace, the teasing smile on her face that had changed into sensual intentness, the sweet weight of her breasts in his palms. He shifted uneasily in his chair. This game was turning into sheer physical torture.

Lenore and Jon were talking about Halloween and the haunted house that the downtown merchants were sponsoring for the kids. Mary Ellen, Ramsey noticed, wasn't joining their conversation. Her face was rigid, expressionless, but he'd be willing to bet that the details of their last poker game were as fresh in her mind as in his. Perhaps, later on, when they were back at Aunt Alma's house . . . He gave himself over for just a moment to imagining that he hadn't been wrong when Mary Ellen had added the wineglasses to the table at dinner, that their feelings for each other were still there, still strong.

"Well," Mary Ellen said abruptly, cutting into the discussion of whether peeled grapes or cooked pearl onions made better ghoul's eyeballs, "I'm folding. My hand's crap." She tossed her cards onto the table. "Listen, I have to go. You all can divide my winnings."

"It's still early," Lenore protested. "You could get better cards. Stay for a few more hands at least."

"My luck won't change, I can feel it." Mary Ellen pushed handfuls of peanuts at each of them. "Besides, I've got a lot of paperwork to do. See you later."

Ramsey got to his feet. "I'll drive you home."

"No, no. You're dealing. I can walk." She wouldn't meet his eyes. He gripped the deck of cards, feeling its edges bite into his palm. "I need the air, anyway," she said.

"It's pretty dark," Lenore began, but Mary Ellen interrupted her.

"This is Dusty Springs, not Berkeley. It's three blocks to the house. I'll be fine." She grabbed her jacket and waved. "Let me know who wins. See you all."

Ramsey stared at the door for a long minute after she shut it, and then at Lenore and Jon's faces. He didn't want to see the sympathetic glances. He didn't want any advice about how to woo his lady back to her rightful spot. He didn't even know if he wanted to try. The potential for hurt was too strong.

No one said anything for a minute, and then Jon punched him lightly on the arm.

"Sit down and deal. You left me stranded in the middle of an inside straight."

WALKING BRISKLY AWAY from Lenore's house, Mary Ellen kicked herself. She had been rude, and maybe hurt Lenore's feelings. But she couldn't stay a second longer, reading the memory of that strip-poker game in Ramsey's face.

He had remembered it. She had seen the exact moment when it had crossed his mind. She'd even been watching for that moment. She, herself, had remembered as soon as she'd seen the packs of cards. She ought never to have said she'd play. She ought to have left before the game started.

She passed Ramsey's pickup, and kicked herself again for taking the shortcut through the park on the way to Lenore's that night, instead of walking through downtown as she was doing now. Then she'd have seen Ramsey's truck down the block. She would have walked on. She wouldn't have had to relive memories that made her feel shaky and empty inside.

The streetlights cast occasional pools of light along the darkened streets. Her footsteps were the only sounds. Dusty Springs shut down at night; all the stores were dark and deserted. She gulped the moist, cool autumn air and shuffled through a few dead leaves, just to make more noise. It was foolish to feel nervous in a town where the biggest news was that high school kids had tepee'd someone's yard.

But she was nervous.

What would be better, she asked herself, *to let Ramsey drive you back and probably put some moves on you? Anyway, it's only nine-thirty, not exactly the witching hour.*

At the instant that thought ran through her head she caught sight of a peaked black hat and a broom, and almost laughed aloud. The store windows she was passing were full of Halloween-related decorations. Obviously that was what had been spooking her.

She stopped to peer into the window of Spencer's Dry Goods, where bolts of orange-and-black had been draped around an assortment of the most hideous rubber masks she'd ever seen. Next door, at the hardware store, a mechanical ghost moved eerily back and forth, while a devil raised and lowered his pitchfork, his pointy teeth displayed in a big smile.

Watching this, she didn't notice the movement reflected in the window behind her, until a hand fell on her shoulder.

Suppressing a scream, she whirled, putting the store wall behind her. It took her a moment to recognize the man who'd accosted her. "Oh, Mr. Markham." She laughed nervously. "You scared me for a minute."

"It's Alma MacIver's niece, isn't it?" Bob Markham smiled genially. "Didn't know who'd be out downtown at this hour. Tell the truth, I thought some kid might be planning a prank." He nodded toward the store window. "Time of year when the kids get frisky."

"I was on my way home and stopped to admire the windows," Mary Ellen said, and then bit her tongue. Nervousness was making her babble. Bob Markham didn't need to know the details of her evening.

"I'll walk along with you, then," he said agreeably. "Doesn't do for a young lady to be out by herself at night, even in a reasonably safe place like Dusty Springs. What's that cousin of yours thinking of, to let you wander around alone?"

Mary Ellen laughed. "He's thinking I can take care of myself, and he's right." She turned off Main Street onto the lane leading up the hill to Aunt Alma's. Bob Markham followed her. "Really, I don't need company. But thanks, anyway."

"Well, if you insist." Bob Markham's genial drawl changed, and Mary Ellen peered doubtfully at him. His face was shadowed. "In that case, let me give you a message for that cousin of yours."

"I'll be glad to," Mary Ellen said civilly. "Would you like him to call you?"

"No need." Again she sensed a coldness underneath Bob Markham's words. "Just tell him, some people around here are getting a little tired of him always stirring up trouble. Maybe he'd better think about letting well enough alone for a change.''

A knot of anxiety twisted in her stomach. "Are you threatening him?" she asked, pronouncing the words with care to keep her voice from shaking.

"Not in the least," Bob Markham replied promptly. "Just wanted to let him know that there's some talk against him in some circles. He should be on his guard if he keeps opposing this Spring Hill development. Someone could get hurt."

"That sounds like a threat to me." The anxiety was growing stronger. Mary Ellen wanted to run, but she made herself stand straight, made her voice even and expressionless.

"No, I wouldn't threaten him." Bob Markham took a step toward her. It was an effort not to retreat. "If I was threatening," he went on, "I'd tell Mr. Ramsey MacIver that he's not the only person who could get hurt. Maybe he wouldn't like to have it on his hands if his pretty little cousin was—damaged in some way."

"I don't know how Ramsey would feel about it," Mary Ellen said steadily, "but I wouldn't care for it in the least. I'd advise you to pursue legal methods to achieve your development, Mr. Markham. Touch me, touch Ramsey or anyone else, and you'll know the meaning of real trouble."

She turned and marched up the hill, praying that the rubbery trembling in her legs was not visible. Behind her, she could hear Bob Markham laughing. But he didn't try to follow her.

CHAPTER NINE

SHE MEANT TO LEAVE Ramsey a note and go on up to bed, but Mary Ellen was still shaken by her encounter with Bob Markham. She poured brandy into a juice glass and gulped it down, sinking into an overstuffed chair in the living room as the reaction set in.

She was still there when Ramsey walked in ten minutes later.

"You're back early." Her words ended the silence that stretched between them as he stood in the living room doorway.

"You're not doing paperwork." He noticed the glass and came over to pick it up. "Hitting the bottle. Something must be bothering you." His eyes moved over her, lingering on her breasts and ending at her mouth. She licked her lips. He closed his eyes.

"Well, you're right," she managed to gasp. "I am— that is, something happened...."

His eyes snapped open, their expression sharpening. "On your way home? Did anyone—" Once more his eyes went over her, but this time assessing her still-buttoned shirt, her neatly buckled belt.

"No one attacked me," she said, sitting up straighter. She felt a sudden flood of warmth from just knowing that Ramsey was here in the room with her, both of them safe. He had his faults, but she would be the first to admit that there was a decency to him that was very comforting. Or maybe it was just the brandy.

"What happened?" He had shuttered his face. The sensuality was gone, or at least banked.

Succinctly she told him what Bob Markham had said, as far as it related to Ramsey. She didn't mention the threats Markham had made at the end to herself. She could cope with that. No need for Ramsey to get worked up over it. In fact, Markham might have been counting on getting Ramsey to do something wild so that his credibility would be destroyed.

Ramsey's face darkened when he heard what Markham had said. "I figured there was someone with more guts behind Arnold," he said, shrugging. "It'll be a cold day in hell before I pay attention to that kind of garbage. What frosts me is that he had the gall to lay it on you! I should go have a little talk with Mr. Markham."

"I'd stay away," Mary Ellen said anxiously. "If there was a fight, he'd say you provoked it, and try to get you into trouble. Just ignore him, Ramsey. But be careful. Maybe you'd better tell Frank Alverez."

"Poor Frank." Ramsey went to the brandy decanter. "He's appointed, you know. He wants to do the right thing, but it could mean his job if he has to investigate Arnold and that bunch."

"Just tell him," Mary Ellen urged him. "He doesn't have to act on it, but it would be better if he knew. Just in case—"

"In case they succeed in eliminating me?" Ramsey smiled derisively. "Those guys are no real threat. If they could scare me they would. Since they can't, they'll back off. Last thing they want is a scandal.

That would end their chance of getting Spring Hill past the county planning department.''

It was a reasonable view, and Mary Ellen breathed a little easier. The same went for what Bob Markham had said about her. He didn't really want to hurt anyone. He just wanted them all to get out of his way.

She was suddenly overcome by tiredness. The emotional wringer was an exhausting place. "Guess I'll see if I can keep my eyes open long enough to fill out those forms," she said drowsily. "Been a long day."

Ramsey looked at her, his face impassive. "Yes, it has," he said after a moment. He held out his hand, and without thinking she put her own into it so he could pull her out of her chair. But he didn't let her go when she was on her feet. Slowly, he brought her close to him until her cheek rested against the soft flannel of his shirt. She wanted to move, to back away, but a sweet lethargy held her quiescent.

They stood together; she couldn't have told for how long. Warmth enveloped her, and incoherently she thought that she wanted it always.

Then Ramsey shifted, and everything changed. Pulled tight against him, she could feel the desire she'd sensed all evening. Her arms went around him and she pressed him to her as strongly as she could. His chest heaved as he gasped for air, and a corresponding breathlessness made her do the same. She felt the wildest need to rub herself against him, as if that would somehow ease the fire that flashed through her, instead of causing it to rage higher. Panting, she lifted her face to his. His eyes burned, but they questioned, too. And she remembered that much was still unanswered between them. Her hand came up to push him gently away.

His arms fell and he took her hands, holding them briefly as he stepped back, then letting go. She felt colder. They stared helplessly at each other before Ramsey turned away.

"Sorry," he said, heading for the door. "I didn't mean to stir all that up. Just thought it would be nice to hold you."

"Nice?" She repeated the word dully, then with more strength. "You think that was nice?" *Stupendous,* she thought to herself. *Overwhelming. Devastating. Not nice.*

"You didn't, I know. I thought—earlier—but I was wrong." He looked back at her, his shutters in place once more. "Don't worry, Emmy. I won't attack you again."

Left standing alone in the living room, she wanted to throw her glass against the wall, stamp her feet, have a loud, noisy temper tantrum. But all she could do was fume. "Damned straight you won't," she said, spitting the words out quietly at the empty doorway. "Of all the stupid, inconsiderate, thick-headed men, you take the cake, you big moron."

The tirade calmed her a little, and she stomped up the stairs, still feeling the traitorous quivers of sensation in various nerve-rich areas of her body. Of course, he was right. She didn't want him to seize her, kiss her, ravish her, tear off her clothes and his, bring her body to the boiling point and then quench the flames with more fire. She didn't want that at all.

But if he'd only opened up, if she'd only gotten him to talk.... If she could have started some kind of dialogue, if he had said—what? What would it have taken to wash away the years of hurt and anger, and let them end up in her big, empty bed?

No, she didn't want to make love with Ramsey until they could build on it. But she didn't want what she got, either, which was a night of tossing and turning and dreaming dreams that were alternately menacing and full of wanton, lascivious pleasure that was always just out of reach.

"WELL, OF COURSE I can handle it." Jeanine's voice was confident over the telephone. "But I don't get it. You could come in but you aren't going to? Do you think your cousin will tear the whole place down if you're gone for a few hours?"

"Not really." Mary Ellen glanced nervously at the kitchen door. She was up early, and had decided to call Jeanine before Ramsey was down. "I just think it would be better if we worked together for the next few days."

"Heating it back up, are you?" Jeanine's voice turned worried. "Be careful, Mary Ellen. Get everything in writing before you commit yourself to anything. Remember that love turns your brain to mush!"

"It isn't love," Mary Ellen protested. "There's been some trouble on the job site, and it would be best if we were both here. That's all."

"Oh. Well, any kind of trouble's better than man trouble." Jeanine sighed gustily into the receiver. "That skunk Derek had someone over here the other day pricing my house and my equipment—for community property, he said. I got this stuff before I even knew him. I ask you! How can a guy get half of things he didn't begin to earn?"

"That's life, I guess." Mary Ellen didn't feel up to a discussion of Derek's perfidy, but she made herself listen and make soothing noises while Jeanine blew off steam.

"This is long distance," Jeanine said finally. "I shouldn't be bending your ear about my personal problems. We'll talk when you come down next week."

"I'll call you about when I can make it." Mary Ellen could hear the floorboards creaking overhead. "Everything else all right?"

"Yeah. Oscar's working out well. The drywall guys got through a day early, so we've already got the cabinets up. The countertop guys are coming today, and then the tile people. We're ahead of schedule, if you can believe it. I can use the time to work on your cabinet order." She paused. "A couple of people have asked for estimates. You want me to take a look?"

"What kind of jobs?"

Just then, Ramsey pushed the kitchen door open and came in. His face was still creased with sleep, and he was scratching at the stubble on his face. He nodded to her and turned the heat on under the kettle, settling at the table with the morning paper.

"A family room addition and a couple of bathrooms," Jeanine said. "One of the bathrooms will be tricky—it's an under-the-stair that was grandfathered in years ago. Probably not up to code anywhere."

"Take a look," Mary Ellen said, turning away from Ramsey. "Tell them it will be several months before we could get to it. Unless you want to do some stuff on your own. I'm trying to scale back until I can see daylight up here."

"I understand." Jeanine was silent for a moment. "I might take on a couple of things, in that case. There's not much left to do on this job except make sure the finish work goes right, and I don't want to sit around, especially with Derek eyeballing my savings account.''

"Be my guest. I'll talk to you later." Mary Ellen hung up the phone and turned to face Ramsey. He was pouring hot water through a coffee filter. She got a tea bag, set her cup on the stove, and he filled it for her.

"Not going down to Berkeley today?" He kept his attention on his cup, pouring carefully, but she wasn't fooled. She could hear the speculation in his voice.

"I'm sticking around here for the next few days." She moved her tea bag up and down and decided to be forthright. "It's probably safer if there's two of us here. In case anyone tries any funny stuff."

His disappointed expression came and went so fast she decided she'd imagined it. "Nothing's going to happen. These people are just full of hot air, that's all."

"In that case we'll get a lot of work done," she said, trying to smile. When she thought about an accident happening to Ramsey, she felt incredible anxiety. *Merely cousinly,* she assured herself. After the previous evening, she wouldn't allow herself to feel any warmer emotions for him. "And don't act like I'm blowing all this out of proportion, Ramsey. After all, you're here because someone bombed your house. That's not exactly friendly behavior."

"True." He rubbed his chin. "I've got to shave, and then I'll get going on the demo in here." He glanced around the kitchen. "Hate to say goodbye to this old room, even though it's gonna be a lot nicer."

"It won't be so different," Mary Ellen promised him. "Same stove, same kind of cabinets, just more of them. A little smaller, easier to get around in. More counter space, but the same great windows."

"I know." He took a long swallow of coffee. "You got the new cabinets ordered?"

"My cabinetmaker says they're almost finished." Mary Ellen crossed her fingers at this white lie. Jeanine hadn't had much time lately for cabinetmaking, given the supervision that had been thrust on her. But she'd get them done all right. "I've ordered the sink and appliances," she went on briskly. "If we get everything torn out in here in the next two days, we could do the reframing in a couple more days and be ready for the plumbers and electricians by the middle of next week. With luck, drywall in two weeks."

"We should insulate and shear-wall," Ramsey pointed out, draining his cup, "while we're down to the studs."

"Right." Mary Ellen refigured the time in her head. "This is Tuesday."

"This is Wednesday." Ramsey grinned at her. "Getting confused, boss lady?"

"Wednesday." Mary Ellen scowled at him. "I've got a lot on my mind, unlike some people, who don't have a mind to have anything on."

Ramsey blinked. "A little incoherent, but I get your drift. We finish the demo and the framing this week. Call in the trades starting Monday. A week from Monday, we should be ready for the drywall. Give them a week. Two weeks from Monday, we'll be putting up the cabinets."

"Who's going to prime the drywall?" Mary Ellen read the answer in his face. "I hate painting!"

"Of course. All contractors hate painting." His voice was very reasonable, but his smile was devilish.

"But we'll be doing it on the weekend, looks like. And real painters won't work then."

"Go shave," Mary Ellen grumbled. "I'm going to pack the rest of the dishes away, and then we can start taking off the trim. Carefully."

"Yes, boss." Ramsey saluted and sauntered toward the door. "It's been a long time since I did so much grunt work," he said, pausing there. "For you, too, I guess?"

"Yeah." She thought about her Berkeley job, where currently subcontractors were working on countertops and floors. Her own crew didn't have much to do. "I could get someone up here to help with the demo," she said finally.

Ramsey nodded. "I could pull someone off, too. Let's get back into supervising. What do you say, boss?"

"I say, get to work." Mary Ellen turned back to the phone. Oscar would be a big help getting the trim off. She would see what she could arrange.

OSCAR AGREED to come up and stay for a couple of days. The thought of his large body and cheerful presence made Mary Ellen feel better—not to mention safer—when she hung up the phone. And just having him there would keep her and Ramsey from slugging it out, at least for those few days. A confrontation was beginning to seem inevitable, but she would feel better prepared for it when she'd had more time to sort through her feelings. *Go on,* she said to herself scoffingly, pulling on her gloves, *how much time does it take?* The feelings were there, but she didn't want to acknowledge them. That was the whole problem.

Ramsey was plugging in a microwave on the dining room sideboard, which he'd covered with a piece of scrap tileboard. He added a portable propane burner to his makeshift counter and stepped back to admire it. "Chili," he told her. "And spaghetti. Stew. There are a lot of one-pot meals we can have. Saves us from the food downtown, anyway."

Mary Ellen had to agree. They got a dolly and moved the refrigerator into the dining room, which would remain essentially untouched. The doorway that opened from the butler's pantry, which was to become a powder room, would be filled in.

They left the stove in the kitchen, just moving it out from the wall and disconnecting it. Ramsey covered it with plastic and a drop cloth. Mary Ellen caught him tucking the cloth in around the stove's base, and she couldn't resist teasing him.

"I thought we could just get rid of this old thing," she said disparagingly, waving toward the stove. "Get a nice, up-to-date cook-top and a built-in oven."

Ramsey turned to stare at her. "That's not on the plan," he said evenly.

"No, but after talking with you I realized I've been too sentimental here. Who wants an old fossil like this, anyway?"

"If you knew anything about cooking," Ramsey said, breathing deeply, "you'd know that these old stoves are the best there are. If I could have found one when I put in my kitchen, I would have one, too. By all means add a wall oven, but this stove doesn't go anywhere!"

"Down, boy," Mary Ellen said, laughing. "I was just teasing you. I feel the same way about those old lavatories and claw-foot tubs, although they're easy enough to pick up on the salvage market." She patted the stove. "So are these, in Berkeley. I've seen them, but they aren't cheap. It can cost you three or four hundred."

"My Wolf range," Ramsey told her, smoothing a last fold of canvas over the stove, "cost a couple thousand. And I'd ditch it in a shot if I could lay my hands on one of these babies. Where did you see them?"

Mary Ellen raised her eyebrows. "I've got the phone number somewhere around. Maybe next time I'm down there, I can pick it up for you. I'll be making a run there anyway to see if they have any moldings to match these before I have some specially milled."

For once Ramsey didn't make a caustic remark about her passion for matching the woodwork. At least that was progress, Mary Ellen figured. She pulled up her dust mask and tied a bandanna over her hair. Her tool belt was draped over a chair; she hooked it around her hips and pulled on a pair of thick gloves. "Well, it's fun time. Gotta tear things up." Picking up her crowbar, she surveyed the depleted kitchen.

Ramsey wore a dust mask too, and a baseball hat turned backward. He disdained gloves. "So you want to save all these casings, huh?"

"Yes." Mary Ellen went to work on one, hammering her crowbar underneath the wood alongside the swinging door. "Saves work in the long run."

Ramsey shrugged. "You're the renovator." He watched while she located the nails and pried a section of casing off them. She took a pencil out of her tool belt and wrote where it had come from on the back of the casing. "Not so hard," she said, flashing him a smile. "See?"

They got the casings off before Oscar arrived, helped by Chris, a lanky young man from Ramsey's crew. Oscar and Chris settled down to pulling the lath and plaster off the framing members, while Mary Ellen and Ramsey took out the trim in the adjoining maid's room.

They worked together in silence for a little while. Mary Ellen was thinking of their encounter the previous evening, but when she stole a glance at Ramsey's face his expression was grim. She hoped he wasn't thinking of her, with that scowl.

"That's the last piece." Ramsey took the apron off a window and marked it. "Now I guess we pull all the nails out."

"You got it." Mary Ellen pushed her safety glasses to the top of her head. "Sounds like the demolition is going well." The muffled thud of plaster hitting the floor came from the kitchen.

"Are we taking all the plaster off in the bathroom upstairs, too?" Ramsey took off his baseball cap and scratched his head. "We could just knock holes in the wall for the plumbing and wiring."

Mary Ellen considered it. "It's not like the plaster is in great shape, or is special in any way," she said. "But it's not much more work to take it down to the studs and put green board up. I don't like the idea of tiling over that old plaster and making any dry rot totally inaccessible."

"Guess you're right." Ramsey stretched and glanced at his watch. "Why don't I go over to the Food Mart deli and pick up some sandwiches for lunch? We've got to feed those guys if we want them to keep working." He looked at her, a grin spreading across his face. "That Oscar is one big dude. Where did you find him?"

"He's a graduate student at Berkeley," Mary Ellen said, sticking her safety glasses into her tool belt. "Getting some money together this quarter so he can go back. He's been a real find."

"I'll bet." Ramsey unhooked his tool belt. "Be back in a little while." He looked longingly at the former bathroom that had adjoined the maid's room. Its sink rested on the floor and the old claw-foot tub had been pulled out. Only the toilet was still working, and it was surrounded by debris. "Guess I'll rinse off upstairs while I still can."

"Good idea." Mary Ellen looked him over critically. "Maybe you should change your shirt. Kinda dirty to go shopping."

"Maybe I should put on my tux." He scowled at her. "Everybody in town is used to seeing me this way. It's my job, Emmy. And we'll get a whole lot dirtier this afternoon when we finish disconnecting all the plumbing."

He stalked out, and Mary Ellen reflected glumly that he was right. Plumbing was always a mess. They had to tear out the old pipes and run new copper through the whole house, including the upstairs, for both the old bathroom and new. Luckily, plumbers were coming in, but she knew Ramsey would expect her to help out to speed things up. And the same with the wiring.

She checked on Oscar and Chris, who were pulling down the ceiling in the kitchen. She had thought about keeping that intact, but Ramsey had pointed out that a lot of the new plumbing for the upstairs bathrooms would be just above the kitchen. Removing the ceiling meant the installation would go easier.

"Good work, guys." She admired the pile of lath and plaster that littered the old linoleum floor. "Ramsey's gone to get us some lunch. We'll break in half an hour or so."

"Maybe we can cart all this out by then," Oscar said, grinning at Chris. "What do you say, my man?"

"You're on." Chris turned to Mary Ellen. "I saw they brought us a nice fresh debris box this morning. Oscar and I are gonna fill that sucker up."

"Right on." Mary Ellen had to smile. She got the nail puller out of her truck and started pulling finishing nails out of the old trim, carrying each piece out to the veranda when she was done. Chris and Oscar trundled back and forth with wheelbarrows full of plaster and lath. It was warm and sunny outside, but somewhere someone was burning autumn leaves.

Mary Ellen dropped each nail she pulled into an old coffee can, and reflected that Ramsey would see that as unnecessary. He would just throw them on the floor and get someone to pick them up later. But she'd decided long ago that it was easier to tidy up as you went along than to try and clean up a humongous mess at the end. Another example of the difference in their thinking.

There he was on her mind again, right where she didn't want him. Lately he'd been invading her thoughts more and more. And it seemed she was making less and less of an effort to get him out of there.

Her feelings were tangled. On the one hand, she couldn't deny he did more to her physically with just a touch than any other man could. During the past five years she'd managed to bury the memory of their loving. She'd even imagined once or twice that she'd met another man capable of wiping those memories out altogether. It hadn't been true.

But sex was only part of a relationship—an important part, she knew, but what about respect? What about equality? Ramsey still had problems with those things. He was always questioning her, always pushing her.

She paused, the nail puller still gripped in her hand. What did she want, anyway? He was paying her the compliment of assuming she could cope with another opinion. Moreover, on this job, where the lines of authority were clearly stated, he'd been pretty reasonable about following her lead. And what if he did tell her every now and then how he would do it? Would she like it better if he didn't let her know when he thought she was making a mistake? Would she, in the same circumstances, not tell him if she thought he was going wrong?

She was still standing, petrified by this revelation, when Ramsey's truck pulled up in the driveway.

RAMSEY HADN'T PLANNED on spending a long time at the deli, but there was a line when he got there. He had to take a number, something that rarely happened in sleepy Dusty Springs. Frowning at the sandwich list, he decided on his order so there'd be no delay when his turn came.

A waft of exotic scent warned him before the touch on his arm. "Ramsey," purred Gloria's throaty voice. "Just the man I wanted to see."

"Hi, Gloria," he growled, wondering if he'd brushed all the plaster dust out of his hair. Not that he

cared if Gloria Gruenwald was offended by his un-
polished appearance. But it did put him at a disad-
vantage when she always looked so immaculate.

She was wearing her trademark white, this time a
lacy sweater and a long, swirling white skirt. The color
did make the most of her creamy tan and dark eyes, he
admitted grudgingly.

"You haven't come to finish my house, Ramsey,"
she said sorrowfully, lifting those dark eyes meltingly
toward him. "I've been expecting you."

"I've been expecting your check," Ramsey said
bluntly. "I can't go on until you've made the milestone payment. We've been over this before, Gloria."

"Yes, we have." She blinked her long lashes. "I
can't pay you until November. I just don't have the
funds. Can't you trust me?"

"It's not a question of trust." He found himself
backing away when she paced slowly toward him. "It's
a business arrangement, Gloria. I work for money, not
for trust."

"I see." Her delicately painted mouth drooped.
"Well, Ramsey, I trust you." She glanced around, and
he thought he glimpsed fear in her eyes. "That's why
I'm going to tell you something I probably shouldn't."
She came a step closer, and this time he didn't back
away. Her hand clutched his arm. "I heard Arnold
talking to that Bob Markham last night. He thought I
was in the powder room. I heard him tell Bob to keep
you away from old man Dalhousie, no matter what the
cost."

Ramsey stared at her. "Old man Dalhousie?"

"Ssh!" Gloria looked around nervously. "If Arnold found out I told you—promise you won't let
anyone know! Promise, Ramsey!"

"Yeah, yeah. I didn't have any intention of going out there, anyway."

"That's wise of you." Gloria stepped back. "I thought you'd see the sense of backing off this whole development thing. I mean, what does it matter where they build those old houses?" She smiled slowly at him, her fear gone. "Just as long as you build mine. You will, won't you?"

"As soon as you meet that payment, Gloria, I'll be out with bells on." Ramsey smiled back at her and moved up to the counter when he heard his number called. From the corner of his eye he caught her glare, but when he turned from giving his order, she was gone.

Her piece of information nagged at him while he waited for his sandwiches and drove back to Aunt Alma's. What could old man Dalhousie have to say? Either he'd tied up the land around Spring Hill so it was development-proof, or he hadn't. There was nothing Ramsey could do about it, whichever it was.

"You could talk to him," his busybody conscience urged. "Find out just what his intentions are. Maybe if the provision isn't binding enough, he could fix that. Maybe he doesn't know what's going on."

Goaded, Ramsey pulled over in front of the building that housed the county offices. He'd applied for enough permits and subdivision maps to know the procedure, and the clerk in charge.

"Morning, Wilma Mae." He smiled at her easily, and she smiled flirtatiously back, patting the rigid, iron-gray curls that defended her scalp.

"Why, it's Ramsey MacIver. What do you want, you wicked boy? Come to break my heart again?"

"Now, Wilma." Ramsey settled himself against the counter. "You know you don't have a heart. Remember, you gave it to that fellow from the State who was out here a couple of years ago." He gazed at her in mock sorrow. "Cut me right out, he did."

"Oh, go along." Wilma Mae laughed. "What can I do for you?"

"Just want a look at the recent filings for subdivision maps," he said casually. "Can't remember if I sent the papers in or not."

"I don't recall seeing your name on anything that's come up in the past couple of months." Wilma Mae came around the counter and pulled a drawer out of one of the filing cabinets that ringed the little seating area.

"Now, don't let me take you away from your work," Ramsey said hastily. "You were probably going to go to lunch. I'll just take a quick look through— won't keep you a minute."

"That's thoughtful of you." Wilma Mae regarded him consideringly. "Tell you what. I was going to lunch, and I don't want to be late. Just close the door when you leave and it'll lock itself." She got her purse from behind the counter and shook a roguish finger at him. "And don't take anything. I'll know who to blame!"

"I'm as honest as the day is long," he said, holding one hand on his heart.

Wilma Mae paused at the doorway, her eyes gleaming. "That's just it, Ramsey. The days have gotten mightily short now, haven't they?"

He had to smile, but she was gone already. Ramsey turned back to the file drawer. Wilma Mae had figured out that he was up to no good. She didn't want to know anything about it, obviously.

He found what he was looking for right away. A subdivision map, filed by the "Spring Hill Development Corporation," with Arnold's name listed as principal. Ramsey used the copy machine behind the counter, and then went over to the county map that hung behind the assessor's desk and worked out the coordinates indicated on the plan. The description of the land to be subdivided corresponded exactly to Spring Hill.

Ramsey refiled the development map, resisting the temptation to put it where it would never be found. If it needed to disappear, he would have to accomplish that some time when he'd been less blatant about wanting access to the files. He folded the copies he'd made and stuck them in his hip pocket. The door locked behind him, just as Wilma Mae had said it would.

On an impulse he bounded up the stairs. Mary Ellen and the guys would be waiting for their lunch, but he wanted to see Frank Alverez. There were things he needed to know.

Frank was just leaving for lunch. "Ramsey! Want to join me at the Blue Willow?"

"No." Ramsey sat down in the chair that faced Frank's desk. "I've got my lunch in the truck, but I wanted to talk to you for a minute, Frank."

"Can't it wait?" Frank asked plaintively. "I missed breakfast because of my daughter's water polo practice." He shook his head. "Seven-thirty in the morning is no civilized time for sports."

"Frank, last night Bob Markham told Emmy that I'd better lay off the Spring Hill thing or something bad would happen to me."

That got Frank's attention. He sat down and pulled a pad of paper toward him. "Tell me."

Ramsey told him, repeating what he could remember of Mary Ellen's conversation. When he was done, Frank looked at him steadily.

"You will take Bob's advice? It sounds like you could be in big trouble, Ramsey."

"Hell, no. I'm not backing down for any tin-pot crooked businessman and his tame politician." Ramsey glared across the desk. "The creep went too far when he threatened Mary Ellen."

"He threatened you, I think." Frank folded his hands across his stomach. "Or warned you. There's no evidence that Bob was talking about himself. Maybe he knows that someone is out to get you."

"I know it's not exactly evidence, but Mary Ellen felt the threat was coming directly from Bob Markham." Ramsey sighed. "There's nothing you can do about it at this stage, Frank. I just wanted you to know."

"I appreciate it, Ramsey." Frank eyed him narrowly. "Anything else I might need to know?"

"Can't think of anything offhand." Ramsey wasn't going to mention the subdivision map. That kind of skulduggery wasn't a matter for the sheriff.

"Tell Mary Ellen I'll stop by on my way home this afternoon and take a statement from her," Frank said, getting to his feet. "It is just as well to have it from the horse's mouth."

"I'll tell her in those exact words." Ramsey's mouth twitched, and after a moment Frank laughed.

"You do that, amigo. Make trouble for me."

"Just one group of people I'm going to make trouble for," Ramsey said grimly. "Isn't there a meeting of the county board of supervisors coming up next week?"

"That's right." Frank looked relieved. "Go through the right channels, amigo. I would hate to have to lock you up for brawling." He added candidly, "You're too old for that now."

"Thanks for the vote of confidence." Ramsey clapped him on the shoulder and took the stairs two at a time. He was expected back, and he didn't want his brawny helpers to get weak from hunger. The better they were fed, the harder they'd work, and the sooner Alma's house would be back together. It bothered him to see Mary Ellen subjected to such primitive conditions, although he had sense enough not to let her see how he felt.

She was standing on the porch when he got to Alma's, her mouth slightly open, her expression that of someone who was about to yell "Eureka!" He wondered what she was thinking about.

She didn't tell him. "Took you long enough," she snapped, grabbing the sack out of his hand. "We might as well eat in the backyard. Too much dust inside."

He followed her around the veranda, wanting to tell her what Gloria had said but at the same time wanting to keep her out of it. All through lunch he was distracted, retaining just enough of his wits to let Mary Ellen know that Frank Alverez was going to stop by.

By four o'clock he couldn't take it anymore. He had to know what old Horton Dalhousie had to say about the subdivision map that had houses all over land he'd promised for a park.

Mary Ellen was flaring the last piece of tubing that carried water to the toilet in the former bathroom. "There," she said. "I'll get the shutoff valves in up above, and we can flush again."

"Yeah." He brushed the dirt off and looked around the cellar. "This isn't as bad as some houses I've worked under, but it still gave me a crick in the neck. I'm going over to Jon's to take a shower."

"So soon?" Mary Ellen stared at him. "I thought we could get copper to the hose bib in the backyard, so we can rip out the sink in the upstairs bathroom. The guys are already demo-ing there."

"I need a break." Ramsey almost told her, but decided it would be better if she didn't know what he was doing. "Besides, you're pretty good at this. We might just do all the plumbing ourselves. You can get the copper out there without me."

"Right," Mary Ellen sniffed. "Have a nice shower."

He left her under the house, muttering, and collected a change of clothes. You just didn't go visiting the Dalhousies with cellar dirt and spiderwebs all over you. He had meant it when he'd said he was going to Jon's to shower. But that was just going to be his first stop.

After the shower, he'd drive up to that elegant white villa in the hills west of town. With luck, he'd get through the gates. With a lot of luck, he might even get to see Horton.

At any rate, he meant to try.

CHAPTER TEN

DALHOUSIE LIVED several miles west of town, off a county road that climbed into the Sierra foothills. Ramsey followed the winding road through hills golden-brown with autumn grasses, past live oaks that spread their dense shade over the road. Here and there a deer bounded away into the underbrush. Hawks circled on thermals overhead. It seemed very lonely, very wild.

The road turned and climbed in a steep switchback. Ramsey hoped no one was coming the other way; his truck took up most of the space. He wondered if anyone besides the Dalhousies lived this far out; in the winter, the road must be damned near impassable. He recalled hearing somewhere that Dalhousie generally spent the winter in the Bay Area.

His truck sputtered a little and he gave it some gas. It surged up a steep slope that soon leveled out. He turned into a driveway leading onto a broad plateau.

The elaborate wrought-iron gates that usually closed off the entrance to Rosedown, Horton Dalhousie's estate, stood open. Ramsey was glad of it, since he didn't particularly want to talk to the intercom built into the brick gatepost.

He slowed, idling between the gateposts for a moment, to take in the scene in front of him. He'd done some work one summer for Dalhousie, building him a fancy greenhouse. But he'd forgotten the grandeur of the place until he saw it again.

Perched on a ridge high above the plain that contained Dusty Springs, Rosedown had been built in the late thirties. At that time its art deco style had been outrageously modern. Now the home's style, with its white stucco facade reminiscent of an Italian villa, was considered timeless. Curved windows and terraces sported custom grillwork. At one end, terrace steps led to a colonnade, where Ramsey glimpsed a pool of blue water reflecting the sun.

The gardens had been laid out in a formal plan, with tall cypress and cedars providing a dark green screen at the back of the house. The driveway circled in front, branching off to the left where the greenhouses and outbuildings were hidden behind the trees. There could have been no greater contrast to the wild solitude of the road.

Everywhere there were roses. Horton Dalhousie, after his retirement from his rather mysterious but obviously highly profitable business, had taken up roses in a big way. His wife, who'd died a few years earlier, had been an enthusiastic gardener, and it was to please her that Dalhousie had added greenhouses and an orchard. After her death, Ramsey had heard, he'd become something of a recluse, spending all his time with the plants.

Ramsey drove his truck around behind the house and parked near an enormous, L-shaped garage. He was over one hurdle, anyway. It might be difficult to get in to see Horton, but at least he'd gotten to the house.

One bay of the garage was open. Ramsey saw feet sticking out from beneath a vintage Mustang convertible. He cleared his throat, and a creeper shot out from under the car. The man on it blinked a couple of times. "Yeah?" His voice was not welcoming.

"Name's Ramsey MacIver." Ramsey looked the man over carefully. He had thick, gray-streaked brown hair receding from a high forehead, dark eyes set under brooding eyebrows, and a mouth that didn't give anything away. His hands, with long capable fingers, were grimy from motor oil. He wore coveralls, also grimy, with the knees torn out. "I'm looking for Horton Dalhousie."

The man's eyebrows went up, forming inverted Vs over his eyes. He sat up on the board, cleaning his hands with a rag. After a moment he said, "Do you have an appointment?"

"No." Ramsey stuck his hands in his pockets. "The gates were open, so I just drove in. I did some work here once," he added, impelled to provide credentials in the face of the other man's flat, suspicious stare. "Greenhouses."

A little of the suspicion seemed to die. "MacIver," the other man said thoughtfully. "That's right. From the town." He directed another searching look at Ramsey, and suddenly smiled. "I'm Clive Dalhousie," he said, rolling off the creeper and standing. He didn't offer his hand, perhaps because he was still wiping his fingers with the rag.

"I remember you," Ramsey said. "You coached a Little League team I was on once." Ramsey did his own staring. Clive was shorter than he remembered, a few inches shy of his own six-two. A ten-year-old kid thought of a twenty-one-year-old as terribly old. But the adult Ramsey saw only a slender man with lines of caution and reserve engraved on his face.

"Were you on the team?" Clive smiled again, but more perfunctorily. "I wasn't a very good coach, as I remember. We came in nearly dead last, didn't we?"

Ramsey shrugged. "At least you weren't a killer. Some of the dads really put the pressure on." He glanced at the Mustang. "Nice wheels."

Clive's expression didn't really change, but Ramsey read affection in the pat he bestowed on the Mustang's fender. "Does okay," he said. "Needs a tuneup, though. That's what I'm doing." He looked back at Ramsey. "Might I ask why you want to see Dad?"

Ramsey hesitated. "Local matters," he said finally.

A flicker of amusement appeared and vanished in Clive's dark eyes. "I'm local," he pointed out. "Can't I handle it?"

Ramsey didn't think so. It had occurred to him that Clive might not like the idea of valuable property being deeded to the town for a park. Clive might be behind the scheme to put houses there.

"I'd rather speak to Mr. Dalhousie about it."

Amusement flickered again in Clive's measuring gaze, this time combined with irritation. He glanced past Ramsey, and Ramsey turned, too. Bob Markham was just coming out of the other wing of the garage. Ramsey figured there was an office there.

"MacIver. An unexpected pleasure." Markham stopped a few feet away, his glance moving from Clive to Ramsey. He wore his usual smooth, unctuous smile, but there was something else in his expression that puzzled Ramsey. "What can we do for you?"

"He wants to see Dad." There was a quality of detachment in Clive's voice, as if with Bob Markham's appearance he'd ceased to be a participant in the scene before him.

Markham frowned. "Mr. Dalhousie doesn't see visitors. Can I help you?"

"I doubt it." Ramsey spoke bluntly, not feeling up to fencing. He'd met Bob Markham a few times around town and never thought much about him one way or another. But when the man had accosted Mary Ellen, he'd put himself beyond the pale as far as Ramsey was concerned. Now his fist itched to plant itself in that round, bland face.

"After all, Dad's the greenhouse expert," Clive said idly. He glanced down the driveway. "The gate's been left open, Markham. Would you see to it?"

Bob Markham's smile lost a little of its cheeriness. "Certainly, Clive. You'll deal with our visitor?"

"Yes." Clive waited until Markham had set off down the driveway before he spoke again. "Dad's out by the hybridizing bed. I'll take you to him."

"Thanks," Ramsey said awkwardly. There were undercurrents here, he decided. None of his business, though.

Clive led the way around the garage. The plateau was several acres wide, sloping gently at the edges before it dropped off in front. At the back, the grounds were bounded by a higher flank of hill. The sky seemed close, the air clearer. Ramsey breathed deeply. Fragrances of roses and cedar mingled on the light breeze.

They passed an arbor that provided a glimpse into a formal garden with a reflecting pond and yew hedge. Beyond it was an orchard, the trees rigorously pruned and beginning to lose their leaves. The greenhouses Ramsey had built were just beyond it. They formed two sides of a U-shaped structure, with a lathhouse as the third side. The center space was marked off into raised beds, most of them containing rose bushes.

Clive called, "Dad!" He smiled at Ramsey. "I'll leave you here. Dad's puttering around somewhere nearby." He hesitated. "I don't know what you've come about, Ramsey, but please don't upset him. He's old, and his health isn't good."

"I'll remember." Ramsey watched the greenhouse door open. Horton Dalhousie came out.

He'd aged in the six or seven years it had been since Ramsey had worked with him on the greenhouses. His wife's death had something to do with that, Ramsey supposed. They had adored each other, and she especially had been concerned with the garden's design. In those days Horton had been energetic and vigorous. Now he stooped, and as he drew closer Ramsey could see the brown spots on his hands and the way his fingers trembled.

"Yes?" Horton peered at them from beneath the brim of a natty panama hat. "What is it, Clive?" His eyes passed indifferently over Ramsey.

"This is Ramsey MacIver, who helped you with the greenhouses, Dad." Clive spoke gently. "He dropped by to chat a little." He turned to Ramsey. "Nice seeing you again, MacIver." This time Clive held out his hand, and Ramsey shook it.

Horton watched his son walk away, and then turned to Ramsey. "I remember," he said, straightening a little. "Your ideas about venting the glasshouses were excellent. Would you like to see them?"

Ramsey didn't really want to. It was after five, he noticed from a surreptitious glance at his watch. But there was still a commanding tone in Horton Dalhousie's voice. He followed the old man meekly into the greenhouse.

It was moist in there, and very warm. "I've had wonderful luck with orchids," Dalhousie said, walking between rows of flowers. Ramsey stared at the blooms, some tiny little things and others big and gaudy. Lenore would go crazy. It was too bad he knew so little about this stuff. All he'd be able to tell her was that Horton had a lot of flowers.

They turned a corner, and it grew cooler. "I'm hybridizing here," Dalhousie explained. "Can't have it too hot for that. Roses like an even temperature." He stopped at a workbench, where wooden trays full of sand held rotten-looking bits of plant matter. "Rose hips," the old man explained. "They're ready now. I'm just getting the seeds out." He took one of the little blackened balls and split it open, spreading the seeds inside on a piece of white paper. He smiled contentedly at them, and then looked straight at Ramsey. "So what is it you want, young man? I know you didn't come here to watch me ride my hobbyhorse."

Ramsey was reminded that Horton Dalhousie had a reputation for having been a very sharp businessman. Now his old eyes were clouded, his hands shook, but the fire was still there.

"I did want to talk to you," he said, taking a deep breath. "About Spring Hill."

"Spring Hill." Horton thought for a minute. "Let me see. That's the place on the northeast side of town, isn't it? Scenic lookout at the top. Yes. I remember now." He shot another sharp look at Ramsey. "What about it, young man?"

"It's been understood in town," Ramsey said carefully, "that your plan was to deed that property to the city as a public park. That was confirmed by Bob Markham at Arnold Hengeman's campaign party last week.''

"That is the plan.'' Horton picked up some of his seeds and dropped them into a glass of water. "If they float,'' he said abstractedly, "they're no good. I only plant the ones that sink.'' He skimmed a couple of seeds off the top of the water and poured what was left into a mesh-covered pot to recover the seeds that had sunk. "What of it?''

Ramsey blinked, not sure if he was being addressed or not. "Well, there's a development map on file in the county office that shows Spring Hill divided into building lots. Big lots, for big fancy houses. Guess it could be pretty profitable for you.''

Horton's rheumy gaze was fixed on him now with a painful intensity. He gripped the workbench edge so tightly his swollen knuckles turned pasty. His face turned a blotchy red. "Get Clive,'' he said, his voice barely intelligible. "Tell Clive to come here.''

"Can't I help you—'' Ramsey was alarmed. The old man looked bad, very bad. "Sit down, here.'' He pushed a tall, padded stool over to the workbench, and Horton Dalhousie sank onto it. Ramsey found an empty jar near the sink, rinsed it out and brought it back.

"Fine,'' Horton rasped, waving him away. "Go— fetch Clive.''

Looking back doubtfully, Ramsey jogged away from the greenhouse. When he got to the garage, Clive was gone. He pounded on the office door, but Bob Markham was gone, too.

Before Ramsey could reach the back door of the house Clive came out. He'd stripped off his overalls, and looked as if he'd never seen the underneath of a car before.

"Your dad's taken ill," Ramsey called. "He asked me to fetch you." He didn't wait for Clive, but turned and legged it back through the orchard. By the time he'd reached the greenhouse, Clive had pushed past him.

The old man was still sitting there, his face set. Clive took hold of his shoulder gently.

"Dad. Did you take your pill?"

Horton shook his head. Clive reached into his father's shirt pocket for a little vial and shook out a pill. Horton opened his mouth obediently for the pill. Clive kept his fingers on his pulse. His eyes, coldly angry, found Ramsey.

"What did you say to him, damn it? Didn't I warn you—"

"Look, I'm sorry." Ramsey felt guilty, but also exasperated. How was he to know he'd cause the old man so much grief with his question? "I just asked him about the development planned for Spring Hill. It didn't seem like such a dangerous thing."

"Spring Hill?" A long look passed between Clive and Horton. "What about it?"

"There's a development map on file in the county office." Ramsey pulled his wad of copies out of his hip pocket. "It shows the whole of Spring Hill divided into building lots. People in town are concerned, because we've always thought your family meant that land for a park." Ramsey shrugged. "Look, if you've changed your minds, okay. But maybe you could give us a chance to raise some money, see if we can buy it from you, before you put houses there. It would mean a lot to all of us."

Clive held up one hand. "Thanks for telling us how you feel, MacIver. Right now, I need to get my dad to bed."

"Let me help." Ramsey came closer. "I'm really sorry to have made so much trouble." He looked at Horton's shrunken frame. "Do you think we could carry him?"

They made a chair with their hands and got Horton into the house. By that time his color was better, and he insisted he could walk, but Clive wouldn't hear of it. With Ramsey's help he carried his father into a sitting room on the ground floor of the big white house.

"I will rest on the sofa," Horton said with dignity. "But you won't take me upstairs to bed, Clive. A little rest and quiet is all I need."

"Okay, Dad." Clive looked down at his father for a minute. "I'll be right outside if you need me."

"I shan't need anything," Horton asserted, closing his eyes and nestling his head into a soft sofa cushion. "Just make sure you go back and shut the greenhouse door. A cold wind could come up."

"Right." Clive jerked his head toward Ramsey, and they left by the side door that led out near the garage and Ramsey's truck.

Outside, Ramsey shifted uneasily. "Listen, I'm terribly sorry." He wanted with all his heart to be in his truck, getting away from the trouble he'd caused. "Can I do anything? Should we call an ambulance?"

Unexpectedly, Clive smiled. "Not really your fault," he conceded. "I didn't know you were going to drop such a bombshell, or I would have taken care of it myself. Thought you just wanted some construction work or something."

"Not just now," Ramsey said, managing a smile. He waited for Clive to bring up the development, but Clive was silent. "Can you tell me—"

"I'll look into it," Clive said abruptly. "There's been a mistake somewhere. I hope we can correct it before it's too late."

Ramsey wanted to make a heated reply, but choked it off. "I hope so, too," he said, trying to sound mild. "There's a county board meeting next week. My guess is that they'll be considering that subdivision map then. Maybe we can get it straightened out there."

"Maybe." Clive shoved his hands in his pockets. "I'll ride down to the gate with you to open it."

"Thanks." Ramsey climbed in his truck and waited for Clive to get in the other side. There was the usual mess of plans and tools on the front seat. He pushed some of it onto the floor and Clive sat down. "You should install a good remote control," Ramsey said, to make conversation. He steered down the driveway.

"We've got one," Clive said, "but I've misplaced my little gizmo that works it. There's a manual switch down here."

Ramsey put on the brakes as he approached the gate. Clive hopped out and flipped open a little door built into the brick gatepost. The gates slid silently open. Ramsey eased the truck forward, raising a hand in farewell to Clive, who reciprocated. He was almost through the gate when Clive called, "Hey, wait, MacIver!"

Ramsey braked again, and Clive came up to the driver's window. "It just occurred to me that you might know a good gardener who could give my dad a hand. It's too much for him, really, but he loves to do it."

"He does all that?" Ramsey looked doubtfully back at the lush greenery.

Clive grinned. "Not hardly. I have two guys coming in every week to give the grounds a going over. It's the roses. This hybridization is his big hobby now—his lifeblood, really. If he couldn't do that he'd get pretty depressed, but I'd feel better if someone else was working with him, so he didn't do too much. The grounds people just aren't knowledgeable enough."

"There's a landscape gardener in town who's really good," Ramsey said. "Lenore Wilson. She worked in Southern California for some fancy landscaping firm for a few years, and she has a degree in horticulture. I'm sure she could handle the roses."

"Great. I'll give her a call. Lenore Wilson." Clive jumped off the running board. "Thanks."

Ramsey put the truck in gear again. In his rearview mirror he could see Clive crossing behind the truck to go back to the gate control, then bend down for a moment to look at something on the pavement.

Before Ramsey could get all the way through the gate, Clive was yelling, his arms waving back and forth. Ramsey stomped on the brake, afraid that he was about to run over a pet.

The brake whispered down to the floorboards. The truck didn't slow.

Ramsey shoved the brake pedal again and again, pumping it, but there was no response from the truck. He was gathering speed now, with the twisting switchback in front of him. He threw the gearshift into first. The engine protested, but the truck finally slowed. The drop-off was steep on the left side of the road, but on the right side there was a relatively shallow ditch with an immense live oak tree shading the road.

As gently as he could, Ramsey steered into the tree. Its low-growing branches scratched the roof of the truck. The radiator grille smacked the tree trunk, and the truck stopped.

Ramsey gripped the steering wheel, picturing his fate if he'd discovered his faulty brakes when he'd already built up some momentum on the downhill slope. Downshifting might have just torn out the transmission if he'd been going too fast. He could have ended up plastered against the hillside or tumbling into a ravine.

He could have ended up dead.

Clive came panting up to the truck. "Thank God," he cried. "I saw you were leaking something, and it smelled like brake fluid. Your brake lines must have gotten loose or something. Looked like total failure there."

"Yeah." Ramsey pushed down on the brake pedal again. "Nothing happening. It's gone." He turned off the engine, carefully, as though roughness might deliver the coup de grace to his truck. "Guess I'd better call the towing service."

"Wait a minute, let's just see what the trouble is." Clive watched him set the parking brake. "Maybe we can fix it if the line's come off. I've got brake fluid at the house."

Ramsey gave Clive a flashlight and squatted beside the truck while Clive rolled underneath to shine the beam beside the tires. He went very still.

"So what is it? Line get broken?"

"Not broken." Clive rolled out from under the truck and sat on the ground. He held something toward Ramsey, and Ramsey took it, a dirty little scrap of what felt like paper. "There's a hole in the line."

"Geez." Ramsey stared down at the scrap, then at Clive's intent face. "I haven't had the brakes checked in a while. Guess the line might have cracked."

"It didn't crack." Clive took back the little scrap. "Someone put a hole in the line, and then taped it shut with this masking tape." He smoothed it on his palm. "The first time you used the brakes, the pressure would pop the tape, and the fluid would start leaking out. After a couple of uses, the brakes would fail."

Ramsey stared at him. "Quite a scenario." He ran his hand through his hair. "How do you come to know so much about it?"

"Had it happen to me once," Clive said briefly. After a moment he added, "It was more in the nature of a prank, but if the humorists who planned it hadn't let it out ahead of time, I might have had a wreck." He glanced at Ramsey, his eyes flinty. "Just like you."

"So," Ramsey said, "this couldn't have been done down there—" he pointed toward Dusty Springs "—or all that would have happened on the way."

"Had to happen here." Clive glanced at him and away. His face was hard. "That's the obvious supposition, isn't it?"

"And if you hadn't seen that leaking brake fluid, I'd have gotten halfway down the hill before I found out I didn't have any brakes." Ramsey thought about it and added, "And you were working on your car when I drove up. So if I had survived, and found out my brakes had been tampered with, I would have put two and two together and come up with your name."

"It could have been that way." Clive handed him back the flashlight. "Is that what you think?"

"I don't know what to think," Ramsey growled. "I just want to get back to town before they start sending out search parties." The sun was sinking now. It was close to six. Mary Ellen would be in a real stew over his defection—two good hours of working time that he'd blown off.

Clive blinked. "Well, maybe I can help. I can patch this up for you—if you trust me to." He gestured back toward the house. "Take me half an hour or so to put on a new line and bleed the brakes. Your tow truck wouldn't get out before then."

"Probably not." Ramsey stared at the other man. "Sure, I trust you. I kind of think you might have saved my life just now."

They walked up the road together. "I'll get my stuff and get on back to the truck," Clive said.

"Guess I'll go shut that greenhouse door for you," Ramsey offered. "Then, after I make a phone call, I can give you a hand."

FRANK ALVEREZ HEAVED himself off of the porch swing. "Well, if that's everything you can remember, Mary Ellen, I'll be going along." He shut the notebook he carried and smiled at her. "You know, I'm sure Mr. Markham didn't mean to frighten you. He's probably heard the same rumors I have and just wanted you to let Ramsey know he should be careful."

"What rumors are those?" Mary Ellen tried to make her voice casual. She sat on the porch railing, her back to the light.

Frank Alverez scrutinized her face. "Just that he was stirring up trouble for property owners. Most everyone realizes that's just not so, but there are a few people here who are always looking to make a killing in real estate, and they get hot under the collar sometimes." He patted her shoulder reassuringly. "We'll get it straightened out, don't worry. You think a lot of your cousin, eh?"

"I think he should concentrate on the job at hand," Mary Ellen said tartly. "This is a big project, and we've both got other irons in the fire. I can't carry it alone, and yet here's Ramsey running off before four!"

Frank Alverez paused on his way down the front steps. "You say Ramsey left early today? Now where could he go that's more important than being with his pretty cousin?"

Mary Ellen brushed the compliment away. "He said he was going to Jon's to take a shower. When he was gone so long I just assumed he'd gone to check on one of his other projects, but Wally Hurtado called up half an hour ago with a question and said he couldn't find Ramsey anywhere." She gazed at the sheriff. "Why? Do you think he's in trouble?"

"Ramsey is like a cat," Alverez said firmly. "He always falls on his feet and strolls away, licking his paw. You don't need to worry about him."

"Well, but, Sheriff—" Mary Ellen grabbed Frank's khaki sleeve, but was distracted when Lenore's truck drove up in front of the house. Lenore got out and bounded up the steps.

"Hi, Frank," she called. "Checking out the big remodeling job? Mrs. Mac isn't going to believe this when she gets back."

"That's right." Frank turned back to Mary Ellen. "What do you hear from your aunt, anyway? I hope she's doing better."

"She seems to be." Mary Ellen smiled at Lenore. "The sheriff was just asking me—" she began, but Frank interrupted her.

"I am curious about Ramsey's whereabouts," he said to Lenore. "Have you seen him?"

"Not since the poker game last night." Lenore frowned. "Why? What's he done?"

"Nothing," Frank said. "But his check for Little League sponsorship is late, you understand. I'm nagging several people about that."

"Well, we'll help you when we see him next, right Mary Ellen?"

"Right," Mary Ellen said hollowly. Frank shook her hand again and walked down the steps to his car. "Tell him to call me if you see him," she yelled, and Frank waved back at her before he drove away.

Lenore flopped down in the porch swing. "Gosh, I'm pooped," she said, pushing her hair back. "I want to take a shower, but I thought I'd stop by and see if you had the same idea. We can take turns."

"Yeah, sure." Mary Ellen got up. "There's no point in waiting around for Ramsey to show up," she added bitterly. "God knows where he is."

"Probably giving a bid or something," Lenore said airily. "Why should you care, anyway?"

"Why indeed." Mary Ellen went into the house, and Lenore followed her. "We're just engaged in tearing up our aunt's beautiful home. Why should he be around to help?"

Lenore walked slowly down the hall, taking in the plaster chunks that littered the cardboard-covered floor and the exposed studs where the butler's pantry had been. "Wow," she breathed. "This is really destroyed! Will you ever be able to put it back together?'' She stopped in the kitchen doorway. The swinging door had been taken down and stored, and the room was stripped of lath and plaster. A naked light bulb dangled from the middle of the high ceiling. The shrouded hump of the stove and the old cast-iron sink unit were all that remained of the fixtures. ''Gee, it looks terrible!''

''Yeah, I know.'' Mary Ellen stared gloomily at the wreckage. ''Usually this stage doesn't bother me, but this time I'm living in it, and it's a big drag. The only toilet that works right now is smack in the middle of everything.'' She pointed through the studs to the former bathroom. Normally there were three walls between Lenore and the toilet, but since all of them had been taken down to the studs, the toilet was visible.

''You need a drape or something,'' Lenore said. ''I've got an old shower curtain you can borrow.''

''Thanks.'' Mary Ellen summoned a smile. ''I'll get my stuff and we can get out of here.''

The short drive to Lenore's was quiet. Mary Ellen worried about Ramsey, at the same time recognizing how foolish it was to do so. He could take care of himself. And if he'd gone looking for trouble, well, it was none of her concern.

At Lenore's insistence Mary Ellen showered first, and she felt a lot better with the plaster dust washed out of her hair. While Lenore was in the bathroom, she wandered through the little house, admiring the pictures and the miniature roses in pots that crowded the wide windowsills. Lenore's house, she thought, was exactly like something you'd expect to find in an enchanted forest.

She repeated this thought to Lenore when her friend joined her in the living room, carrying a bottle of wine and two glasses. Lenore laughed.

"It was a wreck when I bought it," she said, pouring the wine. "That's why I could afford it. Ramsey worked it over for me. He wanted to put in new everything everywhere, but I don't really mind the old fixtures, and I kind of like that funky little kitchen. What matters is that the roof doesn't leak anymore and the foundation is secure." She nodded toward the backyard. "There's a nice garden out there, too. I was lucky to find it before the housing prices went through the roof."

"Was this when you came back from L.A.?" Mary Ellen asked the question idly, but Lenore's tight-lipped nod piqued her curiosity. "Don't tell me if you'd rather not," she said, sipping her wine, "but what happened down there? Why the big mystery?"

"It isn't a big mystery." Surprised, Lenore looked at her, and then down at her wine. "I guess I never have talked about it, but that was because—well, you were all wrapped up with Ramsey when I got back, and it was just too fresh then. I simply couldn't even bring myself to think about it. Later on, you went off to Oakland, and there was no one else around I felt like confiding in." She sighed. "It got to be a habit—ignoring it, hoping it would go away."

"I'm here now." Mary Ellen topped up Lenore's glass. "Confide," she said persuasively.

Lenore hesitated. "I'll get some bread and cheese," she said finally. "If I drink much more on an empty stomach, I'll be tipsy."

Mary Ellen bided her time. When Lenore brought back a cheese board with a sliced baguette and Gorgonzola on it, she took some and curled up in a corner of the sofa, waiting.

"I met a man in Los Angeles," Lenore said abruptly. "It was ten years ago, but it still seems like yesterday. I was working for Putnam's, this big landscaping contractor, and we did a lot of fancy places—stars' houses and such."

Mary Ellen nodded, but she didn't interrupt. After all, if Lenore hadn't talked about this since it had happened, she really needed someone to listen to her now.

"It would be nice if I could say I was young and naive." Lenore smiled ruefully at Mary Ellen. "I was twenty-six. I'd had lovers before. I was looking for romance, like any woman that age—thinking it was about time I settled down. Putnam's sent me out to Max Moreau's place."

"Max Moreau." Despite herself, Mary Ellen whistled. "He's so—whoo." She shook her head. "Remember that movie—which one was it—where he shows his tush for just a few seconds? I got it from the video store once and Jeanine and I played that part over and over. He's got the nicest-looking tush—"

"Yeah, I know." Lenore picked up a slice of baguette and began to shred it into crumbs.

"He's supposed to have all kinds of privacy police around—never goes anywhere without a bodyguard." Mary Ellen stopped babbling. "You mean—you and Max Moreau—"

"We—got involved." Lenore stared down at the pile of bread crumbs on her coffee table as if she didn't know how they got there. "He does have a mania for privacy. He'd just bought this new place then—ten-foot walls everywhere, and surveillance cameras, although I didn't know that at first. I went there with a crew to begin with, supervising the plantings around his pool. One day I came back alone to fine-tune some vines. He came out and started to talk to me. He was lonely," Lenore said simply, "and I was, too. I didn't know too many people down there, and I'd been working long hours. Before long he made a pass at me, and I ran away. He called Putnam's and told them he wanted me put on retainer. I tried," Lenore said softly, "to avoid it, because I knew it was going to be grief, sooner or later. But he had a powerful magnetism."

There was silence for a few minutes. "Gosh," Mary Ellen said finally. "Why didn't you say something about this before?"

"Because it hurt so bad. It still does." Lenore twisted her fingers together. "I lived in a little cottage in back of his house, and worked on his roses and his tropical plant collection, and he visited me when he wanted my company. For five years I accepted that, because I was so desperately in love with him." She jumped to her feet and walked around the little room impatiently. "I thought I was helping him. I thought he needed me, too. I didn't care about the money he paid me, although it was a lot for a gardener. I just wanted him."

"Oh, Lenore." Mary Ellen grabbed one of the clenched hands. "You're not the only woman to let a man take advantage of her," she whispered. "You're strong. You're okay."

"I know." Lenore sat back down and gulped her wine. "I was addicted to him," she admitted. "I thought I couldn't live without him. Then he got married."

"Yeah, that's right. He married some TV cutie, didn't he?"

"Monica Sarton." Lenore said the name tonelessly. "He liked that she had the initial *M*, you see. He told me all about it, said nothing had to change between us. It was like I really saw him for the first time. He'd been using me, he didn't really care about me. Maybe he even found it amusing," she said, her voice tortured. "Making love to the gardener—what a hoot!"

"Lenore, don't." Mary Ellen sat next to her friend on the sofa and put her arm around her. "He wasn't worth a second of your time. And he probably knows that now."

"I heard from him after they got divorced," Lenore said dully. "He wrote me care of Putnam's and they forwarded the letter. Asked me what went wrong, why didn't I come back. I never answered." She stared into her empty wineglass. "I have this terrible thought that maybe I'm still in danger—that if I saw him again, I'd lose it. I never even watch his movies."

"That's where you've gone wrong," Mary Ellen said. "We should rent a couple of them tonight. If you stopped seeing him as a lover and saw him as an aging hunk who doesn't act very well, you'd be okay. You just have to adjust your thinking. That's how I did it." She stopped short.

"Yes," Lenore said, summoning a smile. "If it's true confessions time, Emmy, let's hear from you. Why aren't you and Ramsey back together again? Don't tell me you don't have the hots for him. I wasn't born yesterday."

"We're not discussing me right now," Mary Ellen retorted with dignity. She filled both their wineglasses again. "We're solving your problems, Lenore. So why don't you hit on Jon? He's nice and cute."

"I've thought about it," Lenore admitted. "But he seems so young to me. I mean, he is young. I'm thirty-six, you know."

"He's not that much younger," Mary Ellen scoffed.

"He is to me." Lenore patted Mary Ellen's hand. "Sometimes I feel a million years old, compared to you and Jon—and even Ramsey, who's had enough troubles to age him prematurely."

"Ramsey. What does he know of trouble?" Mary Ellen gulped down some wine. "He simply walks through anyone or anything that gets in his way."

"I don't see him like that." Lenore smiled at her. "He just doesn't have much patience. A woman who loved him would have to learn to deal with that."

"That and a thousand other unpleasant traits." Mary Ellen lifted her wineglass. "To women," she cried. "How have we managed to endure men long enough to keep the human race alive?"

"To men," Lenore retorted. "The few good ones that are out there somewhere."

"I'll drink to that." They clinked glasses and sipped. When the phone rang, Mary Ellen sloshed some of her drink on her clean jeans.

"It's Ramsey," Lenore reported, covering the mouthpiece with her hand. "He wanted you to know he's had truck trouble and won't be in till later."

"How very thoughtful." Mary Ellen raised her glass again. "To thoughtfulness," she said, and drank more.

Lenore laughed. Mary Ellen could hear Ramsey's deep voice coming from the receiver. "Tell him not to worry his pretty little head about me," she said grandly. "I am spending the evening with my friend Lenore."

Lenore, laughing harder, relayed this message and hung up the phone. "We might as well finish off this wine," she agreed. "Then I can walk you home."

"We can have a slumber party," Mary Ellen said, much struck. "You lend me some pj's, and we'll tear everyone we know to shreds. There's no fun back at Aunt Alma's house, anyway."

Lenore, hiccuping, agreed to this. "I'm glad you're here," she said, sobering. "Really, Mary Ellen. This has done me a lot of good."

"Great." Mary Ellen reached for the cheese. "Let's eat some of this and then go get those movies. We'll find so much to cut up in Max Moreau it'll keep us in stitches all night!"

CHAPTER ELEVEN

MARY ELLEN FINISHED nailing up Lenore's shower curtain around the one working toilet and winced as a particularly loud crash of plaster sounded from the second floor. She was feeling just a little fragile after a night spent pumping up Lenore's self-esteem. Somehow that had involved drinking quite a bit of wine.

At least the aversion therapy seemed to have worked; they'd found any number of faults in the on-screen personas adopted by Max Moreau, and had poked holes in his famous magnetism, as well. Lenore had seemed very lighthearted that morning, up early to make French toast. The memory of the French toast made Mary Ellen shudder. It had been good, but her stomach had not yet totally decided to accept breakfast.

Ramsey didn't seem in a much better mood. Of course, he'd gotten up to plaster dust and no working sink; that would cramp anyone's morning cheer. But it didn't altogether account for the way he snapped at everyone.

He'd gone out soon after she'd gotten there, muttering about picking up some breakfast downtown and seeing Wally Hurtado. She hadn't been able to muster enough energy to question him about where he'd been the previous evening, but she'd get around to it. In the meantime, all she wanted was to crawl into bed with an ice pack and be surrounded by total peace and quiet.

"Just drag it on out," Oscar bellowed upstairs, and a scraping, thudding noise followed. It sounded as if the whole bathroom was being turned inside out. She crept up the stairs for a look.

Oscar and Chris were moving the old claw-foot tub into the middle of the bathroom, dragging it over the broken tile of the floor in a hideous cacophony. She tried to smile at them, but knew it came out as a grimace.

"You okay, Mary Ellen?" Oscar let go of the tub and straightened to look at her, his expression concerned.

"Just a slight headache," she said, glancing around the room. "You've really made some progress here."

"Almost finished," Oscar assured her. "We couldn't get at that last piece of plaster without moving the tub, though. Chris has the water shut off and everything."

"Ramsey said the plumber's coming any time," Chris volunteered, pushing his straight brown hair out of his eyes and grinning at her. "Said he's gonna figure out some way to hook up the kitchen sink temporarily so we can have water—hot and cold." He shook his head. "Too bad Ramsey's place is out of commission too. Course, the bedrooms and the bathrooms are okay—you'd think he'd want to at least sleep there, wouldn't you?"

Mary Ellen caught a glimpse of Oscar's foot aimed at Chris's leg, and the abruptness with which Chris stopped talking told its own story. So Ramsey's house was actually habitable, except for the kitchen? Well, she'd guessed it might be. The knowledge that he was staying at Alma's for no good reason should have infuriated her. What did infuriate her was the warm glow she felt on hearing it.

"Well, let's finish up with the plaster in here. If the plumber's coming, maybe he can get copper in here today and get us that much closer to closing the walls."

"Yeah, good plan." Oscar turned back to the tub, laying his big hands on it again. "Let's get a little more working room here, Chris."

They dragged the tub, and it sounded like giant fingernails on a giant chalkboard. Mary Ellen fled.

She checked the little bedroom where the new upstairs master bathroom was to go in, and on an impulse slipped into her aunt's bedroom next door.

Here everything was undisturbed. They would break through the wall for the door to the new bathroom last thing, and until then Alma MacIver's domain would remain as it was when she left. The faint scent of her rose potpourri drifted through the still air. Her poster bed, with its crocheted canopy, her cedar chest, serpentine highboy and dresser, all seemed to be waiting for her.

The noise of construction was muted here. Mary Ellen knelt by the cedar chest, put her head on a quilted cushion and said a little prayer for her aunt's health. When she was done, she felt much better.

"DEFINITELY SABOTAGED," Ramsey told Frank Alverez. "Clive reckons it was done while I was there."

"Does he?" Frank leaned back, causing his desk chair to shriek. "And he's something of a mechanic, you say?"

"Seemed to be." Ramsey stared at Frank. "He replaced it. But he gave me the damaged line, and I showed it to Luis at the garage when I got back to town. He confirmed that it was sabotage." He took a deep breath. "I don't think Clive was responsible, although I agree that he could certainly have done it. But why would he stop me from heading down the hill? It's because of him that I didn't crash, maybe end up dead."

"I understand this," Frank said, bringing his chair down with a thump. "It would have made an awful lot of trouble if you had wrecked your truck—maybe he decided too much."

"More likely it was Bob Markham who rigged the brakes," Ramsey growled. "The man has already threatened me. What more do you want?"

"Frankly, a good deal more." Alverez spread his hands. "Against any of them. Bob Markham is a respected businessman here. Horton Dalhousie is very old and very, very rich. And Clive has powerful friends in Sacramento." He shrugged. "Until there is proof—real proof—against one of them, I can do nothing, amigo. If I tread on toes, I may be ousted. And the next sheriff might not be willing to listen to you at all."

"Yeah, I know." Ramsey got up. "I don't really expect you to arrest Markham, Frank. Just keep an eye on him. And if anything happens to me—"

"Now don't be melodramatic," the sheriff ordered him. "And nothing will happen to you, Ramsey, if you take care of yourself. So please do that. Not just for my peace of mind, you understand. Your pretty cousin would be devastated if these plots against you were to succeed."

"Mary Ellen?" Ramsey stared at him. "I don't know where you got that idea. She barely tolerates me."

"Myself, I would have said that she was worried about you last night," Frank said softly. "More worried than she cared to admit. Did she not fall on your neck when you returned?"

"She wasn't even there—that's how much she cares." Ramsey shook his head. "So much for your romantic theories, Alverez. If you're no better at detecting criminals than you are at figuring out women's feelings, God help us all."

Frank bounded to his feet. "Ah," he said, grinning. "I happen to be very good at both of those things. Think about it, amigo."

Ramsey thought about it while he stomped down the stairs. By the time he reached his truck, he was smiling.

"Hey, Ramsey!" Jon Hsui came out of the bank and crossed the street toward him. "How you doin'? Gonna need another shower after work?"

"I hope not." Ramsey shook himself out of his reverie. "The plumber is supposed to be putting in temporary connections to the kitchen sink so we can at least wash up."

"Well, if it doesn't seem too appealing, just come on over." Jon glanced behind Ramsey. "Spending a lot of time with the sheriff, aren't you?"

"He's been dunning me about my Little League check," Ramsey said easily.

"Try that on someone else," Jon invited him. "What's happened now?"

There was the usual crush of business people on the street. "Get in," Ramsey said, opening the truck door. "I'll tell you about it."

"Where are we going?" Jon hopped into the truck and settled in. "I told my dad I was just going out for coffee for a few minutes."

"Around the block." Ramsey filled him in while he drove around the four sides of the central green.

"Someone's really got it in for you," was Jon's succinct comment. "And no matter what you say, I don't trust the wealthy Clive any more than Frank does. The rich are different, buddy. They tend to think that they're allowed to dispose of anything in their way."

"I know." Ramsey ran his hands through his hair. "I just wish I could figure it out." He pulled up in front of the bank. "Listen, you know some people in Sacramento. Could you ask around, see if you can get a line on this? Arnold may have finagled the legal end of it—started condemnation proceedings or something."

"He can only do that if the government needs the land," Jon said doubtfully. "Can't he?"

"Yeah, but he could be up to something. And it turns out Clive has something to do with government stuff in Sacto. See if you can dig anything up, okay?"

"Sure." Jon got out of the truck. "Just take care of yourself, buddy. Keep a low profile."

"You bet," Ramsey said. "I don't think anyone but you and Lenore has figured out I'm living at Alma's now."

"If anyone's watching your house they must know you're not there."

"Someone's there." Ramsey grinned. "The guy in Emmy's crew—Oscar. He wanted a place to stay and thinks he's in the middle of a thriller. I told him nothing's likely to happen—these guys never seem to repeat themselves—but he's on the alert."

"Good thinking." Jon raised a hand. "Get back to you with whatever I can find soon. Watch your back."

I plan to, Ramsey thought, heading out toward his spec house, where he'd meet Wally Hurtado. He wasn't too concerned that his enemy, whoever that was, would succeed in taking him out. What bothered him was the possibility that he'd put Mary Ellen in danger by moving in with her.

Of course, she was in danger, anyway, if Bob Markham's behavior was any indicator. At least Ramsey was in a position to protect her by living at Alma's with her. He only wished he could be guarding her a little closer—say, from the same bed.

He thought about Frank's observation, that Mary Ellen was worried about him. And maybe she was. But she was also mad at him. She wanted this project done with, and he'd quit early instead of working until he dropped. He hadn't stuck around that morning long enough to gauge her mood, except to realize that it hadn't been good.

Well, he'd finish with Wally and go back to face the music. Maybe the plumber would have arrived. Hot water on tap would soothe any woman's mood, he thought. But to be on the safe side, he'd stop and order pizza for dinner that night. Maybe they could eat together, get a little relaxed. Maybe he could find out if what Frank had said was true.

OSCAR CLATTERED DOWN the front steps and drove away, whistling, and Mary Ellen walked around the house, relishing the silence. It had been a productive day. Once a couple of pain relievers had taken care of her headache, she'd rather enjoyed knocking the last of the plaster down. The plumber had brought helpers, and they'd made excellent progress, managing the temporary connections in the kitchen and getting the copper to all the bathrooms. He'd even put the toilet back in the upstairs bathroom, making life that much easier, although the tub and sink wouldn't be hooked up until the wiring was done and the green wall was in place. The way things were going, that would happen before she'd thought it possible. In two weeks they would be taking showers.

Frowning, she amended that thought. *She* would be taking showers. Ramsey would be gone by then. The plumber had chattily told her that he'd made the connections at Ramsey's place the day before, and the cabinets had arrived just as he was leaving. He'd told Ramsey, too, who was apparently out there now, supervising their unpacking. Oscar had agreed to spend the next couple of evenings hanging them, and she supposed Ramsey would work with him.

The house felt empty, too empty. Without plaster, the whole back area echoed, and the rooms were simply blanks, darkened by the studs and siding.

She shook off her depressed mood. At least with Ramsey out of the way she could rinse off the construction dirt. She didn't want to keep running Lenore's water bill up.

Her bedroom was a warm oasis from the construction. She was tempted to flop down on the bed, but the thought of getting plaster dust all over it deterred her.

She gathered up soap, shampoo and towels, some clean clothes, and went back to the kitchen.

The bulb dangling from the center of the room gave off too harsh a light, she decided, so she cut the power and left the room dark and shadowy, lit only by the last of the sunset glow. As if it were a ritual, she covered the old sink's drain board with a towel and laid out her toiletries. She stripped off her shirt with a sigh of relief; the dust was itchy, and she had perspired freely during the day. Her jeans followed, then she tossed the dirty clothes over a chair and unhooked her bra.

The water was hot. She blessed the plumber, who'd set the water heater up outside the back door and made it functional. Starting at the top, she washed her hair and wound it in a towel, then lathered her washcloth with iris-scented soap. It was blissful to scrub her face, get all the gritty bits off her neck.

Leaning against the sink, she soaped her breasts. The sensual rasp of the washcloth against her tender skin made her close her eyes, imagining... When she opened them, she was looking straight at Ramsey.

His face was shadowed, but she could almost feel the heat in his eyes. The silence stretched between them. Her soapy skin cooled and tingled.

"I didn't hear you drive up," she whispered finally.

"Oscar dropped me off down the block," Ramsey said. His voice was idle, but when he stepped forward his face moved out of the shadow. The hunger there made her gasp. "So... how's the hot water?"

"Fine." She swallowed, trying to moisten her dry throat. It seemed absurd to try to cover herself, and yet that was her impulse. "I'm bathing now."

"I noticed." He cleared his throat, but his voice still sounded hoarse. "I showered at home."

"That's nice." He came another step closer, and she flattened herself against the sink. "Ramsey. Go away now."

"I can't." His hands reached toward her, then dropped. He might as well have touched her. Her nipples contracted; her breasts felt heavy and ripe. Her skin was flushed with heat, shivery with cold. She couldn't speak. "Emmy—you're so beautiful." He searched her face, his eyes devouring her. When he looked at her mouth, she ached for him to kiss her. "Please—let me..." He was right in front of her now. She closed her eyes and lifted her face to his.

The touch of his lips was gentle, wondering. He held her face between his hands and pressed sweetness on her mouth. Something that had been locked tight within her sprang free. Tears welled up behind her closed eyelids and overflowed.

"What's this?" Ramsey caught the tears in his fingers. "Oh, Emmy. I never meant to cause you sorrow. Darlin'..."

"Don't mind me." She blinked up at him. "I don't think it's from sorrow. Only if—if this doesn't work—"

"I'll do whatever it takes," Ramsey said simply. "Don't leave me again. I love you so, Emmy. I'm just an empty building without you."

"Ramsey." She locked her hands behind his head and pulled, and this time when their lips met it was fire and lightning. She felt it to the ends of her fingers, to the tips of her toes. When she moaned, he caught it in his throat, plunging his tongue into her mouth. When he growled, she bit his lip gently and rubbed her wet mouth across his.

He knew about the place just above her collarbone, and used the knowledge shamelessly. In turn, she found the spot on the rim of his ear and sunk her fingers delicately into it.

They were both gasping for air by the time the kiss ended.

Ramsey's hands drifted down her naked back, pulling her tightly against him. "So," he said, his breathing ragged, "don't let me interrupt your bath. In fact, I could help you."

"Could you?" Mary Ellen ran her hands along the broad shoulders with an exhilaration she never remembered feeling before. The room was dark now, only faintly illuminated from the garage's outdoor light. "How would you do that?"

"First," Ramsey said, bending to search one of the drawers of the old cast-iron sink unit, "I'd get the ambience right." He straightened. There was a faint scrape, and a match bloomed in the darkness. Ramsey's face, frowning in concentration, swam into view. He had found a box of small votive candles. Lighting them, he clustered them at the edge of the drain board, out of his way.

Mary Ellen watched him, feeling as if she were floating in a sea of cool, flickering flames. He turned back to her, and she shivered deliciously at the thought of causing that expression on his face.

"You're cold." He became solicitous, turning on the hot water and picking up her washcloth. "I'll finish what you started." His voice thickened. Holding her with one arm around her shoulders, he ran the warm washcloth over the tops of her breasts. "You didn't get a chance to get this soap off, after all." The words came out hoarsely. "Wouldn't want you to get—dry skin..."

Mary Ellen sucked in air when the washcloth closed warmly over first one breast, then the other. She stared at Ramsey's intent, aroused face as he circled her nipples with the washcloth. She had to wind her arms around his neck to support herself; her knees kept wanting to buckle.

"Ramsey," she whispered finally. "Please—"

"I want to," he growled back. "I want to please you every way. Emmy..." He dropped the washcloth and lowered his head, letting his tongue flick out to tease and torment her tender flesh.

She couldn't bear it. His mouth wove tantalizing patterns over her breasts and his free hand slipped down her hip, disregarding the panties she still wore to find its way into the soft patch of hair at the apex of her thighs. Moaning, she sought revenge, tearing at the buttons of his shirt with shaking fingers. His chest was a study in contrasts, crisp hair over warm flesh. She scraped her fingernail lightly over one of his nipples. His arm tightened around her, and he straightened.

"Bedtime," he said huskily.

"Yes." She rubbed her breasts against his chest, enjoying the sensation and the way it affected him. "Can we make it upstairs?"

"You bet," he said, laughing a little. "I'd like to make it with you in every room in the house. But it's not exactly habitable down here right now."

She wound her arms around him, which impeded their progress out of the room. Finally he picked her up and carried her up the stairs, despite her protests.

"Just like—Rhett Butler," he grunted, dropping her on her bed.

"I'm surprised you know who he is." Mary Ellen folded back the quilt and scrambled beneath the sheet, suddenly shy.

"Lenore made me watch that movie for hours one night." Ramsey wasn't paying much attention to what he said; his eyes were fixed on Mary Ellen. She swallowed when he tossed his shirt to the floor and unbuttoned his jeans. Five years hadn't changed his masculine magnificence. He was broad-shouldered and muscular without being muscle-bound; his waist was trim and his hips slim. Her gaze centered on his groin, and she suppressed a groan of longing. That, too, was just as she'd remembered it, which she'd done all too often in the empty nights that followed their parting.

Naked, he knelt on the bed beside her, his face serious. "Emmy, I mean what I say. As far as I'm concerned, this is for keeps. I couldn't handle it if we made love and you left me again."

"I know." She ran one hand down the side of his face, feeling the smoothness of his recently shaven cheek. "I couldn't stand it, either, Ramsey. I think I've always been in love with you. Trying to suppress that just doesn't work."

"I've imagined you so often, like this, waiting for me." The roughness of his voice made her breath come faster. "Your pale, silky skin. Your hair spread on the pillow." He tangled his fingers in it and cradled the back of her neck in his hand. His mouth came closer and her eyes drifted shut, the better to appreciate the fireworks, she thought hazily. Certainly there were fireworks, everywhere his hands went, and his hands were everywhere. His clever hands, so apt with tools and blueprints, built a raging inferno within her. She made forays of her own, down his muscular flanks, around his flat stomach, finding the thrusting strength of him. But then he would nibble on some hidden bud and make it flower with passion, and she would become limp and quiescent, needing him to fill her, needing to bring the circle around to completion, and so close it.

Every touch of his mouth, every brush of his hand, made her moan with pleasure. In the dark room, with the scent of roses drifting through the casement windows, she felt that she floated above the ceiling, above the house, encased in the velvet darkness with only the successive bursts of fireworks for illumination.

At last, when she was hot and wet and unable to lift a hand for the passion-shot languor that enveloped her, he placed himself between her opened legs and raised her hips to receive the gift he brought her. She cried aloud when he slid into her, and he shouted, and then the languor turned to fierce, furious motion, and everything exploded, and the black velvet was littered with stars.

RAMSEY SIGHED DEEPLY. Lying in Mary Ellen's bed, with her warm, silky skin against his, he was totally happy for the first time in a long while. He smoothed the hair back from her forehead and felt her smile. "That was a world-class experience," he whispered.

"Think we could ever do it again?" She snuggled against him, and he knew there'd be no problem with that.

"After dinner maybe. I'm hungry."

"So am I," she said, yawning. "But I'm too relaxed to do anything about it."

"You don't have to." He turned his head for a
glimpse of her clock. "A pizza should be arriving any
time now."

"Pizza? Really?" She sat up in bed, making him
feel cold. He reached to pull her down again.

"Yeah, I ordered one for seven o'clock. I was going to use it as bait to get you to talk to me."

"But you didn't need it, did you?" She nuzzled his
cheek. "Is that why you're all shaved and everything? I wondered if you'd planned this."

"I couldn't have planned it," he said, hoping she
wasn't looking for ulterior motives on his part. "I
didn't know I'd walk in on you half naked and looking like some pagan goddess in the moonlight."

"Ramsey, you're so poetic tonight." Emmy planted
a wet, enthusiastic kiss on his cheek. "I didn't think
you'd be back. Thought you were hanging cabinets
with Oscar."

"He doesn't need my help." Ramsey stretched and
decided, reluctantly, that he should put his pants on.
He didn't want to have to scramble for them when the
pizza arrived. "Listen, I'm going to get dressed for a
minute. But you don't need to."

"And deny you the opportunity to take off my
clothes?" Emmy raised her arms above her head and
arched her back. "I feel terrific. Are there going to be
anchovies?"

They set the table in the dining room, retrieving the
candles from the drainboard with much tender kissing. Ramsey felt young and foolish, and terribly vul-
nerable. Every time he saw Emmy smiling at him with
love shining on her face, he was afraid. Afraid he'd do

something stupid and blow it, again. Afraid it was just a dream, and he'd be kicking himself awake anytime.

The pizza arrived and was duly shared. It wasn't until they were clearing the table that things got awkward.

"So why did Oscar drop you off down the block?" Emmy put their paper plates into the pizza box and licked a speck of tomato sauce off her finger. Ramsey wanted to lick her finger, too, and the rest of the body it was attached to. He forced himself to pay attention to her words.

"Oscar? Oh, he's going to drive the truck back here tomorrow. I didn't want anyone to know I was staying here tonight."

He sensed her withdrawal before she said, "Oh?" The single syllable carried a wealth of question.

"That's right, you don't know the latest developments, do you?" He hadn't really wanted to tell her, but he knew if he didn't, she would be terribly hurt when she found out. And she would find out. In a small town, very little could be kept secret. Eventually, by some kind of osmosis, everyone in town would know that Ramsey MacIver's brakes had been tampered with at the Dalhousies'.

So he pulled her into the living room and down onto the dust-sheeted sofa, and told her all about his trip to Rosedown the previous day.

She heard him in silence, but her hand gripping his was proof that she wasn't angry. When he finished, she looked up at him, and the same vulnerability he'd felt earlier was mirrored in her face.

"I don't like it," she said slowly. "You have to be careful, Ramsey. Really careful. If I lost you now—"

"Don't worry." He nestled her against his side, putting his cheek against her hair. "That's why Oscar's keeping my truck at my place. And they've put the phone lines underground, so the security system is damned-near impregnable now. Oscar should be safe enough. I don't want whoever's doing these things to come here looking for me and find you."

"Is it Bob Markham?" She shivered. "I didn't like him one bit."

Ramsey wound her fingers in his. "Frank doesn't think there's enough evidence to pin it on anyone, not Markham, not Clive Dalhousie, not even Arnold, who's certainly in this thing up to his neck." He tilted her face up to meet his. "Don't worry, Emmy. I'm going to keep a very low profile until the county supervisors' meeting next week."

She met his kiss eagerly, and he made the pleasant discovery that she'd put her clothes on very haphazardly, not bothering with underwear. He hadn't bothered, either, which made the activity he had in mind much simpler.

They didn't speak of marriage, or business, or any of the problems that they both sensed would be difficult to resolve. They merely forged as strong a bond as they could, to get them through whatever problems would come later.

And it was strong, Mary Ellen thought hazily as they lay limply together on the sheet-covered sofa. It was very strong, indeed.

CHAPTER TWELVE

BUCKY SCHNEIDER SQUATTED beside the door to the bathroom and screwed a red wire nut onto the electrical outlet he was wiring. "Sure helps a lot," he grunted, "y'all drilling all these holes for me. Might get around to the whole upstairs today."

"That would be great," Mary Ellen said. She wiped her hot face with a bandanna and stuck it back in her pocket. She hefted the right-angle drill again and started out of the room. "I'll do the new bathroom. You're stringing the wire from the junction box above the kitchen, right?"

Bucky agreed absently, and Mary Ellen went down the hall. In the last two days, they'd really thrown themselves into the plumbing and wiring, and the results were visible. The back part of the downstairs, and the upstairs bathrooms, were still shells, with walls of bare studs and no fixtures. But now there was an air of purpose about them, and the spaces between the studs bristled with plumbing connections and were festooned with swags of electrical cable, switches and outlets.

Ramsey came up the steps, carrying two cups. He handed one to Mary Ellen and took a swig from the other one. "Tea," he told her, his eyes warm on her face. "Know you don't care for coffee that much."

"One cup in the morning's about my speed," she agreed, sipping from her cup and smiling at him. "Thanks."

"You're welcome." For a moment they basked in each other's approval. Mary Ellen felt a flush of pleasure when she looked at him, memories of the past three passion-filled nights coming to the fore. She was dizzy and filled with a fragile kind of exultation, underneath which was concern. They hadn't yet taken time to set ground rules or make long-term plans. She had no doubt that Ramsey meant their reunion to be permanent, and she, too, wanted that. But there were things she needed to know, two businesses to talk about. *Soon,* she told herself. *When we get this house done, we'll have time to talk, we'll be relaxed enough.* Until then, she would take things as they came.

Ramsey, too, seemed to feel an urgency to complete their project. He had brought a couple more people off his crew in to help string cable for Bucky. Sipping her tea, Mary Ellen eyed the circular metal reel that Ramsey had brought upstairs by wearing it like an outsized bracelet over his arm. "We gonna fish some wire?"

Ramsey nodded. "I don't want to have to open up the walls unless it's absolutely necessary. I'll fish from the attic if you'll feed in the Romex. We need to do the rest of the bedrooms up here. I already took out the fuses." He shook his head. "Sure is gonna be good to bring the twentieth century into this place. I'm surprised that old fuse box hasn't caused a fire."

Mary Ellen pulled the cordless screwdriver out of her tool belt and took off the switch plates in the bedrooms. Bucky whistled in a mournful monotone, the sound bouncing off the bathroom walls.

Ending up in Aunt Alma's bedroom, she un-
screwed the ancient switch and pulled it out, along
with the ancient wire. She flicked the switch a couple
of times to make sure the power was off. They were all
using extension cords plugged into outlets on two circuits, the last ones to be rewired. She didn't want to
think about the couple of days ahead of them; the old
wiring would be totally disconnected before the new
electrical service was installed.

She used her lineman's pliers to cut the old wiring.
"Well, I haven't been electrocuted yet," she muttered, cleaning out the electrical box that had held the
switch. The box was old, but it could probably be re-
used, which would save having to chip away the plaster around it to take it out and put in a new one. If the
old boxes had to be replaced, rewiring the house would
take even longer. And living without electricity was
right up there with loss of plumbing on her list of dis-
comforts to avoid whenever possible.

Actually, she thought, the speed with which things
had gone on this project was nothing short of phe-
nomenal. Of course, it helped that there were two
contractors, and that both were extraordinarily dedicated to Alma's house. Wally Hurtado had stopped by
the previous evening to complain that his work was
going very slowly with most of the crew having been
pulled off by Ramsey. But it wouldn't be for long. And
if there were delays, the crew could go back to the spec
house.

Ramsey's voice came through the ceiling, muffled.
"Send up the fish tape."

"Okay." Mary Ellen pulled at the end of the metal
reel, unrolling some of the flat, narrow wire that was
coiled around it. The end of the wire was bent to form
a hook. She pushed it through the hole at the top of

the electrical box, feeding more of the fish tape through. "It's coming."

"Wish I were." Ramsey's words were still muffled, but she knew what he was saying.

"Yeah," she muttered under her breath. Now that she wasn't trying to repress all her feelings for Ramsey, they threatened to overwhelm her. It was a miracle they got any work done at all, considering the way his hot gaze made her feel, or the urges she got when she saw the way his worn jeans lovingly hugged his rear.

"I got it," Ramsey said. Even through the barriers of plaster and wood she felt the vibrations he was putting out. "I'm pushing it in. Take it, darlin'. All the way."

She wound the fish tape back, hearing it scrape down between the walls, bringing the electrical cable with it. "Keep it coming," she called. "We're almost there."

"Grab hold, Emmy." More scrabbling came from the walls.

"It's here! I've got it." Mary Ellen reeled in the last of the fish tape, with the end of the electrical cable fastened to it. She pulled the end out and unfastened the fish tape.

"Was it good for you?" Ramsey was laughing, she could tell.

"Fabulous," she called to him, and turned to bump into Bucky.

He leered at her and winked. "Ready for me in here?"

"Just about." She heard Ramsey coming down the attic stairs. "There's some more cable to pull." She could tell from the heat in her cheeks that her face was red.

Ramsey bounded expectantly into the room, stopping short when he saw Bucky. "Ah," he said, clearing his throat. "I wasn't sure where you were going to put your junction box in the attic, Bucky."

"I'll just go up and take a look," Bucky said, plodding toward the door. He dug his elbow into Ramsey's ribs before vanishing.

Mary Ellen had to laugh. "Guess we aren't very subtle about the change in our status here."

"Guess not." Ramsey grinned and grabbed her, pulling her hard against him. "Can't help it if I get a hard-on every time I'm around you."

She rubbed against him, and their tool belts clanked in unison. "Kind of hard to be romantic when you're wearing fifteen pounds of metal," she muttered.

"You know," Ramsey said, adopting a serious expression, "I think we need to check some stuff out at my place. Let Oscar help Bucky with the lights."

"Yeah." She followed him down the stairs. Oscar was just finishing drilling the holes Bucky had marked for the electrical wires in the downstairs powder room.

"Oscar," Ramsey said, "Bucky needs some help in the attic. That stuff up there should keep you both busy for an hour or so. We've got an errand to run out at my place." He put one arm possessively around Mary Ellen.

"I see." Oscar glanced shrewdly from Ramsey's hand, which slid up and down Mary Ellen's arm in an absent caress, to the blush that she could feel coloring her cheeks. "I'll get right to it, then." He went up to the attic, his cheerful whistle joining the lugubrious drone of Bucky's.

"Oscar guessed we're up to hanky-panky," Mary Ellen said with a nervous laugh.

"Good. He'll be sure to stay out of the way." Ramsey charged down the hallway. "We're out of here."

"Um—why don't we take my truck?" Mary Ellen glanced at the heap of papers, tools and empty lunch bags that littered Ramsey's front seat.

He hesitated. "Well, okay," he said slowly. "Whatever you say, honey."

Mary Ellen unlocked her truck and watched out of the corner of her eye as Ramsey got in. He looked very tall, sitting there, his arms folded over his chest. She drove decorously, wondering if he remembered, as she did, that some of their most spectacular fights had arisen over their differing concepts of what constituted order.

"I'm not slamming your truck or anything," she blurted out, just as he began to speak.

"I just wanted to say how much I admire your sense of organization," he said after a moment. "I know I've been messy in the past. But working with you has shown me that it doesn't take that much more time to clean as you go. Makes the job site a lot easier to work at, too."

Mary Ellen heaved a huge sigh of relief. "That's big of you, Ramsey." She turned into his driveway and waited for him to activate the gate. "I was afraid you thought I was nitpicking again."

"Nope." He grinned at her. "My truck is a mess. I admit it. And I have nothing against being driven around in your nice clean truck. Chauffeur me anytime, darlin'."

Mary Ellen parked at the side of Ramsey's house, in front of the garage. She'd been out to the place once since the fire. This house carried a lot of baggage for her; Ramsey had built it after she'd left, after selling the place she thought of as theirs, which she'd helped him fix up. At first sight she'd hated it. Its stark presence had grown on her, but she didn't know if she'd ever find the place comfortable. She preferred the houses she worked on in Berkeley, with their gracious details and sense of history.

Ramsey unlocked the back door, and they entered the kitchen. There was no more evidence of the firebomb. But Mary Ellen looked around nervously. "So what do you think they'll do to you next?"

"Who?" Ramsey ran one hand along the wall. "Good job of taping," he said with satisfaction.

"Whoever it is that's trying to kill you."

He turned, taking her into his arms. "No one's really trying to kill me," he said soothingly. "They're just hoping I'll take the hint. Do you think I'd let Oscar sleep here if there was any danger?"

"And have you taken the hint?" She searched his face, already knowing that the integrity that was such a big part of him wouldn't let him back away from a moral stance.

"As far as they know," he said, unfastening the clip that held her hair in a knot. It tumbled over her shoulders, and he buried his fingers in it. "The county supe's meeting is the day after tomorrow." His voice thickened. "I'll...lay low till then. Emmy—"

She pulled his head toward her and kissed him, fiercely, feeling that she was fighting fate for her lover. Surely no harm could come to him now, when she had claimed him.

"I wanted to show you my bedroom," he whispered. "We could...do some electrical work."

"You mean—?" She bit his earlobe delicately, and enjoyed his shiver.

"I mean, the male plug...seems to short-circuit...when the female receptacle—"

"I see." She stopped nibbling on his chest and smiled up at him. "Show me the problem."

No short circuit here, she decided hazily a little later. The equipment was obviously all in working order. Perhaps it was a case of too much power—definitely a circuit overload. The kind of problem that would have to be repeated often before it could be fixed—if ever.

AUNT ALMA'S DINING ROOM seemed very romantic lit by flickering candles. Mary Ellen spread place mats on the table and smiled at Ramsey, who was busy at the sideboard. "It's a good thing we still have the outlets," she said, sniffing the savory aroma. "Otherwise we'd have to eat at the Blue Willow."

"We won't have them much longer." Ramsey brought a skillet of chili to the table, and reached for a basket of sliced sourdough. "But Bucky will be finished with them sometime tomorrow."

"New electric service on Thursday?" Mary Ellen took a spoonful of chili. "This is terrific," she said appreciatively. "What a deal—a great lover and you're good in the kitchen, too."

She thought Ramsey blushed, but the light was too dim to tell. "Yeah," he said, passing her the bread. "Actually, he said if the last two circuits go fast, he might be able to install the meter and get the power in tomorrow afternoon."

"Wonderful." She nibbled on her bread. "Maybe we should go out to your place tomorrow evening to get cleaned up before the big meeting."

Ramsey shifted uneasily. "I don't want to be there at hours when people think I might be there," he said, stirring his chili.

"Real clear," Mary Ellen said lightly, but she felt cold inside. So Ramsey still thought there was danger, despite his efforts to downplay it. "So, it's okay to go over during the day, but not when you'd be getting off work?"

"Right." Ramsey smiled unhappily. "Not for long, darlin'. After this meeting, there won't be much point in trying to shut me up, since I'll have said my piece. Everyone will simmer down, and we can live at my place while we finish up here."

"Meanwhile," Mary Ellen said, trying to make her voice light, "we can consider it part of your strategy not to shower. Might empty the room that way."

"Then we'd lose our supporters as well as our enemies," Ramsey pointed out. "But I hate to impose on Jon anymore."

"Likewise, with Lenore." Mary Ellen crumbled her bread.

"Well, we'll just have to wash each other off," Ramsey decided. "After all, tomorrow will be the one-week anniversary of our getting back together." He gave her a devilish look. "I vote we always remember the date by being naked and wet."

"You have the best ideas," Mary Ellen said, batting her lashes. "But can we risk it? This meeting is important. We don't want to be late."

"We'll get rid of the crew and start early." Ramsey reached across the table and took her hand. "I can't tell you how happy it's made me, being back together with you." His voice was quiet, but his tone heartfelt. "It's like the last five years was a bad dream, and now I'm awake again."

"I know what you mean." Mary Ellen blinked away the tears that unaccountably welled in her eyes. She tightened her grip on his hand, then let go. It was time to talk about the future.

"I learned a lot in the last five years, just the same," she said slowly.

"You certainly have." Ramsey gave her an admiring look. "It's going to be wonderful having you on the team here. Maybe the paperwork will get under control, and I'll be able to see the upholstery on my truck again."

Mary Ellen sat up straighter. "That's not exactly what I meant, Ramsey." The sick feeling in her stomach made her feel as though she was on an express elevator going down fast. "But let's talk about it anyway. I have my own business and it's been profitable. You seem to assume that I'm going to give it up and work for you."

Ramsey set his spoon down. After a moment he said, "I didn't realize you were planning to keep your business in Berkeley. That will be a lot of driving for you. That is, if you were going to live with me."

The thinly veiled sarcasm in that last statement goaded Mary Ellen, but she decided that this time she was going to get through the issues instead of getting angry. "Since we haven't talked about any of this, I don't know what I'm planning. Are we getting married?"

Ramsey shoved his chair back and came around to pull her out of hers. "Emmy," he whispered into her hair, "don't let's fight about anything. I couldn't bear to lose you now."

She clung to him, swallowing the tears that threatened her. "I don't want to fight, Ramsey. But we have to talk about these things. We have to make decisions that are good for both of us. We can do that without fighting, can't we?"

He let her go, keeping his hands on her shoulders. "I don't know," he said, smiling grimly. "We couldn't before."

"We will this time." Mary Ellen pushed him back into his chair. "Let's eat some more of this excellent chili and talk like rational people."

"We will," he promised, and pulled her onto his lap. "But first I have to ask you, will you marry me?"

Mary Ellen took his face between her hands. "I want to," she said, kissing him gently, then drawing back. "But maybe we're going too fast. Maybe we should talk about the blueprint before we jump into the contract."

His shoulders slumped. "You're probably right," he said dully. "We should be practical."

"We should be together," Mary Ellen corrected him, unable to bear the desolation in his voice. She kissed him again, pouring the fire of her feelings into it. He came alive under her lips, his mouth growing eager, his tongue engaging hers in a duel they could both win. She fastened her hands in his hair and lost herself in the passion that built between them.

His hands slid down her arms and found the aching weights of her breasts. His fingers trembled as they circled her nipples through the thin cloth of her T-shirt. She moaned, and he tore his mouth away from hers, pulling her up until her knees straddled his hips. He pushed her T-shirt up and took one swollen nipple into his mouth, licking, sucking, gently tugging. She clenched her fists on his shoulders, arching back when he treated her other breast to the hot, lavish caresses. His hands invaded her sweatpants, pushing them down. Blindly she followed his whispered instructions. Blindly her hands sought and found the buttons on his jeans, pushing ineffectually until he managed to free himself from them. He tossed aside her T-shirt, then his.

And at last she was settled onto him, her legs dangling on either side of the chair. Their groans of pleasure rent the air almost simultaneously. He was deep, deep inside her, a part of her that could never be denied. Each movement of his made her shudder; each delicate contraction of hers wrung a cry of pleasure from him. He stroked her breasts and the sides of her hips; she steadied herself with one hand on his shoulder while her other hand made teasing forays to the heated places where they were joined.

When his mouth fastened avidly on her nipple again, she dissolved, her body a shivering mass of pleasure, her soft cries of delight mingling with his shout of satisfaction as he plunged upward again and again, until at last she collapsed, cradled in his arms, his head bowed against her breast.

There was no more talk of the future that night. Mary Ellen thought about it, snuggled sleepily against Ramsey in her tower bedroom. She would bring the topic up the next day, gently, so as not to imply that she was giving Ramsey an ultimatum.

He mumbled a drowsy good-night, his arms tight around her. She felt safe, secure, well-loved. Smiling, she drifted to sleep.

"I THOUGHT WE WERE working well together." Ramsey jammed his hands into the pockets of his jeans and stared at her. Mary Ellen decided too late that it was a bad time for the confrontation she could see looming ahead. But she'd waited all day to bring up the touchy subject of combining their two businesses.

She should have waited longer. The county supervisors' meeting was that evening, so after the crew had left, she and Ramsey had shared a hasty dinner of leftover chili. And then, because it was on her mind, Mary Ellen had blurted out her doubts.

Now she stood stiffly in the living room, flipping the new light switch while the ceiling light flashed on and off.

"We are," she said, wanting to maintain her cool. "These past few days have gone really well."

"Then why don't you want to come into my business?"

"Why," she said, drawing a deep breath, "don't you want to come in with me in Berkeley?"

The question took him by surprise. "Well—this is home," he said awkwardly. "For me, and for you, too, I thought."

"It was home," she agreed. "But there are more business opportunities in Berkeley. I've built up a clientele. Why shouldn't you join me?"

"Well—just because." He ran one hand through his hair and glared at her. "Okay, I know what you want me to say. Damn it, Mary Ellen, I think of you as an equal. We are equals. I just don't want to give up my business."

"Then you can understand how I feel." She left the light on and prowled restlessly around the room, standing in front of the portrait of her uncle, Ramsey's namesake. Scottie MacIver glared down at her, as outraged by her defiance as his nephew was.

"Sure I understand." He shook his head as if bewildered. "But you wouldn't be uprooting yourself to come back here. These are your roots. Whereas I—" He glanced around helplessly. "Berkeley is foreign territory to me."

"That's a point," she agreed thoughtfully. "So what's the compromise here?"

"I don't know." He grabbed his hair again. "You're setting me up, Emmy," he growled. "I know damned good and well that if I say the wrong thing it'll go on my permanent record. So tell me what the right thing to say is."

"I guess it's unreasonable of me to want you to know what the right thing is without my telling you," she whispered.

"I've asked you to marry me. I want to be with you forever," he said desperately. "I want to have children with you and watch them grow up. I want to get old and decrepit with you, for God's sake! What more do you want?"

"How could I want more than that?" Mary Ellen was shaken by the intensity of his speech. "Truly, Ramsey, those things matter more than almost anything."

"But not enough?" He turned away, glancing at his watch. "Time for the hearing," he said quietly. "We'd better get going."

They climbed into Mary Ellen's truck, although the county offices were less than half a mile away. Mary Ellen parked at the curb, noticing that most of the spaces around the town square were filled. "Looks like a popular meeting," she commented.

"People hope to see some fireworks," Ramsey said, his smile grim. If his mood was any indication, Mary Ellen thought, fireworks were almost assured.

Inside the meeting room, people milled around, greeting each other and exchanging gossip. Mary Ellen nodded to Mrs. Fordice and slipped into a seat beside Lenore. Ramsey and Jon were in a corner, conferring, and she realized she didn't know the strategy for the evening. She and Ramsey had had other things on their minds.

Lenore seemed to know all about it. "So," she said gaily, "my spies tell me that you and Ramsey have finally come to your senses."

"If you mean we're having a hot, tempestuous affair..." Mary Ellen paused for a moment, and then grinned. "Yes, you're right."

"Great!" Lenore gave her a quick hug. "So when are the wedding bells going to ring?"

"Oh, I don't know."

"You're not going to get married?" Lenore scowled at her. "Mrs. Mac will not be pleased to hear that. You don't know what she'll do next if you two don't oblige her."

"That is a terrifying thought," Mary Ellen said faintly. "Thanks for sharing it with me." It was true that their aunt would see all her finagling as a waste of time if no marriage took place.

"Any time." Lenore looked toward the dais in front of the room, where the supervisors sat behind a curved table. Arnold was busily shuffling papers, smiling broadly, but he wasn't quite as relaxed as he pretended, if the way his forehead glistened was any indicator. "What's going down here? We've sure got a first-class audience." She turned in her chair to survey the room, and Mary Ellen did, too.

There was a momentary hush as two new arrivals came through the doorway. The old man looked very frail. He used a cane and leaned on the arm of his companion. Lenore studied them with interest.

"I think that's old Mr. Dalhousie," Mary Ellen said, recalling Ramsey's description. "That must be his son Clive with him. I didn't really expect them to come."

"If they've come to say they're opening Spring Hill for development, they'd better beware of the rotten tomatoes." Lenore nodded toward the table. "Looks like Arnold didn't expect them, either." He was staring at the Dalhousies while he patted his face with a snowy handkerchief.

"Oh, there's Bob Markham." Mary Ellen spotted the stocky man standing well back in the room, far away from Ramsey. She saw Markham notice the Dalhousies, then exchange a long look with Arnold.

There were a couple of men standing behind Bob Markham who seemed familiar. After a moment Mary Ellen placed them. "Hey," she said, nudging Lenore. "Those guys were at Arnold's party. I remember they left right after the dustup between Arnold and Ramsey. Markham said something to them, and they dashed away. Do you know them?"

"I seem to remember them from the party," Lenore said slowly, looking the men over, "but they're not local." She grabbed the arm of a passing man, and he stopped, smiling. It was Frank Alverez.

"You ladies have come for the excitement, too?" His words were genial, but there was something watchful in his attitude.

"Frank, do you know those two guys?" Lenore jerked her head toward the back of the room. "Standing near Bob Markham?"

Frank glanced casually around and turned back to Lenore. "No, I don't. Do you?"

Mary Ellen told him about seeing them leave the party at Arnold's house. "No doubt I'm leaping to conclusions," she said, "but Markham told them something, and they left, and soon after that Ramsey's house got blown up. Maybe those things are related."

Frank pursed his lips. "You're very observant," he told Mary Ellen. "I'll keep an eye on them. It may be necessary for me to inquire as to what their business is in town." He moved off, and shortly afterward Lenore whispered that a couple of the men standing in the crowd by the door were part-time deputies. Frank was taking no chances.

The meeting was called to order. Jon and Ramsey ended up sitting across the room from the two women, uncomfortably close, in Mary Ellen's opinion, to Bob Markham and his friends. Those two sported no expressions at all beyond blankness and boredom. Under the circumstances, she told herself, that made them seem pretty sinister.

"I gather most of you here have come about agenda item number thirteen, approval of a subdivision map," said the board chairman, an earnest and rotund attorney. "I suggest we move that item up to first place."

"Good idea," snapped a choleric-looking woman on Arnold's right. "Maybe some of these spectators will go home then."

"Perhaps we should simply table the item," Arnold suggested, blotting his forehead with a crumpled handkerchief. The crowd muttered.

The chairman seemed unimpressed by that idea. "There's no reason to table it, unless the application is incomplete in any way." He turned to the county clerk, Wilma Mae, who sat at the foot of the curved table with her tape recorder and note pad. She shook her head.

"It's all there, Mr. Garrison."

"Fine. Is there a motion?"

The choleric woman glared at the audience. "I so move."

"All in favor of moving agenda item thirteen up to number one?" There was a murmur of approval from

the board members. "Opposed?" Arnold shot a
nervous look at the crowd, opened his mouth and
closed it without speaking. "Motion carried. We'll
dispose of old business, and then take up agenda item
thirteen."

Mary Ellen didn't listen to the drone of minutes being accepted, votes being taken. Her mind drifted to
her own concerns, and she saw Ramsey's face again,
when he'd made his impassioned declaration. Warmth
and panic battled within her whenever she thought of
it. She was definitely in love.

Lenore poked her in the ribs, and with difficulty she
brought her attention back to the conference room.
There was a stir throughout the audience. "This is it,"
Lenore whispered.

The development map was displayed on an overhead projection screen that pulled down from the wall
behind the dais; it was blurred and pale, difficult to
see. But a pile of papers were circulated through the
room—copies, Mary Ellen saw, of the map. She took
one and passed the rest on.

Wilma Mae droned out the legal description of the
land. It meant little to Mary Ellen, but on her map
someone had lightly sketched in the contours of Spring
Hill. The development didn't miss an inch of it.

The board considered the application and found it
complete. Horton Dalhousie was mentioned as owner
of record. Finally Mr. Garrison picked up a last piece
of paper.

"I have here," he said, glancing around the room,
"a request for a restraining order, based on the prem-
ise that there is a conflict between this use of the land
and a previous legal designation of it as parkland."

Arnold tried to look surprised. "Does the development encroach on the proposed parkland?"

"You know it must, Mr. Hengeman." The chairman sounded testy. "According to this subdivision map, you are a member of the financing group putting this together."

Arnold looked down at his papers, refusing to meet the eyes of anyone in the room. "Nevertheless," he said, "the owner of record has agreed, in writing, to the subdivision."

This caused quite a stir in the room. Horton Dalhousie rose.

"I would like to speak," he said, his voice quavering a little.

"I was just about to open the meeting to public comment, Mr. Dalhousie," the chairman said courteously. "All in favor?"

Arnold's mouth moved, but he said nothing when the rest of the supervisors acquiesced. He used the handkerchief on his damp forehead again, looking unhappy.

"That man there," Horton said, pointing at Arnold, "approached me a couple of years ago about allowing development on Spring Hill. Of course I told my business manager to refuse. My dear wife and I always planned to leave it to the city for parkland."

"Mr. Dalhousie, I—"

"Please don't interrupt, Hengeman." The chairman gestured to Horton. "Go on."

"Well, last year Mr. Markham came to me in great distress. He said this man—" again Horton pointed to Arnold "—was threatening to expose some very—unsavory business deals I'd been engaged in long ago, during the Second World War." Horton stopped talking, his mouth working. The room was silent. "I would have regretted that very much," he went on.

"I'm not proud of that period of my life, and I didn't want my son to know what I'd done."

Clive, still seated, took his father's hand and squeezed it. His low-voiced comment could not be heard, but Horton's voice gathered strength.

"No, I can finish, Clive. I just want to say that at Markham's urging, I considered throwing the land around the base of the hill open to development, but had not yet agreed to. I have seen the consent-of-sale documents that purport to have my signature on them. It is not my signature. I will not give up Spring Hill for development."

Horton sat down. There was a moment's stunned surprise, and then applause broke out. The old man took out a spotless handkerchief and wiped his face. He looked shaken. Clive handed him a small pillbox, and he swallowed something out of it.

Mary Ellen's throat was tight. Horton Dalhousie had been such a gallant figure. It must have cost him a lot to admit to having been nothing less than a war profiteer.

"This is a serious allegation against you, Hengeman," said Mr. Garrison. "As an elected official, you are barred from benefiting in any commercial development."

"I was not concerned with personal benefit," Arnold protested, "but with the welfare of the town and county." His voice squeaked, and he took a breath, steadying it. "Our tax base is stagnating and our business districts lose revenues to the urban areas. We need more development." He spread his hands and tried a conciliating smile. "Granted, this was unfortunately placed. I was told it was to encompass only the land near Spring Hill."

"By whom were you told this?" Mr. Garrison looked over his spectacles. Arnold eased his collar away from his throat and hesitated before speaking.

"By Mr. Bob Markham. When he first approached me about the development." Arnold adopted a righteous air. "Naturally I explained my interest was only in what would benefit the county."

"Naturally." Mr. Garrison's tone was skeptical. "Mr. Markham, what basis did you have for starting this development idea? The land wasn't yours to dispose of and had been earmarked for other purposes."

Bob Markham's round, genial face wore a look of amazement. "Mr. Hengeman has taken me by surprise," he said, glancing innocently at his surrounding neighbors. "He was the one who came to me suggesting that Spring Hill be developed, I told him the hill itself was out of the question. This is all a total fabrication." He addressed himself primarily to Horton Dalhousie's back. The old man wouldn't turn around, but Clive twisted in his seat, and his expression boded no good for Markham.

"That's a lie," Arnold shouted, springing to his feet. He was shaking. "It was Markham's idea from beginning to end. He even had his goons blow up Ramsey MacIver's house to stop him from asking questions."

Frank moved then, but he was too late. Markham and his men were pushing through the crowd at the door.

"Sheriff wants to talk to you," one of the volunteer deputies said, trying to stop them. Markham shoved him, the deputy shoved back, and almost immediately a fight broke out, with the enthusiastic participation of several locals.

Mary Ellen and Lenore got hastily to their feet and pressed against the walls, along with some other members of the audience, while the fight raged through the room. Chairs were overturned, and Mr. Garrison finally gave up banging his gavel on the table in front of him, although when a seething mass of brawlers threatened to overrun the dais, he used it on one of them.

"All right now, stop it!" Ramsey climbed on a chair and bellowed. The brawlers, tiring of their fun, quieted. "This is not the place for fighting. Those of you who want to continue, step outside." Men exchanged sheepish looks with their neighbors and began setting the chairs back up. "Let's let the supervisors get about their business, which is to vote on the issues before them."

"Thank you, Ramsey," Mr. Garrison said. "I believe we'll close the meeting to public comment at this point." A ripple of laughter ran over the room. Horton Dalhousie tottered into a seat again. Lenore sat, too, but Mary Ellen remained on her feet. She had just noticed that Arnold no longer occupied his place on the dais.

Mr. Garrison noticed it, too. "Looks like our esteemed colleague has had to step out," he said, keeping his face straight. "We won't wait for him." He put the Spring Hill development map to a vote, and it was unanimously defeated.

The room broke into spontaneous cheers, and Ramsey was surrounded by well-wishers, with Jon and Lenore in the lead. Mary Ellen didn't feel like being one of the crowd. She would congratulate Ramsey later. Right now, she wanted to be alone.

She slipped unnoticed out the door. The town square was deserted. Ramsey wouldn't need a ride after the meeting. She got into her truck and drove aimlessly away.

After a little while she realized she wasn't going back to Alma's house—not yet. She would drive up Spring Hill, and be the first to celebrate its freedom.

There were no other cars in the parking lot at the top of the hill. She got out and leaned against the hood, relishing the cold breeze that whipped the leaves off the trees and sent them scuttling along the gravel. The moon was waning, and the stars were thick and bright.

Below her the lights of Dusty Springs were sparse in comparison, but Ramsey was right. It was her home. The Bay Area had many opportunities for contractors, but her family and friends lived in the little town spread out at her feet.

Absorbed in her thoughts, she didn't at first pay attention to the sounds behind her, until it sank in that the noise had come from her truck. She turned to find Arnold Hengeman climbing out of the bed of her pickup.

"What in the world are you doing?" Gaping at Arnold, she didn't at first take in his distraught expression.

"I hitched a ride. Hope you don't mind," he said, civilly enough. "I thought Ramsey would be with you."

Mary Ellen swallowed. Arnold had reached into his pocket and pulled out a gun. The starlight shone on its barrel. It was small, ornate. But she didn't think it was a toy.

CHAPTER THIRTEEN

RAMSEY GRINNED AT JON, who pounded him enthusiastically on the back. "You did it, boy!" Jon shouted to be heard over the ruckus in the meeting room. "We won!"

"I didn't do anything," Ramsey protested. "Arnold did it to himself."

"Yeah, him and that crook, Bob Markham." Jon stepped aside when Lenore elbowed him.

"Great work, Ramsey." She grabbed him around the neck and planted a big kiss on his cheek. "I think they want us to clear the room."

"Probably." Ramsey glanced toward the dais. Mr. Garrison, although he smiled benevolently, was pounding his gavel on the table. Mary Ellen wasn't visible; she must have already left. He felt a little coldness at that thought. Their earlier disagreement surged back into his mind, and he wondered if this night of triumph would turn out a disaster, after all.

Jon and Lenore dragged him out the door. In the hallway Horton Dalhousie was surrounded by a crowd of exuberant townspeople. Clive, watchful as ever, stood beside him.

Ramsey paused in front of Horton and cleared his throat, not knowing what to say. They looked at each other for a moment.

Lenore's clear voice broke the silence. "You're a very brave, very sweet man," she said to Horton, shaking his hand. Impulsively she kissed his cheek, too. He flushed with pleasure.

"Thank you, young lady." He turned to Clive. "My son gave me the courage to go through with it. I'm afraid Markham might have gauged my fear of disclosure accurately if not for Clive."

Ramsey wanted to introduce Clive to Lenore, but he was swept away by the press of the crowd before he could do so. And it didn't seem like exactly the right time for networking. People were shouting and cheering. By the time he got outside his shoulder was sore from congratulatory slaps.

The town square was full of people, all talking briskly as they went to their cars. Ramsey didn't see Mary Ellen anywhere.

"Where's Mary Ellen?" Lenore came up to stand beside him. She was also scrutinizing the crowd.

"I don't know. Thought she was with you."

"We got separated during the riot." Lenore turned to Jon, who had been talking with Clive Dalhousie.

"Clive said the folks in Sacramento will be glad to see Arnold gone. He was an influence peddler from the word go," Jon announced. "Say, where's Mary Ellen?"

"We were just wondering that." Ramsey walked along the sidewalk, dodging the chattering knots of people, smiling absently at their greetings. When he got to the space where Mary Ellen had parked, he stopped. Her truck was gone.

"Hmm." Jon and Lenore grasped the situation. "She ditched you, eh?"

"She probably didn't want to hang around," Ramsey muttered. "Can you drop me at Alma's?"

"I'm parked over here." Jon went back the way they'd come, and Ramsey followed him impatiently.

Lenore, trailing at the rear, was still looking hope-fully around.

"I thought she'd want to have a victory celebration with us," she mourned. "Why would she leave early?"

Jon cleared his throat. "We can celebrate any time," he said quickly.

"We had an argument," Ramsey told Lenore. "Just before the meeting. Guess she's still mad."

"Maybe she just wanted some time to think," Lenore said, dodging a group of men.

One of them turned and shouted after them. "Ramsey!"

Ramsey stopped. Frank Alverez came up to them. "I thought you should know," he began, his fore-head creased with a frown, "that your good friend Arnold Hengeman has disappeared. Also Bob Mark-ham. This concerns me a little, since they may blame you for their troubles. Be careful, amigo."

"I'll be careful," Ramsey promised absently. "They're probably halfway to Mexico by now with all the spare cash Markham could get his hands on. You should tell the Dalhousies to shut down any funds he might have access to."

"That's a good idea." Alverez looked at Lenore. "We got those two men."

"Oh, good." Lenore lingered. "Have they con-fessed?"

"They don't actually have to, as their fingerprints came up on the FBI's list of outstanding warrants. I have hopes of getting a story from them."

"What two men are these?" Ramsey broke in im-patiently.

Lenore told him what Mary Ellen had noticed. "We told Frank about it just before the meeting."

"She uses her eyes, your sweetheart," Frank said approvingly. "Where is she? We may need her to provide a statement."

"She's already gone." Ramsey glanced at Jon, who was unlocking his car.

"Well, tell her to stop in sometime in the next couple of days. And watch your back."

There wasn't much talking in Jon's car during the short drive to Alma's house. The mood was flat, like day-old champagne. Ramsey barely waited for Jon to slow down in the drive before he vaulted out of the car. "Thanks for the ride," he said. "Talk to you guys later."

After they'd driven away, he realized that Mary Ellen's truck wasn't in the driveway. He walked around to the back, just in case she'd decided to park out of sight. That faint hope was dashed. Her truck was nowhere around.

He went inside. The light was on in the hall, but the house felt empty. "Emmy?" He knew she wasn't there, but he had to call, anyway. His voice rang through the living room, the dining room. He took the stairs two at a time and pushed open the door to her room.

It, too, was empty. He wandered disconsolately over to the window seat in the tower and yanked the curtain back. From here he could see most of Dusty Springs, now just clusters of lights along the grid of streets. None of the vehicles on the road turned into Alma's driveway. No sign of Mary Ellen anywhere.

A sudden fright hit him, and he jerked open the closet doors, breathing a sigh of relief when he saw her clothes still on hangers. A faint, sweet scent wafted toward him. Closing his eyes, he breathed it in.

Where was she? He checked Aunt Alma's bedroom, the two chaotic bathrooms upstairs. No sign of her. It seemed obvious she hadn't been back since the meeting.

He should wait there for her; she was bound to return when she'd hammered things out with herself. But he was too restless to sit meekly. He got his truck keys and locked the front door behind him. He would drive to Lenore's and then out to his place, in case she'd just felt like taking a shower or giving Oscar some instructions. He'd drive over every square inch of the town, if need be. She wasn't going to get away from him.

Giving the old pickup some gas, he roared away to begin his search.

MARY ELLEN LOOKED from the gun back to Arnold's face. There were lines of strain on his forehead; his mouth was folded tightly. "Where's Ramsey?" The gun wavered in his hand when he turned to look at the bushes, as if Ramsey might be hiding behind one. *I wish he was,* Mary Ellen thought fervently, and then took it back. She didn't want Ramsey anywhere near this gun-toting maniac.

"I left him at the meeting." She noticed that Arnold's suit coat had a smear of dirt on the sleeve. His tie was skewed under his ear.

"The meeting!" Arnold laughed wildly. "A pretty total humiliation for me, wouldn't you say? My political future is washed up!"

Mary Ellen hoped so, but she didn't like the way Arnold kept waving that gun around. "Just a setback," she murmured soothingly. "Nothing that a lot of politicians haven't gone through and come out of unscathed."

"You think so?" Arnold came closer, peering into her face in the dark. "No, no. You're wrong. It's over."

"Now, Arnold." Mary Ellen tried to put conviction in her voice. "Wait a minute!"

Arnold seized her arm and dragged her to the edge of the cliff. There was a railing there, but it only came up to her knees. He would have no problem pitching her over it, especially if he put a bullet in her first. "It's pretty far," he said, considering. "Would you say it's far enough to kill someone?"

"I—I don't know." Mary Ellen's teeth began to chatter. "Probably not. Why do you ask?"

He dropped her arm impatiently, and she stepped back. "Well, because I'm thinking of jumping, of course! No point in jumping if I'll just break a leg or something. It has to be the whole enchilada, don't you think? I always kind of despise people who can't even succeed at killing themselves."

"Arnold, wait!" Mary Ellen groped desperately in her mind for what to say. It didn't sound like he planned to kill her, but he was definitely unbalanced. And she didn't want him to kill himself, either. "You're going to take the easy way out?"

"You think this is easy?" Arnold grabbed her arm again. "Why don't you try jumping off a cliff?"

"I don't want to." Mary Ellen dug her heels in. "And yes, it is easier to jump off a cliff and end up in the hospital, maybe a vegetable for life, than it is to work at reestablishing yourself as a man of integrity."

Arnold laughed again. "I've never been a man of integrity," he shouted. "Didn't Ramsey tell you?"

"Well, it's not too late to start." Arnold stood beside the railing that blocked off the cliff, one foot resting on top of it. She tried to think of some way to talk him out of suicide. "Really, there's no use, Arnold! You'll break your leg and miss the skiing season, that's all that will happen."

For a moment he stared over the cliff. Then he heaved a sigh. "You're right. It's not high enough to ensure death." His shoulders slumped, he walked toward her. "I guess I'll have to use the gun."

She had almost forgotten the gun. Mary Ellen watched, horrified, while he raised it to his head. "Arnold, really! Have a little consideration." She kept her voice from shaking, injecting indignation into it, instead. "You're going to blow your brains out here, right in front of me, probably causing me terrible mental anguish, and make a mess where all the high school kids come to park? Isn't there somewhere better?"

Disconcerted, he lowered the gun. "Well—I don't know. This is pretty appropriate, really. The site of my downfall and everything." He looked around. "Might be kind of neat to haunt the place, scare off the lovebirds."

"Oh, right." Mary Ellen was too frightened to notice how sharp her voice sounded. "After you send your brains flying all over the parking lot, believe me, Arnold, you will no longer be in any condition to care about what happens next. I'm the one who will have to cope with that."

"You're supposed to be talking me out of this, aren't you?" Arnold regarded her doubtfully. "I read an article once. You're supposed to point out how much I have to live for and all."

"I tried that." Mary Ellen shrugged, realizing that she was keeping him off balance. Sooner or later someone would probably drive up the hill, especially in light of its reprieve from development. If she had some help, she might be able to overpower Arnold. Single-handed, she doubted it. "You didn't want to listen."

"Well, tell me again." Arnold leaned against the hood of her truck. "I'll listen this time."

"Okay." Mary Ellen edged closer. "Why don't you let me hold your gun while I tell you?" She made the suggestion brightly. "I'll give it back if you decide you're really going to shoot yourself."

Arnold hesitated. "It's not really my gun," he said. "I borrowed it from Mr. Dalhousie's collection when I was at Rosedown once. He wouldn't like me to lend it."

"I won't take it anywhere." Mary Ellen spoke soothingly. "It's just hard to concentrate when you have to take care of a gun."

"Well..." Arnold looked down at the gun, then at her. "Okay, I guess." He held it toward her. Hardly daring to breathe, Mary Ellen reached for it.

"Drop it!" The command came from the dark, leafy cave that was the entrance to the trail winding down the hill. Arnold, unnerved, spun around and waved the gun.

Mary Ellen was flooded with relief—then anxiety that Arnold would shoot. She launched herself at him, hitting him in the small of the back and knocking him flat on the gravel. The gun flew out of his grip. "It's okay," she called toward the trailhead. "He's down."

Footsteps came quickly from the path. She sat on Arnold, who wriggled protestingly, and groped for the gun, which had landed just out of her reach. Before she could grab it, a gloved hand picked it up. "Thanks," she grunted, pushing the hair out of her eyes. She looked up, smiling gratefully.

Bob Markham stared down at her. The gun's round, cold black eye was trained on her heart.

"No—thank you," he said politely. "Get up, please."

Slowly, she stood. The gun moved, too, as she rose. Arnold stayed facedown on the gravel, emitting faint sobs.

"Well, Ms. Saunderson, we meet again." Bob Markham was smiling. Mary Ellen wondered why so genial an expression should be so frightening, and decided it had something to do with the gun. "Where's the boyfriend?"

Mary Ellen wanted to say that Ramsey would be meeting her almost immediately. But what would that really accomplish? "He isn't here," she said at last, feeling that it was stupid, that Markham could see that for himself.

Markham frowned. "I really wanted to get him in on this," he muttered. "That would have made it perfect. Star-crossed lovers—everyone would believe it." He glanced down, chewing his lip, and his face cleared. "Oh, well, Arnold will do. He's already been pretty useful. I brought my own weapon, but it's so much better to use one with his fingerprints all over it."

A louder sob escaped Arnold at that, and Bob Markham kicked his supine body contemptuously. "Get up, Arnold. I can't shoot you while you're lying down."

"Why not?" Arnold turned his head and shouted. "Go ahead. Shoot me while I'm down. Stab me in the back, why don't you? That's more your speed."

"You're the traitor," Markham said sharply. "Trying to put it all on me, when it was your idea in

the first place. I'd kill you for that, even if there wasn't
any other reason.''

Mary Ellen wanted to believe that it wasn't real. She
wasn't standing on a deserted hilltop while two men
quarreled over who was the biggest crook. There
wasn't a gun pointed at her chest. She looked at the
scene in front of her and blinked. Actually, there
wasn't a gun pointed at her chest. In the heat of his
argument, Bob Markham had swung the gun around
so that it was pointing at Arnold.

It was difficult to make her body respond; her feet
were frozen to the ground, and very rationally she
thought, ''That's because I'm terrified.'' But some
part of her, detached from the terror, was thinking feverishly. She forced her feet to move. She took a cau-
tious step back, and another. Her truck was just a yard
or two away; if she could get behind it, she might be
able to dodge the bullets that seemed pretty likely to
fly.

''Go on, get up,'' Markham snarled. ''This has got
to look just right.'' He glanced over at Mary Ellen,
and she froze, trying to assume an innocent expression. Her heart hammered painfully. The air on her
face was cold, with a hint of dampness. Leaves rustled on the trees and drifted to the ground. She was
filled with the hopeless realization that she was going
to die here, on this dark autumn night, before she'd
had time to live her life or pay attention to what was
really important.

''You, come here.'' He gestured with the gun, his
earlier courtesy gone. Mary Ellen crept forward on
stiff feet. ''Arnold's going to kill you, see,'' Markham told her, his face intent. ''Then he'll commit suicide. That's what it'll look like. That'll take the heat
off me. The paper trail will show he's stashed the

money in a Swiss account, and they can spend all their time ferreting it out. Meanwhile, I've got a nice little place in Mexico to disappear to."

That roused Arnold. "What money? You haven't even paid me yet!" He sat up on the gravel, looking deeply offended. "And I'm not going to kill Mary Ellen. I don't care if you kill me—I'm not a murderer."

"It'll just look like you killed her," Markham explained patiently. "I'll do it for you. It's a good thing I didn't pay you—would have wasted my money, wouldn't I? Although I planned to use Dalhousie's money." He chuckled. "That old man didn't take nearly enough interest in keeping track of his money."

Mary Ellen tried to speak but nothing came out. She cleared her throat and tried again. "Nobody has to kill me," she said, surprised at how normal her voice sounded. "I'll just promise not to say anything and be on my way." She tried a smile and backed toward her truck.

"Nope. You have to go." Markham raised the gun, and she froze again. "I'd have killed your boyfriend, too, for starting all the trouble. But since you're handy, you'll do. That'll be punishment enough for him, I reckon."

The sound of a car engine drifted through the night air. Markham seemed not to hear it, so Mary Ellen tried to keep from alerting him. She prayed that it was on its way up the hill and that it would by some miracle be Ramsey or Frank Alverez or both of them— heavily armed, of course, perhaps leading a small army. Desperately she pulled her mind away from such hysterical thoughts.

Markham gestured at Arnold again. "Come on, get up. The police can tell where you were standing when you fired the shot. Here, missy, you come and stand over by Arnold.''

Mary Ellen shuffled her feet loudly, trying to conceal the car sounds coming nearer. She was hallucinating, she decided; the engine roared just like Ramsey's old pickup. But whoever it was, he or she would be welcome.

Arnold wasn't cooperating. ''Make me,'' he said to Markham. ''I'm staying right here. I might as well be comfortable before I die.''

''You moron!'' Markham lost his temper. He pointed the gun at Arnold and tried to kick him in the side. Arnold grabbed his foot, jerking him off his feet. The gun went off.

Mary Ellen's eyes squeezed shut for a second. The gun sounded incredibly loud to her, and in the silence that followed its explosion, the approaching car was plainly audible. Markham scrambled upright, hearing it. Arnold didn't move. He was crumpled on the ground. She couldn't tell if he was dead or not, but there was blood oozing from his head, dripping on the pale gravel of the parking lot.

''Damn,'' Markham swore, noticing the blood. ''That's physical evidence. Can't do anything about it.'' He stared at Mary Ellen. ''Someone's coming.''

''I don't hear anything.'' All she could hear was her teeth chattering. Then she realized that the car or whatever had stopped. ''Guess they parked somewhere.''

''Spooners.'' Bob Markham looked disapproving. ''Well, can't risk another shot. They might hear it.'' He looked at the gun in his hand, then down at Arnold. Mary Ellen looked, too. Arnold seemed very still. The blood was still oozing, but slowly. She'd read somewhere that dead people didn't bleed.

Arnold must be dead.

I'm next, she thought. She wanted to do something to save herself, but couldn't think what that would be. She didn't know how to disarm anyone. If she screamed, chances were good the parking couple would hear, but also good that they would assume it was youthful high spirits, and not bother to investigate. And she could be dead by then, with Markham halfway down the hill.

Tearing her gaze from Arnold, she found Bob Markham watching her. He looked worried. "Gotta plan this," he muttered. "You. Go over and stand by the railing there."

Mary Ellen went, wondering if she should dive over the cliff and take her chances. Markham stood between her and her truck, so there was no possibility of getting into it before he could shoot her. And she didn't doubt he would. Despite not wanting to use the gun again, something in the way he clutched it made her sure he would shoot if she provoked him.

At least she still had her car keys. She'd half expected him to ask for them, since his car must be parked at the bottom of the hill. If he killed her, he would have a hard time getting away. Unless he thought to ask for her keys.

"Let's see." Markham talked aloud, still pointing the gun at her. "Arnold's shot there. If you shot him, your prints will have to be on the gun. You wrestled it away from him, killed him, and then jumped over the cliff out of remorse. That sounds pretty good."

He was going to make her put her prints on the gun. Maybe she could grab it then. Mary Ellen watched him walk toward her, smiling that affable smile. He stood beside her and looked over the cliff. "Not too far down," he observed, and suddenly his hand lashed out, gun butt first.

She was too startled to dodge, but she did jerk her head aside. The blow landed on her shoulder, making her cry out with the sharp, sudden pain. It cleared her head, though. When he grabbed at her, she managed to elude him.

"Wait," she said breathlessly. "You haven't thought. If they find a bruise on me, they'll know someone knocked me out and tossed me over the cliff."

"No, missy." He grabbed for her again. She slipped on the gravel, falling to her knees, and he pinned her against the railing. "You'll more than likely bump into a lot of stuff on your way down," he pointed out. "Enough to cause that bruise. Enough to break your neck. See, you might survive, unless you're dead when you go over."

He gripped her shoulder, right where the blow had landed. The pain was terrible. Again he brought the gun up like a club. "I'm knocking you out first," he whispered. "It's more humane that way."

His expression was one of concentration, as if she was an unwanted animal to dispose of.

"Markham!" The shout came from the trail that led down the hill—the same one Markham had come from. He spun around, letting go of Mary Ellen. She wanted to yell a warning about the gun. But all that came out was a frightened, wordless shriek.

Markham fired a couple of shots toward the trail entrance. Ramsey hadn't shown himself, but Mary Ellen knew it was him, waiting there, trying to figure out his approach. Her own mind worked feverishly. Markham's attention was focused on the new threat; he peered at the dark shadows of the trailhead. Any moment he would remember she was there and use her as a shield or a hostage. She couldn't let that happen.

She tried to crawl backward, but thick underbrush held her against the fence. Markham stood in front of her, facing the trailhead. If she tackled him, his gun would more than likely go off, and perhaps hit Ramsey. But if she didn't—

Before she could think too much about it, she launched herself for the second time that night, trying to aim her uninjured shoulder at the small of Bob Markham's back.

Some noise she made alerted him, and he turned, firing wildly. She felt a stinging fire in her arm, and then her head connected with his midsection.

With a pained exclamation, Markham went down. She sprawled on top of him, out of breath herself. She could hear Ramsey's footsteps thudding over the gravel. Markham heard them, too. He raised the gun again, glancing at it as if surprised to find it still in his hand. His eyes met hers, and a trace of his old genial smile crossed his face. He pointed the gun straight into her face and pulled the trigger.

It clicked aimlessly on an empty chamber.

For one long, frozen moment Mary Ellen held his gaze. Then Ramsey's fist fastened on Markham's collar, and he was pulled to his feet.

With a sigh of relief, Mary Ellen fainted.

RAMSEY SAT BESIDE the hospital bed, studying his love's pale face. There was an angry red scrape down one cheek. Her eyes were closed. They had anesthetized her to dig the bullet out of her arm and set her broken collarbone. That had been just after the ambulance had brought her to the hospital, and she hadn't yet woken. He wanted her to, but ached at the thought of the pain she'd suffer when she did. It would be awhile before she could pick up a hammer.

The door whispered open and Lenore tiptoed in. "Jon just called me," she said in a low voice, staring at Mary Ellen in the bed. "I can't believe it. Is she— will she be—"

"She's fine, the doctors say. Just superficial stuff, according to them." Ramsey's jaw tightened. "A superficial broken collarbone, a superficial bullet hole in the arm— God, I wish I'd killed that bastard!"

"From what I hear," Lenore said with the ghost of a smile, "you nearly did. You mangled him good, Frank said."

"Is Frank out there?" Ramsey glanced over his shoulder. "Did he say how Arnold was?"

"He'll live." Lenore shrugged. "Just a graze, evidently. He filled Frank in on all the hanky-panky. Put all the blame on Markham—for firebombing your house and booby-trapping your brakes . . . you forgot to tell me about that one."

He flushed under her accusing stare. "Didn't see any reason to alarm you, since it didn't work." He added defensively, "I told Frank."

"At least you had that much sense." Lenore was silent for a moment, watching Mary Ellen's chest rise and fall. He watched, too, finding her steady breathing immensely comforting.

Lenore yawned. "It's all been very exciting, but I have fifteen crepe myrtle to plant tomorrow—today, rather," she said, glancing at the clock on one wall. "All this turmoil is bad for my beauty sleep. How long does she have to stay here?"

"Probably just tonight." Ramsey took Mary Ellen's limp, cold hand in his. "They want to check her out tomorrow, and then they'll let her go."

"I'll stop by tomorrow afternoon, then." Lenore stood, stretching. "Let me bring you something for dinner. You sure she can take the turmoil at Alma's?"

"During the day she can stay in the living room." Ramsey had already thought about it, during his long, quiet wait. "We'll go to my place for the night. My kitchen should be done pretty soon, and then we'll just move in there while I finish up Alma's."

Lenore raised her eyebrows. "You've got every little thing planned, I see. Does it occur to you that Mary Ellen might have different ideas?"

"She'd better not." Ramsey tightened his grasp on her hand. "After tonight, she'll have one hell of a time getting rid of me."

"Well, I'm with you." Lenore walked over to the door. "But a word of advice, buddy. Ask her about it, don't tell her. Even in her battered condition, she won't take kindly to being told what to do."

"Yeah, yeah." Ramsey waved Lenore away, but when she was gone, he thought about her words. He'd gotten into a lot of trouble with this woman, telling her what to do. But for the past few weeks, while working on Aunt Alma's house, he'd come to enjoy sharing decisions with Mary Ellen, not carrying the whole load on his shoulders. And, although he would never admit it aloud, it was even relaxing to let her be in charge, to follow orders and eschew responsibility.

He raised his eyes from brooding contemplation of Mary Ellen's hand, and found that she was looking at him, a faint crease between her brows. Her lips shaped his name.

"Emmy!" He wanted to kiss her, but the bandages put him on his guard. It would be terrible to hurt her. He contented himself with kissing her hand. "Thank God you're all right."

"Am I?" She glanced around. "Why am I in the hospital, then?" A shadow crossed her face. "Oh, yes. I remember. He shot me, didn't he?"

"Got you right in the arm." Ramsey tried to speak naturally, but the words sounded funny when he ground his teeth. "You'll have an interesting scar— like an extra vaccination mark, the doctor said."

"What about you?" Her eyes examined him worriedly. "Did he hurt you?"

Ramsey coughed. "Not exactly." The shoe was definitely on the other foot in that respect.

"He had another gun." Mary Ellen was still concerned. "He mentioned it when he took Arnold's. I was going to tell you to be careful, he had another gun." She shuddered. "I thought I was going to die."

He gripped her hand tighter. "You're okay now, Emmy." He tried a smile. "Should have another fifty years, easy, if you wear your seat belt and don't take up smoking."

Her eyes drifted shut. "Yes," she murmured, then said it louder, looking straight at him. "Yes."

He was puzzled. "Yes? Yes, what?"

"Yes, I'll marry you. Tomorrow, if you want. Tonight. I want those fifty years with you. I want to have a golden wedding anniversary, and everything in between."

He had to kiss her, he just couldn't help it. He did it as gently as he could, leaning over, not touching anything but her lips. She seemed incredibly sweet and precious, and his triumph at winning her was mingled with fear of losing her, not to disagreements or divorce, but to that scythe-carrying figure he'd nearly glimpsed at the top of Spring Hill. Her mouth was warm and comfortingly alive. He didn't try to call back the tears that slipped from under his eyelids. Total happiness was worth crying about.

A nurse pushed the swinging door open, meaning to check the patient's vital signs and be sure she was coming out of the anesthetic nicely. She stood there for a moment, and then quietly retreated. Judging from the look of things, the patient's pulse would be tumultuous and her temperature might be up. But her vital signs were fine.

CHAPTER FOURTEEN

Mary Ellen sat on the front porch, basking in the autumn sunshine while she carved pumpkins into jack-o'-lanterns. From the house behind her came the sounds of hammering and occasional shouted questions. She missed being in the thick of activity, but Ramsey and the doctor were adamant that her arm and collarbone should heal completely before she put on her tool belt again.

She added a toothy smile to the jack-o'-lantern, which was wedged in the crook of her left arm since she couldn't use her left hand very well. Looking at the carved smile, she shivered. Somehow the pumpkin resembled Bob Markham, just before he'd tried to blow her head off. She still saw his awful smile, relived that scene in dreams that no amount of reassurance could totally erase. The dreams came less frequently now, and always when she woke, trembling and drenched with sweat, Ramsey was there beside her. That had helped to overcome her fear.

So she stuck out her tongue at the jack-o'-lantern and gave it menacing, scowling eyebrows. "There, Bob Markham," she muttered, setting it on the porch next to the two others she'd carved. "You're nothing but a pumpkin head. And when Halloween is over, I'm going to compost you!"

She gathered up pumpkin scraps, wincing when she moved her left arm a little too much and jarred her collarbone. The pain was minimal now, but it would be a couple of weeks before they let her take off the strapping.

The bullet wound had healed faster, although the doctor had warned her against doing anything strenuous that might reopen it. It was just about her speed to carry scraps to the compost bin. For the first week she'd done nothing more than sit at a desk and catch up on paperwork, both hers and Ramsey's.

Now the paperwork was done, and she was antsy. She'd tried supervising the placement of cabinets and tile, tubs and toilets, but it was maddening not to be able to lend a hand, and that morning she'd been kicked out of the kitchen when she absently tried to heft a cabinet.

Dumping the pumpkin scraps, she stood on the sidewalk in front of the house, admiring the bronze foliage of the bridal wreath around the foundation, and the last of the climbing roses nodding over her tower window. Most of the construction debris had been disposed of, and the old place looked lovely in the golden light. They would paint the exterior, she thought, before Aunt Alma returned. The interior was already scheduled for painting next week; Mary Ellen had sadly informed Ramsey that the state of her health precluded her lifting a paintbrush, and he'd agreed.

"Excuse me." The husky voice was vaguely familiar. Mary Ellen turned to see Gloria Gruenwald standing behind her, wearing a white leather jacket. She looked pinched and uncomfortable.

"Mrs. Gruenwald, isn't it?" Mary Ellen would have offered her hand, but Gloria didn't seem like the type to relish a friendly handshake. She nodded, instead.

Gloria's eyes were fixed on the arm that was strapped to her chest. "You're—hurt?"

"Just a broken collarbone." Mary Ellen stepped back a pace. "Would you like to come in?"

"I don't—well, is Ramsey there?" Gloria looked past her to the house.

"If you listen closely, you'll hear him bellow." Mary Ellen looked curiously at the other woman. Ramsey hadn't said much about her beyond the fact that she owed him money, but Mary Ellen had picked up a few slivers of gossip from the crew.

"I won't come in." Gloria dug her hands into the pockets of her jacket. "He hurt you, didn't he? That Markham character."

"Yes." Mary Ellen met her eyes steadily.

Gloria was the first to look away. "I didn't know," she said suddenly, her voice for once unstudied and full of real feeling. "Arnold said—well, I thought they were just shading the law a little. I would never have gotten mixed up with them if I'd known—"

"How were you mixed up with them?" Mary Ellen watched her curiously. "You were seeing Arnold socially, I know."

Gloria glanced away, and even backed down the driveway a couple of steps. Then she squared her shoulders.

"Arnold asked me to make sure Ramsey went to visit old man Dalhousie." She spoke rapidly and tonelessly, not looking at Mary Ellen. "I didn't know they were going to try to—hurt him. I just thought—"

"You told Ramsey." Mary Ellen's lips tightened. "You got him to go out there."

"Look." Gloria held up one hand. "I've felt really bad, you know? I told Arnold to take a hike when I heard Ramsey's truck had been tampered with. I may not be Miss Lily-white, but I don't do that kind of stuff." She fished in one pocket and brought out a piece of paper. "Here." She held it out, and after a moment Mary Ellen took it. It was a check. "That milestone payment Ramsey talked about. He can work on my place again—just like the contract specified." She darted a glance at Mary Ellen. "I'm going out of town for a couple of months. Maybe he could finish it before I get back."

"Maybe." Mary Ellen held onto her temper. She wanted to pick up a jack-o'-lantern and ruin that pristine white leather. The savage impulse frightened her a little.

"You two are getting married, I hear." Gloria lifted her chin. "Good luck. You might need it."

"I think we already have it," Mary Ellen said. She had a brief flash of sympathy for Gloria, but she quelled it firmly. The woman deserved whatever troubles she had.

Gloria turned away abruptly, and Mary Ellen watched her go down the street before she tucked the check into her pocket. She wouldn't tell Ramsey anything more than Gloria had dropped it off, she decided. If he knew how she'd manipulated him, he might get dangerous.

"Looking very nice," said a dry voice at her elbow. She turned and saw Mr. Featherstone standing there, impeccable as usual, carrying his briefcase.

"How nice to see you." Mary Ellen urged him up the walk. "Would you like to check the progress inside?"

He eyed her strapped-up arm. "Have you had an accident, Mary Ellen?"

"Nothing serious," she said hastily. They had tried to keep the events of that night out of the news, but it was, Mary Ellen suspected, pretty generally known around town. Mr. Featherstone's knowing look corroborated this, but he didn't say anything.

She showed him the new powder room, its tile fresh and sparkling, the textured drywall above it ready for painting. The kitchen was a seething mass of workers, with Jeanine overseeing the installation of her beautiful cabinets. Their glass-paned doors were stacked carefully to one side while Oscar and Chris muscled the bases into place.

At the back of the hall was the door to the new apartment. Here Ramsey worked busily, putting doors on the cabinets that had been installed earlier. The apartment consisted of a large, airy sitting room, a bedroom, a tiny kitchenette and a newly refurbished bathroom. Intricately patterned mosaic tiles on the bathroom floor carried out the turn-of-the-century look established through the rest of the house.

"Mr. Featherstone." Ramsey put down his screwdriver and shook the lawyer's hand. "It's all coming together, eh?"

Mr. Featherstone took off his glasses and polished them. "You have certainly done miracles in the short time you've been busy. Almost finished, are you?"

"Well, not quite." Mary Ellen checked off the tasks on her fingers. "The floors need refinishing—that's a horrible job. The place needs painting everywhere—including the exterior. Not just because of the new siding. The gingerbread trim is peeling."

Ramsey nodded. "Good idea. Then there's that terrace Lenore wants to put in, and some new landscaping around it. If we don't get that done before the first frost, it'll be next spring before we get to it."

"We've still got our work cut out for us," Mary Ellen told the elderly lawyer. "But a lot of it will be done by subs."

"Subcontractors," Ramsey clarified, taking her hand. "Mary Ellen's not doing any bricklaying for a while."

"Brute." Mary Ellen wrinkled her nose at him. "I love bricklaying."

Mr. Featherstone cleared his throat again, and they stopped gazing foolishly at each other, although Ramsey didn't let go of her hand.

"I did, as you asked me, send word of your proposed nuptials to Mrs. MacIver," Mr. Featherstone said. He set his briefcase on the counter and opened it. "I received a faxed message from her today, which I have taken the liberty of bringing. She also sent me some instructions."

"Shall we go to the living room?" Mary Ellen led the way, a little nervous about what her aunt would say. Aunt Alma would be delighted, no doubt, that they'd decided to cooperate with her and get married. But what new demands would she make?

When they were seated in the living room, Mr. Featherstone gave them a piece of paper.

Dearest Emmy and Ramsey,

Nothing could please me more than to hear that you intend to get married. You have probably guessed that I hoped this would be the outcome of my request for you to jointly undertake the renovation of my house.

Unfortunately, I will not be able to come back to Dusty Springs for your wedding. I tried to get permission to leave, but they're worse than jailers here, and my doctor pointed out that it would be foolish to endanger all the progress I've made by interrupting the treatment. You must not consider waiting five more months, when you've already waited five years! You certainly have my blessing, children.

I have another proposition to make, and have asked Jamie to explain it to you. It is entirely voluntary on your part, and you may reject it if it seems unpalatable to you.

Again, congratulations, and my grateful thanks for making my dream come true. Now, don't wait too long to have children!

Mary Ellen had to laugh when she read that last line.

Mr. Featherstone folded the letter. "Your aunt," he said in his precise voice, taking another sheaf of papers from his briefcase, "left instructions for me, in case this contingency should arise—that is, the two of you planning marriage. She has asked me to put this proposal before you, emphasizing that it is only a suggestion, and you are not bound by it in any way."

"What's she up to now?" Ramsey's expression grew suspicious.

"She offers you this house." Mr. Featherstone let the words fall into the sudden silence before he continued. "Her proposal is that she transfer ownership to the two of you, with lifetime tenancy for herself included. She plans to live in the apartment you've been fixing, giving up the rest of the house to you and your children. The plan would include provision for her care in the nursing home of her choice at such time as it becomes inevitable."

Mary Ellen was thunderstruck. Ramsey, too, she could tell. They stared at each other.

"I never expected such generosity," Mary Ellen said helplessly. "We ought not to accept. It's too much."

"Excuse me, but your aunt is very well aware that she would benefit the most from this plan." Mr. Featherstone tapped his papers into a precise rectangle atop his knees. "After all, her health is uncertain. Being on the ground floor would be advantageous for her, as well as having her family living with her. Her main concern is the lack of privacy you might experience. For that reason, she wishes you to be free to refuse."

Again Ramsey and Mary Ellen looked at each other. "We'll have to discuss it," Mary Ellen said finally. "Could we call on you later today, or tomorrow?"

"Please take all the time you need." Mr. Featherstone gave them the stack of papers and shut his briefcase. "Call me with any questions you might have. And, once again, best wishes on your upcoming marriage." He permitted a moment of human curiosity to appear in his gaze. "When is the wedding to be?"

"We—haven't really decided," Mary Ellen told him, still dazed. "Soon. There's been so much work—" she gestured toward the sound of hammers coming from the kitchen.

"Well, please send me an announcement." Mr. Featherstone rose, and Mary Ellen accompanied him to the door.

When she came back to the living room, Ramsey was glancing over the papers Mr. Featherstone had left. "We should take off this afternoon and discuss this," he said, looking at her with a worried frown. "We still haven't really settled how we're going to combine forces, Emmy. We're going to have to talk about it."

"I know." Mary Ellen sat on the arm of the sofa and ran her fingers through Ramsey's hair. She had put off discussing the details of their future, hoping that things would work out without any confrontations. It had been so sweet to be close to Ramsey, to bask in his solicitous regard. She'd never had anyone take care of her the way he was doing, not since childhood, anyway. It had been seductive—and dangerous. But now it was time to face the future.

"We'll have a picnic," Ramsey said. "I'll fix some sandwiches."

"Okay." The check in her pocket rustled, and she pulled it out. "Before I forget, that Gloria Gruenwald was here. She said she's going away for a while, and you can finish her house while she's gone."

Ramsey glanced at the check and pursed his lips. "Hmm. Wonder if she still wants that wet bar in the dining room."

"Just like the contract, she said."

"Great." Ramsey stuck the check in his pocket. "We can get going there after we're done here. I'll just go make that lunch."

"Let me have a word with Jeanine." Mary Ellen stood up. "I'll tell her we're going out."

The kitchen was quiet; Oscar and Chris were sitting in the backyard with their lunch coolers. Jeanine was marking level lines on the walls. She straightened. "You can get the counter people in tomorrow," she told Mary Ellen. "It's coming together like a dream."

"The cabinets are wonderful." Mary Ellen admired their glossy white paint, while Jeanine picked up one of the glass-paned doors and held it up to the wall cabinet so she could get the finished effect. "Just perfect with this room."

"It's a nice room." Jeanine nodded at the ceiling. "I like the light fixtures. Great stove, too." She pat-

ted the Wedgewood, which was back in place with a
new stainless-steel vent hood gleaming above it.

"So Jeanine, how are things going in Berkeley?"

Jeanine leaned against the sink counter. "I wanted
to talk to you about that," she said, her face serious.
"I've been giving some bids, and a couple of people
want me to contract their projects. You would have
gotten those jobs, Mary Ellen, if you'd been down
there. Are you going to be coming back to Berkeley
when you're done here?" She eyed Mary Ellen
shrewdly.

"Well, here's the problem." Mary Ellen wandered
over to the stack of cabinet doors, running her fingers over the muntins that separated the panes of
glass. "Ramsey and I are getting married."

"That's good news, isn't it?" Jeanine looked worried. "I must say I've been impressed with him these
past couple of days. You can learn a lot about someone by the way he works with a crew, and your Ramsey seems like a good guy. But will he be a good
husband? Marriage changes some men."

"And some women," Mary Ellen reminded her. She
hugged her elbows, feeling the stretch in the newly
healed skin around her bullet wound. "I want to
marry him," she said, low-voiced. "I found out that
that matters more than anything else. But I don't want
to put more strain on our marriage than it can take,
particularly when it's new. So I don't think I'll be
coming back to Berkeley. It's a long commute for me
from here, and I want to spend more time with Ramsey."

"Understandable." Jeanine nodded. "Well, then,
how about me buying out Victorian Visions? I can't
give you much money up front, but I could pay it off
over the long haul. The name has come to have some

value in our neck of the woods, and it would be a help
to me in starting as a contractor.''

''No.'' Mary Ellen shook her head, and Jeanine
looked crushed. ''I'm not selling it. I was thinking I
would open a branch of it up here, maybe do some
work in Sacramento and Davis. I want you to run the
Berkeley branch. We can draw up a partnership
agreement if you want, although myself I lean toward
incorporation for tax purposes. And we can help each
other through the lean times, or write in dissolution
clauses if either of us gets sick of it. But you won't
need any up-front money. You've already helped me
tremendously by taking on so much this past month.''

Jeanine brightened. ''That sounds great. I like the
part about no up-front money especially, considering
how Derek's taking me to the cleaners.'' Her face
clouded. ''He wants to reconcile now. My lawyer said
that's because his lawyer has probably advised him
that he'll lose in court.'' She sighed. ''I hate thinking
that I was just a meal ticket where he was concerned,
and not a very good one, either.''

''Well, you'll be independent now.'' Mary Ellen
patted her awkwardly on the shoulder.

''That's right.'' Jeanine smiled.

Ramsey appeared in the doorway, carrying a big
paper bag, with a blanket draped over his arm.

''We're out of here,'' he announced. ''You're
hereby appointed chief slave driver, Jeanine.''

''Yes, I know.'' Jeanine winked at Mary Ellen.
''You two have a good time, now. And congratulations. I recommend a water-tight prenuptial contract.''

Ramsey was scowling as they left the house. Mary
Ellen wasn't allowed to drive, but in deference to her

he'd kept his truck clean. "What did she mean by that crack?"

"She's getting divorced, and her husband claims her woodworking tools are community property."

That got Ramsey's sympathy. "Well, we each have our own tools, so that wouldn't happen to us," he said firmly. "Besides, we won't be getting divorced."

Mary Ellen agreed, but absently. She felt a sense of unease when Ramsey took the southeast road out of town. "Where are we going?"

"Spring Hill." He glanced at her, then turned his attention back to the road. "Might as well check it out."

"Check what out?" Mary Ellen turned on the seat to face him. "Ramsey, I don't want to go there right now."

"When, then?" He turned onto the twisting road that led to the top of the hill. "If you're going to live here, you can't avoid it forever. Especially now that it's going to be a park."

Mary Ellen didn't answer. Her hands twisted together in her lap. True, in the gentle sunlight of a late October day, the hill looked serene. Leaves drifted from the sycamores and the liquid-amber trees showed brilliant color.

The parking lot at the top was empty. Ramsey came around and opened her door, and reluctantly she stepped down from the truck. She stared at the railing beside the cliff edge. Nearby was the trailhead. It wasn't dark and sinister, just a shady, tree-dappled path.

She walked swiftly over to the railing and looked straight down. The cliff wasn't so high, or so steep. And the view was spectacular; it led her eyes past the town, past the hills where Horton Dalhousie's villa glinted like a shard of quartz, catching the sun on its windows. Behind it rose more hills, and the distant, hazy blue of the Sierra.

"If we had binoculars," Ramsey said, coming to stand beside her, "we could almost tell what Oscar and Chris are having for lunch." He pointed to the small dot that was Aunt Alma's house.

"You'd need pretty good binoculars." She turned to face him. "Too bad we can't see your house from here."

"My house." He looked at the picnic table where he'd left the lunch. "I can't think on an empty stomach. Let's eat and figure out what the hell we're going to do."

The sandwiches were good. "If we moved into Alma's," Ramsey said thoughtfully, offering Mary Ellen an apple, "I could use that fabulous stove. I'll give you this, Mary Ellen. You did a great job of designing the kitchen. A person would almost think you liked to cook."

"Tell you a secret," Mary Ellen said, munching on an apple. "I did a kitchen last year that a fancy designer had drawn the plans for. It had all that stuff in it—the pullout trash drawer, the wall convection oven, the tray cupboard and the walk-in pantry. I just rearranged it for Aunt Alma."

"Well, you did a good job, anyway." Ramsey threw his apple core into the bushes. "I get the feeling you like Alma's place better than mine."

"Yours is very comfortable." Mary Ellen spoke carefully. She didn't want to hurt Ramsey's feelings.

"So will Alma's be, when we're finished with it." He took one of her hands, holding it warmly. "Now it's time for my confession. When I built my house, I was still angry at you." He squeezed her hand. "I made it the exact opposite of everything I knew you liked. Stark, modern, minimalist—I really got into it." He let go of her hand and shrugged. "I don't even like it all that much myself anymore. I've been feeling for the past few months that it mirrored a phase I was going through."

"So if we sold it, that would be okay with you?"

"Sure." He smiled at her. "Matter of fact, I've had a couple of people from Sacramento express interest in it."

"Would you mind sharing a house with Aunt Alma?"

"Not at all," he said promptly. "She'd have her own place there, and you know, Emmy, she's busy when she's home—lots of clubs and meetings and things. I don't think we'd have trouble."

"I like the idea, myself." Mary Ellen spoke softly. "What I missed most about Berkeley was that feeling of connection to relatives and a community. Dusty Springs is a pretty nice place."

"So you'll be working here?" Ramsey looked up hopefully from repacking the lunch bag.

Mary Ellen braced herself. "Not really. I've talked to Jeanine, and I want to open a branch of my business up here, working mostly in Sacramento and Davis." She reached over, in turn, for Ramsey's hand, not liking his sudden stillness. "Don't you see, Ramsey? There's not a whole lot of work in town, not of the kind I like to do. And I don't want to cut into your work."

"You could work with me." He curled his fingers around hers. "I thought we'd be working together."

"We can, some. I expect to help you with your jobs, and to get your help with mine. We can do paperwork together every evening." She tried a smile. "I'll help you bid if you'll be my concrete expert."

His hand relaxed a little under hers. "It sounds complicated."

"Not really. Separate but equal." She reached up to cup his face. "Maybe down the road we can combine our businesses. But it's too great a strain to try and do everything all at once. We both like being in charge too much."

"You're right about that." He studied the initials carved in the picnic table for a moment, then raised his head to smile at her. "If this is what you want, Emmy, I won't complain. As long as we have time to spend together."

"Time when we're not working," she amended. "If we always worked together, we'd probably never stop. This way, we'll be taking weekends off. Do you know I've never stayed at a bed and breakfast?"

"Don't think I have, either." He scratched his head. "What's the big deal?"

"They're romantic, that's what." She tightened her grip on his hand. "A beautifully furnished room with a big brass bed, a walk on the beach at sunset—get the picture?"

"Yes, I see." He jumped to his feet and pulled her up, gently. "Except for the brass bed and the ocean, sounds a lot like my house. Shall we go check it out?"

Mary Ellen made a show of looking at her watch. "You're suggesting a nooner? I believe I can fit that into my busy schedule."

Ramsey tossed the paper bag into the trash can and boosted her into the truck. "Speaking of vacations," he said, when they were driving down the hill, "were you thinking what I was thinking when we heard Aunt Alma's letter?"

"I don't know," Mary Ellen said demurely. "I was thinking that we didn't have to get married up here."

"Exactly." They smiled at each other. "We'll just take the show to Pasadena. A first-class schemer like Aunt Alma ought to get to see the fruits of her labor."

IT WAS NOVEMBER, but the sun still shone brightly in Pasadena. It had been cloudy the previous night, and Mary Ellen had worried that the rainy season would start the day she got married. But she stood looking out at the courtyard of Aunt Alma's clinic and blessed the blue sky that beamed light on the Spanish tiles surrounding the pool.

Beside her, Lenore looked cool and serene in an off-the-shoulder dress made from layers of cotton gauze dyed different shades of gold. She had done the bouquets herself, from her own garden, and brought them over on the plane. Her own was a collection of old-fashioned flowers: daisies, black-eyed Susans, larkspur, stock and wallflowers, in shades of gold and white. Lenore hadn't said one word about her fear of coming back to L.A., but Mary Ellen had known how her friend must have felt. Still, Lenore had worked tirelessly, making arrangements with a Pasadena florist for the magnificent arch of autumn leaves and flowers at the far end of the pool. The colonnade that enclosed the courtyard was festooned with gold-and-white ribbons. In the shade, on either side, were chairs for the guests. All the residents of the clinic were there, enjoying the wedding.

Mary Ellen turned to smile at her aunt. Alma MacIver stood at her other side, magnificent in a beautifully cut suit of nubby gold silk. For her, Lenore had devised a corsage of chrysanthemums, and a wreath of them to twine around the creamy veiling of her gold hat. Beneath the hat, her white hair curled crisply. She held herself erect and looked more vigorous than Mary Ellen remembered her being in years.

"You look wonderful, dear," Aunt Alma said, and Mary Ellen looked down at herself complacently. She had suggested at first that she and Lenore wear suits, but Lenore had scornfully vetoed that idea. And she had to admit that her dress made the occasion even more special—quite a change from her work wear. She wore an ankle-length gown with a handkerchief hem, made from an opalescent silk shot through with gold threads. Her feet looked stylish and unfamiliar in gold pumps. Lenore had made her bouquet from showers of gold-and-white roses; their fragrance made her dizzy with pleasure. More roses nestled in her hair. She did look wonderful, she knew, but no more so than Ramsey, standing beside Jon in front of the archway at the far end of the pool. His dark suit made an elegant stranger of him.

"I can't tell you," Aunt Alma said, "how pleased I am that you're getting married here. You and Ramsey have made me very happy, my dear."

"You've done so much for us," Mary Ellen said warmly, kissing her aunt on the cheek and then rubbing off the lipstick smear with a laugh. "We're looking forward to seeing you next spring when they finally let you out."

"Oh, didn't I tell you?" Alma beamed fondly at her. "I've made friends with a delightful lady here—she's sitting on the other side of the pool, dying to be introduced to you. Beatrice has traveled all over the world—made me feel quite provincial, never leaving California. After our treatment is over, we're going to travel together and hit all the health spas she can think of." Aunt Alma's eyes grew dreamy. "Just think—Baden-Baden, Bath, Santoríni, that place in Japan, the hot springs of New Zealand—what an experience! It may take a year."

Mary Ellen frowned. "You're sure you'll be up to that? It sounds strenuous."

"This place is making a new woman of me," Aunt Alma declared stoutly. "And if it gets to be too much, I'll just hop on a jet and come home. Beatrice's granddaughter is a travel agent, and she's already making arrangements for us."

The pianist switched from Bach to Lohengrin, and Lenore straightened. "My cue," she said, and paced deliberately through the French doors and down the colonnade beside the pool.

"I hope nobody slips and falls in," Mary Ellen muttered to herself.

"Don't worry." Aunt Alma smiled serenely, offering her arm to her niece. "I had them put down the piece of Plexiglas they cover the pool with when we have dances. No one can fall in."

Mary Ellen linked arms with her aunt. "Thank you for thinking of that. And thanks for giving the bride away."

"I could give the groom away, too," Aunt Alma pointed out as they walked toward the archway. "Doesn't he look handsome?"

"He looks wonderful." Mary Ellen fastened her gaze on Ramsey. Despite his spiffy turnout, he was still his down-to-earth self. His dark eyes held heat and promise as she came closer.

Afterwards, she didn't remember much about the ceremony. What she remembered was Ramsey's hand clasping hers, the cool metal of the ring he slid on her finger, and how his ring stuck for a panicky moment on his knuckle. When they kissed at the end, a collective "ohh" went up from the clinic residents.

The party afterward passed in a blur, too. There were many toasts, some to people who hadn't been able to make it to the wedding, such as Oscar, who was planning his next semester's courses, and Jeanine and Frank Alverez.

Lenore and Jon would be flying back that evening. Mary Ellen had assumed that she and Ramsey, too, would take a plane home. But after they'd cut the cake and passed it around, accepting compliments and meeting Beatrice, Ramsey swept her toward the door.

"Where are we going?" Mary Ellen hung back, looking over her shoulder at Lenore, who was laughing gleefully.

"Have fun." She waved, and Jon waved, too. Aunt Alma gave them a glowing smile.

"We're going on our honeymoon, of course." Ramsey looked down at her. "Did you think you could get out of that?"

Mary Ellen blinked. "I didn't know we were having a honeymoon. I thought we had to get back and start moving."

"It can wait." He pulled her toward the door again.

"Wait a minute, now." She dug in her heels, and at once he stopped.

"Did I hurt you? I'm sorry," he said anxiously.

"No, you didn't hurt me. I'm totally well. But there's something you're forgetting." She turned back to the room full of people. Pulling one perfect golden rose out of her bouquet, she lifted it high.

The room stilled. "For the next bride," Mary Ellen called out, and tossed her bouquet.

It fell straight into Lenore's hands. Surprised, she looked at it, then at Mary Ellen. "Hey," she said. "This must be for someone else."

Mary Ellen grinned and shrugged. "It seems to be yours, sweetie." She waved and let Ramsey lead her out of the room.

In the clinic's sweeping driveway a rental car waited. "At least there aren't any old shoes tied on it," Mary Ellen said when Ramsey seated her in it. "Aren't we supposed to change before we leave?"

"We should bask in our elegance as long as possible," he remarked, getting behind the wheel. "To tell the truth, I kind of liked getting dressed up." He picked up a fold of her dress. "And you," he said, his voice husky, "look like a princess."

"Why, thank you, my prince." She gazed at him, and then looked at the road. "Where are we going?"

He smiled. "There are a lot of outstanding bed-and-breakfast places between here and home," he murmured, pulling onto the highway. "I figured we'd hit as many of them as we could."

Mary Ellen let her gaze travel over his face, his hands sure and competent on the wheel. "Well," she said, settling back in her seat. "I sure hope it's not too far to the first one."

EPILOGUE

ALMA MACIVER climbed out of the taxi and looked up the walk. On either side a wide flower border bloomed with all the brilliance of June. At the end of the walk the house stood proudly, lavish details picked out by gleaming paint. Roses climbed over the veranda and up the tower, nodding creamy blossoms at the open windows.

She paid the driver and left her bags on the sidewalk. The house drew her, but she took her time going up the walk. It had been a long time—too long, really, but she'd enjoyed every minute. She glanced down fondly at the gaily colored hibiscus blossoms that spattered her Hawaiian muumuu. She'd had more fun than a seventy-eight-year-old woman was ever supposed to, she thought. But coming home was the best part.

She bent over the flower border, noting the new roses, greeting the old ones. The lawn was lush and well-tended; the bridal wreath and hydrangea shrubs were fountains of bloom. A mockingbird sang from the weather vane atop the tower. Bees flew drunkenly from blossom to blossom. She drew a deep breath of the mingled fragrances of flower and freshly mown grass, and smiled. Yes, indeed, it was good to be home.

At the foot of the steps she paused, relishing the thought of greeting her niece and nephew. There had been countless letters and postcards, but she'd been more than willing to allow them a first year and a half of marriage without her interference. Not that she meant to interfere now, she told herself virtuously. It was just that she wanted them to get started on a family. Ramsey would be a wonderful father, she knew, and Mary Ellen the kind of mother every child deserved. And she herself was ready and willing to play grandma.

The steps were freshly painted, as if she'd been expected home. The front door, she saw, was open behind the elaborate screen door.

She was almost up the steps before she spotted it.

Standing in front of the porch swing, shaded by a clematis vine, was a gleaming baby carriage.

Alma tiptoed over. The baby sleeping inside, wrapped in soft blue blankets, couldn't be more than three months old. He scowled in his sleep, his tiny mouth disapproving of something in his dream.

He was the image of Scottie. "Oh, lad," she whispered. "How could your mommy and daddy not tell me?"

The screen door burst open behind her, and she was suddenly enveloped in a hug. "Aunt Alma! You're back!" Mary Ellen was laughing, but there were tears in her eyes. "We missed you so much! How do you like our surprise?"

Ramsey was right behind her. "You shouldn't have stayed away so long," he said, grinning at her while he wrapped his arms around her. "We tried to get him to wait, but he insisted on being born."

"Oh, children." Alma had to sit on the porch swing. Ramsey picked the baby up as if he'd been doing it all

his life and handed him to her. She held the precious
bundle and felt the tears streaming down her face.

"I think she likes him," Ramsey told Mary Ellen.
She, too, was frankly crying.

"Welcome home, Aunty."

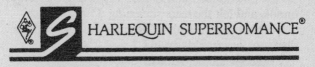

HARLEQUIN SUPERROMANCE®

COMING NEXT MONTH

#546 AFTER THE PROMISE • Debbi Bedford
Despite all his knowledge and training, Dr. Michael Stratton could
only stand by helplessly as his small son, Cody, battled for his life.
But something good might come of this—Cody's illness had
thrown Michael and his ex-wife, Jennie, together. While others
worked to heal his child, Michael could heal his marriage.

#547 SHENANIGANS • Casey Roberts
Paul Sherwood was a man with a mission: to take over ailing
cosmetics giant Cheri Lee. Lauren Afton was a woman with a
goal: to save her mother's self-made empire. Lauren knew she was
a match for Paul in the boardroom, and she had a sneaking
suspicion they'd also be a pretty good match in the bedroom....

#548 THE MODEL BRIDE • Pamela Bauer
Model Jessie Paulson had been on the jury that convicted
Aidan McCullough's father of murder, yet now the verdict was
beginning to haunt her. Aidan, too, was haunted by his father's
conviction. Not only had it uncovered a past best left buried, it
was standing in the way of his future with Jessie.

#549 PARADOX • Lynn Erickson
Women Who Dare, Book 5
Emily got more than she bargained for when she decided to start a
new life in Seattle. Her train crashed and she woke up to find
herself in the year 1893, at the home of rancher Will Dutcher.
Trapped in time, Emily had to discover a way to return home. But
how could she abandon the man she loved?

AVAILABLE THIS MONTH:

Following the success of WITH THIS RING and
TO HAVE AND TO HOLD, Harlequin brings you

JUST MARRIED

SANDRA CANFIELD
MURIEL JENSEN
ELISE TITLE
REBECCA WINTERS

just in time for the 1993 wedding season!

Written by four of Harlequin's most popular authors, this
four-story collection celebrates the joy, excitement and
adjustment that comes with being "just married."

You won't want to miss this spring tradition, whether
you're just married or not!

**AVAILABLE IN APRIL WHEREVER HARLEQUIN
BOOKS ARE SOLD**

JM93

HARLEQUIN SUPERROMANCE®

HARLEQUIN SUPERROMANCE NOVELS WANTS TO INTRODUCE YOU TO A DARING NEW CONCEPT IN ROMANCE...

WOMEN WHO DARE!
Bright, bold, beautiful...
Brave and caring, strong and passionate...
They're women who know their own minds
and will dare anything...
for love!

One title per month in 1993, written by popular Superromance authors, will highlight our special heroines as they face unusual, challenging and sometimes dangerous situations.

Next month, time and love collide in:
#549 PARADOX by Lynn Erickson
Available in May wherever Harlequin Superromance novels are sold.